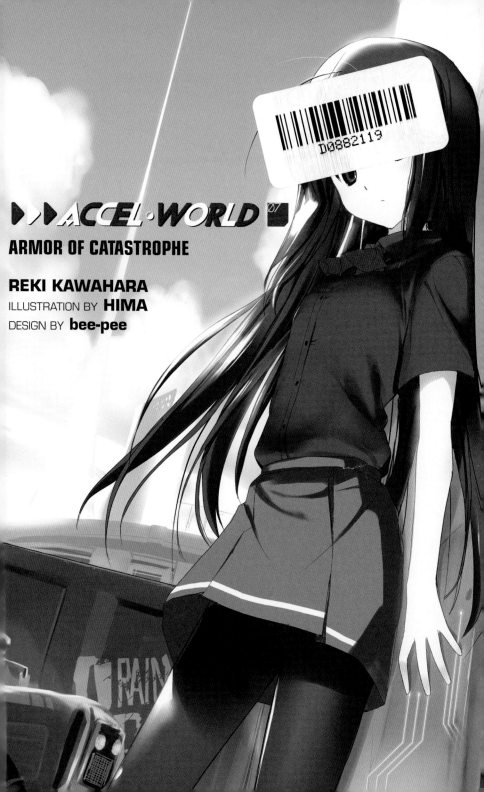

▶▶▶ACCEL·WORLD 07

ARMOR OF CATASTROPHE

REKI KAWAHARA
ILLUSTRATION BY **HIMA**
DESIGN BY **bee-pee**

"Yeah. I'll work something out. We're going home alive... to everyone waiting for us in the real world."

HARUYUKI

Controls Silver Crow, the duel avatar polluted by the Armor of Catastrophe. Boy in the lowest school caste.

"I believe
I told you:
that true
strength
is moving
forward
without
giving up,
even if you
lose or
fall down
or fail."

UTAI SHINOMIYA

Controls the duel avatar
Ardor Maiden, a member of
the old Nega Nebulus.
Grade four student.

"I apologize for my rudeness. But please believe me. I haven't the slightest intention of fighting you."

TRILEAD TETROXIDE

Mysterious, young samurai-type avatar encountered in the Castle.

TAKUMU

Controls duel avatar
Cyan Pile, a member
of Nega Nebulus.
Haruyuki's classmate
and good friend.

"Taku...Ever since
I can remember,
I've wanted to be
like you. So that's
why...I'll fight you
now to show
you that."

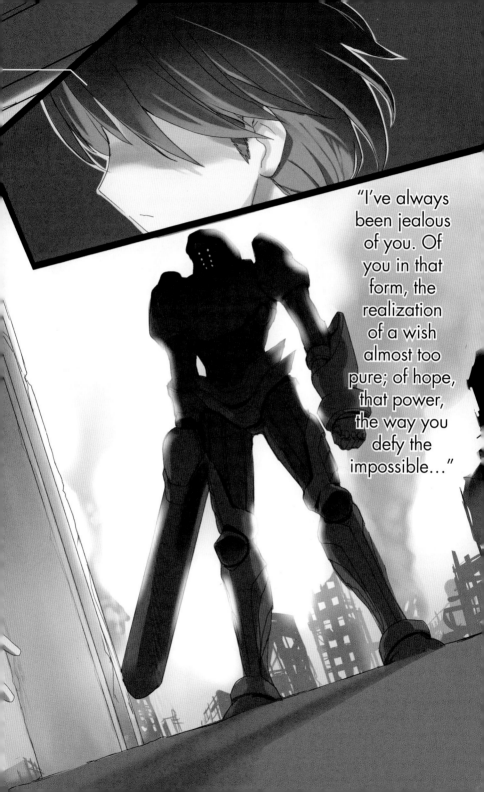

"I've always been jealous of you. Of you in that form, the realization of a wish almost too pure; of hope, that power, the way you defy the impossible..."

ACCELERATED WORLD LEGION DISTRIBUTION MAP

ITABASHI WARD

ADACHI WARD
YELLOW LEGION
CRYPT COSMIC CIRCUS

KITA WARD

NERIMA WARD
RED LEGION PROMINENCE

KATSUSHIKA
WARD

ARAKAWA WARD

TOSHIMA WARD ● SUNSHINE CITY

SUMIDA
WARD

SUGINAMI
WARD

BUNKYO WARD
BLUE LEGION LEONIDS
SHINJUKU WARD

TAITO
WARD

BLACK
LEGION
NEGA
NEBULUS

● KOENJI STATION

● TOKYO SKYTREE

● UMESATO JUNIOR
HIGH SCHOOL

CHIYODA WARD

EDOGAWA WARD

● GOVERNMENT
OFFICE

■ IMPERIAL PALACE

SHIBUYA
WARD

CHUO WARD

KOTO
WARD

MINATO
WARD

PURPLE LEGION AURORA OVAL

GREEN LEGION
GREAT WALL

● OLD TOKYO TOWER

SETAGAYA
WARD

WHITE LEGION
OSCILLATORY UNIVERSE

MEGURO
WARD

SHINAGAWA
WARD

OTA WARD

ACCELERATED WORLD

Imperial Palace

This building sits in the same, corresponding location as the Imperial Palace in the real world. Considered impregnable, it has not once allowed entry to a Burst Linker since the birth of the Accelerated World. With gates rising up to the east, west, north, and south of the Castle, and invisible barriers above and below its walls, entry is impossible.

Each gate is guarded by one of four "God-level" Enemies, the strongest of the strong. These Enemies—the Four Gods—are an absolute presence, boasting a strength far greater than that of Legend-level Enemies, and unless all four are defeated simultaneously or a Burst Linker manages to slip past their watch, the Castle cannot be infiltrated. Some Burst Linkers say that one condition for clearing Brain Burst is to steal the points of five level-nine Burst Linkers, and to then reach level ten. Breaching the Castle's center is perhaps another condition for winning.

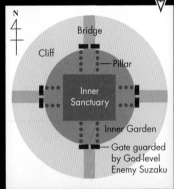

N

Bridge

Cliff

Pillar

Inner
Sanctuary

Inner Garden

Gate guarded
by God-level
Enemy Suzaku

▶▶▶*ACCEL·WORLD*

ARMOR OF CATASTROPHE

Reki Kawahara

Illustrations: HIMA

Design: bee-pee

YEN
ON

NEW YORK

■ Kuroyukihime = Umesato Junior High School student council vice president. Trim and clever girl who has it all. Her background is shrouded in mystery. Her in-school avatar is a spangle butterfly she programmed herself. Her duel avatar is the Black King, Black Lotus (level nine).

■ Haruyuki = Haruyuki Arita. Eighth grader at Umesato Junior High School. Bullied, on the pudgy side. He's good at games, but shy. His in-school avatar is a pink pig. His duel avatar is Silver Crow (level five).

■ Chiyuri = Chiyuri Kurashima. Haruyuki's childhood friend. Meddling, energetic girl. Her in-school avatar is a silver cat. Her duel avatar is Lime Bell (level four).

■ Takumu = Takumu Mayuzumi. A boy Haruyuki and Chiyuri have known since childhood. Good at kendo. His duel avatar is Cyan Pile (level five).

■ Fuko = Fuko Kurasaki. Burst Linker belonging to the old Nega Nebulus. One of the Four Elements. Lived as a recluse due to certain circumstances, but is persuaded by Kuroyukihime and Haruyuki to come back to the battlefront. Taught Haruyuki about the Incarnate System. Her duel avatar is Sky Raker (level eight).

■ Uiui = Utai Shinomiya. Burst Linker belonging to the old Nega Nebulus. One of the Four Elements. Fourth-grade student in the elementary division of Matsunogi Academy. Not only can she use the advanced curse removal command Purify, she is also skilled at long-range attacks. Her duel avatar is Ardor Maiden (level seven).

■ Neurolinker = A portable Internet terminal that connects with the brain via a wireless quantum connection and enhances all five senses with images, sounds, and other stimuli.

■ Brain Burst = Neurolinker application sent to Haruyuki by Kuroyukihime.

■ Duel avatar = Player's virtual self, operated when fighting in Brain Burst.

■ Legion = Groups composed of many duel avatars with the objective of expanding occupied areas and securing rights. There are seven main Legions, each led by one of the Seven Kings of Pure Color.

■ Normal Duel Field = The field where normal Brain Burst battles (one-on-one) are carried out. Although the specs do possess elements of reality, the system is essentially on the level of an old-school fighting game.

■ Unlimited Neutral Field = Field for high-level players where only duel avatars at levels four and up are allowed. The game system is of a wholly different order than that of the Normal Duel Field, and the level of freedom in this Field beats out even the next-generation VRMMO.

■ Movement Control System = System in charge of avatar control. Normally, this system handles all avatar movement.
■ Image Control System = System in which the player creates a strong image in their mind to operate the avatar. The mechanism is very different from the normal movement control system, and very few players can use it. Key component of the Incarnate System.
■ Incarnate System = Technique allowing players to interfere with the Brain Burst program's Image Control System to bring about a reality outside of the game's framework. Also referred to as "overwriting" game phenomena.

■ Acceleration Research Society = Mysterious Burst Linker group. They do not think of Brain Burst as a simple fighting game and are planning something. Black Vise and Rust Jigsaw are members.
■ Armor of Catastrophe = Enhanced Armament, also called Chrome Disaster. Equipped with this, an avatar can use powerful abilities such as Drain, which absorbs the HP of the Enemy avatar, and Divination, which calculates Enemy attacks in advance to evade them. However, the spirit of the wearer is polluted by Chrome Disaster, which comes to rule the wearer completely.
■ ISS kit = Abbreviation for "IS mode study kit." IS mode is "Incarnate System mode." The kit allows any duel avatar who uses it to make use of the Incarnate system. While using it, a red "eye" is attached to some part of the avatar, and the overlay that is the sign of Incarnate use is emitted as a black aura.

▶▶▶ ACCEL · WORLD

1

Blackout.

Spotlight.

In the circle of white light: an enormous matte column, painted scarlet. Leaning back against its curved surface: a small doll, not a real person. The doll's body is covered in metal armor of a silver hue, head encased in a helmet of the same.

A faint light grows to illuminate the surroundings. Nighttime. Countless bonfires flicker silently. The initial red column is not the only one; similar pillars stretch out in a seemingly endless row. The ground is blanketed by snow-white gravel. In the distant background, the silhouette of a massive palace looms. The silver helmet moves to gaze at the faraway castle.

...It's not "absolutely impregnable." Not even close.

He couldn't help grumbling to himself, even though he was only too aware that this was totally a "reap what you sow" kind of situation.

He couldn't voice this complaint out loud. Actually, he couldn't even allow himself the soft *crunch* of a single footstep. The instant he made the slightest sound, the terrifying samurai-type

Enemies parading around within the fortress might descend on him and attack all at once.

Each samurai was at most three meters tall. Enemies five times that size in the Beast class that lived in the world outside were not at all unusual. But the samurai, strutting through the long hallways and the tops of the castle walls in groups of three or four, armor clanging, emitted a concentrated pressure greater than Beasts, on par with Legends—or even the Four Gods standing guard at the gates of the palace.

Naturally, the fact that he had been able to get into the inner sanctuary of the palace—the solemn Castle reaching to the heavens in the center of the Unlimited Neutral Field—was precisely because he had breached the guard of those Four Gods. That said, however, this in no way meant he would be able to defeat even one of those samurai. Rather than breaching the guard of the Gods, it would be more accurate to say he had found a gap to sneak in through or, perhaps, made it inside through mere chance.

There has to at least be a leave portal in here, he told himself silently, to push back the fear and anxiety filling his heart.

Reflecting the light of the torches inside the Castle, his metal avatar was frozen right through, his heart echoing as it pounded beneath the somewhat dull silver of his armor. He was clearly in a desperate situation, the biggest crisis of his life as a BB player.

Still, he couldn't deny that he felt just the tiniest bit excited.

It had already been eleven months since the birth of the Accelerated World—since Brain Burst, the full-dive fighting game application created by an unknown developer, had been distributed to approximately one hundred first-grade students living in the heart of Tokyo. Many players, after reaching level four during that time and thereby earning the right to dive into the Unlimited Neutral Field, challenged the massive palace enthroned in the center of this world. Given that it was in a location that corresponded to the Imperial Palace in the real world, and the supreme gravitas of the structure (surrounded as it was by cliffs), it obviously had to be the final objective of the game—in the words of a child, the last boss's castle.

But the challenges of every Burst Linker had been knocked aside with a single breath by the terrifying super Enemies, the Four Gods.

Genbu in the north. Seiryu in the east. Byakko in the west. And Suzaku in the south. While each was an independent Enemy with a five-level HP gauge, they also had the ability to support and heal one another. Specifically, the Gods not in combat sent buffers and heals to those fighting at the other gates with alarming force, which meant that players could not focus their fighting strength to crush each God individually. They also had to split their forces up and simultaneously attack all four. But that sort of large-scale strategy was not possible when the total number of Burst Linkers still had not reached five hundred, and these few players were divided into countless tiny Legions that were constantly wrangling with one another. In some cases, players who dared to challenge the Gods had taken a small-scale squad to charge one of the gates, only to die well onto the bridge, where they fell into Unlimited Enemy Death—although the term was not coined until later—and lost all their burst points.

Given all this, it only made sense that he'd be the tiniest bit thrilled at being inside the Castle, despite the fact that he hadn't actually defeated the Four Gods.

If he could push on and reach the depths of the palace to get his hands on the final flag item there—whatever it was—perhaps his name would be forever etched into the narrative of the Accelerated World as the first person to clear Brain Burst.

He, a subdued metal color possessed of no significant abilities, was never paid any particular attention by anyone. His name—
Chrome Falcon.

Although his avatar name was kind of cool with the falcon bit, or maybe because of that, Chrome Falcon's abilities and appearance had long been deemed to not live up tò that name. And not just by his duel opponents; he thought so himself.

The only part of his avatar that resembled a bird of prey was the mask, which tapered to a sharp point at the bottom in the shape of a beak. His face was a smooth silver with no eye lenses, and he couldn't shake the impression that this made him look like someone's underling. His body was long and slender; his limbs had nothing in the way of weapons. Naturally, there was nothing that even hinted at wings on his back.

The only person who said his duel avatar—which had nothing but the attack abilities of Punch and Kick, the speed that came from being small, and the hardness of his body—was "amazing" was his tag-team partner, Saffron Blossom. He believed her sincerity in saying so, but at the very least, he wished he had something to complement her abilities.

Blossom had, as her name suggested, the power to make flowers bloom. She shot different kinds of seeds from a small stick in her right hand and embedded them in the Enemy—or an ally avatar. The flowers that bloomed after a certain period of time manifested a variety of effects, such as eating up health or special-attack gauges, stopping legs, or, conversely, applying buffer effects or removing debuffing effects. Critical gossips called this a "parasitic attack" and other unpleasant things, but even among other yellow colors, a duel avatar as all-purpose as she was was hard to find.

Of course, if a player had that much power, then naturally some other part of their skill set would have to be sacrificed, and in Blossom's case, it was her fairly unreliable defensive power. To compensate for this weakness, she tag-teamed with the hard, metallic Falcon, and even after nearly six months of fighting together, that anxiety still lived in his heart. The anxiety about what would happen if someone even harder came along and invited Blossom to partner up.

The metallic color wheel, separate from the so-called normal color wheel, had the precious metals platinum and gold on the far left, and the base metals steel and iron on the right. Precious, base—regardless, the potential was the same if the level was, with placement on the left side being stronger against special attacks with poison, acid, or corrosion, and the farther right you went, the stronger the avatar was against physical attacks from punching or swords.

Chrome was basically in the center. Not having much resistance one way or the other, this metallic color existed in no small numbers, excelling only in the simple hardness of its armor. In fact, it wouldn't be at all strange to come across a better shield among the normal colors, in the defensive-oriented green line.

In other words, given that all he had was the fact that he was a hard metal, he had no idea when Blossom would be taken from him.

He himself couldn't quite grasp what this feeling was blocking his chest. While he had somehow managed to survive up to that point in a stronghold in the bay area of the Accelerated World, and other players had recently given him the nickname Black Eagle, when he burst out, he was still just an eight-year-old boy in second grade. Or maybe that was just an excuse, too: He had already spent nearly five years of subjective time in this world of no time limits since earning the right to dive into the Unlimited Neutral Field.

So he did actually understand it somewhere in his mind. Understand why the other day, when he finally reached level five and obtained a certain special attack, he had immediately thought of the Castle…And why he had acted on that idea, why he was in this tight spot now, holding his breath, surrounded by countless terrifying Enemies. All of it was for his love of Saffron Blossom and his desire to monopolize her.

If he didn't move soon, one of the samurai groups that moved around within the palace in a fixed pattern would show up in this hiding spot. He poked the edge of his mask out from the shadow of the crimson pillar and took a quick peek at the situation.

His current location was a corner of the main road that connected the Suzaku gate and the main entrance of the palace itself.

It was in the southern area of the Castle's inner garden, which in and of itself was a circle fifteen hundred meters in diameter. On both sides of the entrance, Enemies sat in wait, looking more like fierce gods than samurai with their extremely vicious countenances; there was no way he could break through them. He decided instead to set his sights on one of the windows in the white walls. Given that this was not an established route, there was a strong possibility that they couldn't be opened from the outside, but if it would just *please* be a real window, he should be able to get inside.

He heard the footfalls of a group of samurai Enemies on patrol approaching from behind. Taking a deep breath, he put his right foot forward and very quietly said the name of his technique.

"Flash Blink."

Perhaps picking up even this quiet utterance with their sharp ears, the samurai quickened into a run.

By then, however, the dark silver avatar had already completely disappeared from behind the pillar. Vanishing temporarily, leaving nothing but a blue afterimage, he materialized silently along the wall of the Castle, thirty meters away.

This was Chrome Falcon's level-five special attack, a pseudo-teleportation. *Pseudo* because it was an extension of the ability to move in a straight line at high speeds, so he could only move to somewhere he could see that was connected in space. But while moving, his avatar changed into a particle with zero mass, and physical and gravitational attacks were completely ineffective.

He reappeared with his back pressed up against the white wall and watched the samurai Enemies swarming the place he had been moments before. Having lost the intruder that was the target of their aggression, they swiveled their heads wildly in an attempt to regain their prey, but eventually, they returned to their original patrol route as if all was forgotten and began walking at a leisurely pace again. He heaved a sigh of relief. The attack AI of the samurai Enemies, at any rate, was clearly not on par with the Four Gods.

Glancing back, he looked up at the large window in the wall behind him.

He had been anticipating this, since the Field's attribute was the Japanese Heian-style stage, but the window was indeed just red latticework incorporated into the wall lengthwise, with nothing resembling glass in it. Since one square was only about three centimeters on any given side, there wasn't a duel avatar out there who could slip through this gap in their given form, but...

He glanced up and checked his special-attack gauge in the upper left of his field of view. Five percent remaining. There was also only 20 percent left in his health gauge, but either way, a single blow from the sword of a samurai Enemy would mean instant death, even if his gauge were full.

He carefully decided on a trajectory, planted his right foot forward, and used up the last of his gauge for a final Flash Blink.

The particulate body of Chrome Falcon slipped through the narrow gap in the frame and finally made it into the actual Imperial Palace.

It was this ability that had made it possible for him to fool the Four Gods and break through the absolutely impenetrable outer walls of the palace. The method he devised had been exceedingly simple: After charging up his special-attack gauge in advance, he headed first toward not the large bridges guarded by the Four Gods but the outer moat filled with infinite darkness surrounding the palace, where he Blinked the maximum distance. That said, even using up his entire gauge, the maximum he could travel was a hundred meters, not even close to being enough to cross the five-hundred-meter-wide palisade.

Because of this, he set his initial trajectory a bit higher up in the sky. The instant he reappeared above the palisade, the indisputable force of gravity caught hold of his avatar and tried to drag him to the bottom of the ravine, crunching away at his HP gauge. However, since this simultaneously recharged his special-attack gauge, he Blinked again diagonally into the sky once his gauge had reached a certain point. Then it was a matter of repeating this to cross the valley.

All that was well and good, but the truth was he had planned to simply experiment today in the name of reconnaissance. Once he confirmed that the cycle of Blink, charge, Blink was indeed possible, he had intended to fall to his death at the bottom of the ravine. He'd be regenerated in front of the palisade, and he could reexamine his plan based on the information he obtained. Once he was certain it was possible to actually implement, he would come back to take on the challenge of the real thing.

That was how it was supposed to go, at least, but here he was on his first try, on this reckless suicide mission, because falling into an infinite valley had been an unbelievably terrifying experience. He completely forgot himself on the first fall and continually and intently Blinked forward, so that before he knew it, he was clinging to the exterior wall in a trance.

The results were exactly what he'd been hoping for, but he didn't get the chance to stand around and pat himself on the back.

While these eleven months since the beginning of the Accelerated World were a history of the fights among the children who became Brain Burst players, they were at the same time also a history of the conflict between all players and the mysterious game developer. The children turned all their youthful enthusiasm toward seeking out holes in the system—finding ways to earn delicious points—and the moment they found one, the developer plugged it up with an update patch. Any point-earning tech that had the faintest whiff of deceit such as Enemy Stalking or Tool Cheating (using external programs in the real world within the game) was dealt with so fast, it was surprising compared with other net games, and they could no longer use it. From the speed of this reaction, more than a few players insisted that it wasn't a human who developed and ran BB, but rather an AI.

At any rate, the unknown developer appeared to be firm in their refusal to allow any back doors or shortcuts. And more than that, this developer sternly demanded payment equal to whatever the player was trying to gain in the Accelerated World.

Which meant that there was absolutely no way the developer was going to approve of Chrome Falcon flying over the moat to break into the impenetrable Castle, rather than going through the proper route through one of the four gates. A patch would be applied soon enough, and the super gravity of that palisade would be able to grab hold of even Flash Blink, a technique impervious to physical and gravitational effects. Maybe it was already being fixed at that very moment.

So this was his first and last chance.

I'm going to get something or do something here, and become a Burst Linker worthy of partnering with Saffron Blossom. So that I won't have to live in fear of losing her anymore. So that I make her happy she chose me.

And, more than anything else, to pay her back for talking to me and reaching out to me, when I did nothing but look down at the ground in this world, just like in the real one.

Once he slipped in through the window frame, he was met with beautifully polished wooden floors and an inside wall made up of sliding *fusuma* doors, adorned with gorgeous color prints. Candlesticks stood at evenly spaced intervals, orange flames flickering quietly. No sign of any Enemies at the moment.

Checking the window behind him, he saw a small latch at the bottom. It wasn't a meaningless decorative object; when he unlocked it and gently pushed on the window, the entire vermilion-painted frame lifted up soundlessly outward. At the very least, if he made it back here, he could get out of the Castle's inner sanctuary.

But there would be no leave point portal there if he did. And he couldn't exactly go home empty-handed after having come all this way. He'd made it to this point; he could only keep going deeper and deeper inside as far as his nerves and his luck would hold.

He held his breath beneath his silver mask and carefully began walking forward, as if his slender avatar were melting into the gloom.

How many hours—or days, for all he knew—had passed?

He had dived into the Unlimited Neutral Field right after he got home from elementary school, so logically, he had the leeway of staying in this world for a few days easily, or even a few months. In fact, he had once spent three months on a dive together with Blossom—or, rather, living together with her.

That said, continuing to advance while avoiding the range of detection of the Shinto priest and samurai Enemies several levels more terrifying than the ones in the garden was a more difficult task than he could have imagined. If Falcon hadn't been a small, lightweight type, it likely would have been an impossible one. At the same time, the assumption of the architecture seemed to be that the palace would be captured by a large army of several dozens or even hundreds. The halls were excessively wide, the ceilings high. Because of this, somehow, he had been able to dodge the Enemy groups on patrol and make his way forward, but his powers of concentration were very nearly at their limit.

Big, deep breath. He used the air to cool his head and tried to pick out where he would go next from the shadow of a thick pillar.

The diameter of the entire Castle was fifteen hundred meters, and the distance from Suzakumon to the main gate guarded by the demon god was approximately four hundred meters. In which case, the size of the inner sanctuary should have been at most about seven hundred meters from north to south. He figured he had already advanced five hundred meters since he made it inside, so he should be getting to the center of the inner sanctuary soon.

Sure enough, at the end of a hallway stretching northward, he could see a remarkable large space and a mysterious light shining in the floor there.

Lined up, two of them. Transparent blue, flickering like the surface of water.

He had seen this color before. There was no mistaking it; this was the light of the leave points—also known as portals—set up in the landmarks of all areas of the Unlimited Neutral Field.

Unconsciously, he let out a sigh of relief before gulping hard. If he simply left now for the real world, not only would he not have the glory of clearing the game, he wouldn't even be able to bring home a single piece of evidence that he had succeeded in breaking into the Castle. But then, why had he Blinked do-or-die toward the infinite palisade wall and endured the tension of this sneaking around for however many dozens of hours...?

No.

His original motivation for this personal mission hadn't been as utilitarian as that. He had simply wanted something, one thing, that could be the core of his self-confidence. Something that would give him the power to keep standing proudly next to Saffron Blossom.

In which case, this was already enough. He had infiltrated the most dangerous area in the Accelerated World, had made it to the innermost sanctum, and would return alive. Even if he was the only one who knew all this, it should give him a certain strength for a long time to come. It was indeed a fact that he had achieved something that even the Pure Colors, currently deemed the strongest in the world, couldn't do.

When he thought about it, there had been absolutely no explicit statement from the system side on what would happen when this magnificent, mysterious game known as Brain Burst was cleared. The name of the person who beat it might be announced to the entire Accelerated World, they might be given a certain amount of points in lieu of prize money and a certain sort of Enhanced Armament in lieu of a prize, and then the game could continue on. It would be nice if that happened, at least, but it wasn't hard to imagine the ending theme suddenly playing as the credits scrolled by, and then THE END flashing in front of their eyes in all caps before the program was deleted from the Neurolinker of every BB player. And since he had naturally never met Blossom in the real and they hadn't exchanged real contact information, if that happened, he'd never get to see her again.

Which was why he was sure that, if he did discover some clear-flag-ish item in this castle, he probably wouldn't touch it. This was enough. Making it back alive through the portal was the greatest reward he could hope for with this mission.

Perhaps the actual god of the Accelerated World took pity on the sober metal color as he made this laudable speech to himself. Because, awaiting him in the open space he mustered up the last of his concentration to sneak into, lay no simple portal.

Two ellipses next to each other, filled with a quivering blue light, the very same light as found in the many leave points existing outside the Castle. But each had a strange object directly in front of it.

Stone pillars about a meter high, lustrous and black. No, perhaps better to call them *pedestals*. Atop each sat an object. On silent feet, he approached the one on the left.

Tilting his head back slightly, he saw enthroned there, bathed in the light of the portal, a single sword—though maybe it was a katana. The reason he couldn't say for sure either way was that, although the workmanship on the guard and the grip looked Japanese, the scabbard was a perfectly straight line without a hint of a curve to it. The whole thing was a mirrorlike silver metal, with exceedingly little decoration.

Still, he could tell at a glance that this straight sword harbored terrifying power. If it was an Enhanced Armament, he had no doubt it was in the strongest class or maybe even beyond that. Just looking at it, he could feel a pressure that possibly rivaled that of a Legend-class Enemy at extremely close range—or even the Four Gods, which he had seen just once before, and they had almost taken his breath away.

With effort, he pulled his gaze away from the straight sword and looked again at the black, granite-like pedestal. A square metal plate was embedded on the front of it, with several shapes and characters carved into it.

The one at the very top was made up of seven connected dots, placed in a shape like a letter *P* that had fallen on its side to the left. He had seen this same shape when they studied the constellations in his elementary school science class: a square drawn by four stars and a tail of a line of three, the ladle-shaped Big Dipper. Staring at it closely, in the center of the dipper part, he saw that the fifth star from the left was the only one drawn larger than the others.

Under the constellation were two kanji characters, rare in the Accelerated World so full of English. They were *jewel* and *point*, and maybe read as *gyokusho*, but he didn't know what they meant together like this. And then farther down was another line, this one in roman letters.

THE INFINITY.

He was pretty sure that meant *boundless*. It was probably the name of this straight sword Enhanced Armament in the system. Rolling the name around over and over beneath his silver mask, he slipped a few steps to the right and looked up at the other pedestal.

If he was forced to describe it, he'd say that sitting on this one was a Western design full-body defensive tool.

Armor.

It wasn't anything oppressive. In a general VRMMORPG, it would likely be classed as light armor. The helmet was a crown type, and the chest, shoulder, and arm parts were also minimal. The lower body was nothing but knee-high boots. But there wasn't a hint of cheapness to it. Like the sword, the entirety of the armor was mirrored silver, and concealed an incredible density of information that seemed like it would repel any and every attack. Even the air around it looked like it was warped somehow. Compared with this, even the armor of metallic Chrome Falcon was a toy.

Suppressing a sigh, he checked the plate on this one.

The overall design was the same as that of the sword pedestal. The upper part was a bas-relief of the Big Dipper. However, the larger star in this one was the sixth from the left. The kanji carved into it was again two characters, maybe read as *kaiyou*. And again, he didn't understand their meaning.

And then the English name at the very bottom was—

THE DESTINY. He was pretty sure this meant…*fate*.

Once he had read that far, he took a step back and finally allowed himself to exhale heavily. Both were probably Enhanced Armaments in the top class in the Accelerated World. Sword and armor.

If he reached a hand out and touched them, they'd be his. He had heard rumors about finding Enhanced Armaments sitting on pedestals like this in the depths of dungeons, albeit in small numbers, all over the Unlimited Neutral Field.

But what bothered him were the portals shimmering immediately behind the pedestals. Obviously, these had to be related. In all probability, when he touched one item or the other, the portal would activate at the same time and forcefully return him to the real world.

In addition to the items being the activation key, these portals were likely one-time use only, and while one was activated, the neighboring pedestal was probably locked. In other words, an individual or a group could obtain either the sword or the armor, but not both at once. At any rate, he was faced with an either/or choice.

Just a few minutes earlier, he had thought just having made it in and gotten back out was plenty, but given this new development, he couldn't come to such complete terms with the idea that he was unable to refrain from stretching his hand out toward the pedestals. His real-world age was eight, after all, and even adding in the time he had spent accelerated, he was still only thirteen.

From the placement, it was clear that he couldn't use either portal unless he touched one of the armaments. But which one?

He had no doubt that he would become markedly stronger than he was at that moment, whether he equipped the sword or the armor. But it was meaningless if Chrome Falcon alone was

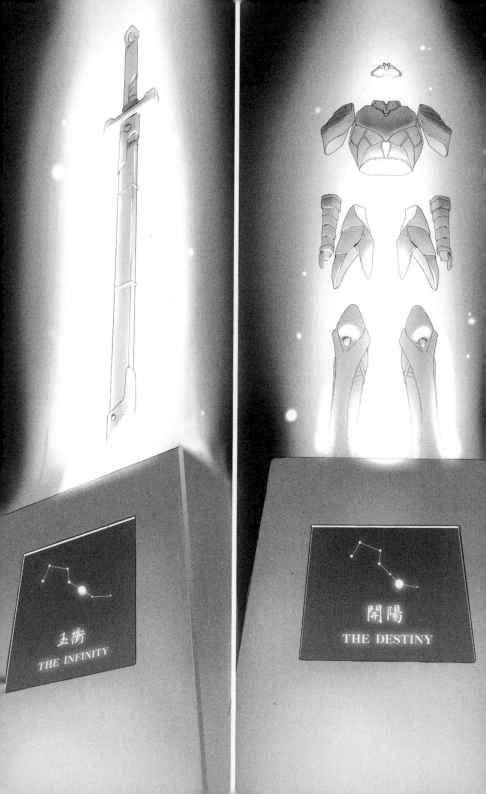

玉衡
THE INFINITY

開陽
THE DESTINY

enhanced. He needed to think about this with the assumption of tag-teaming with Saffron Blossom. The meaning of his existence was to protect her. So then the sword. Becoming any harder than he already was as a metal color, a defensive type to begin with, was gilding the lily. He turned toward the INFINITY pedestal, and legs that had begun to take a step toward it froze on the spot.

He had to protect Blossom. If that was his sole desire, then there was an even more optimal solution. A way to remove her weak point, her thin armor, and make it so that she could endure the fiercest of concentrated attacks.

Clenching his right hand into a fist, he banished the reluctance and desire that beat hard once in the center of his chest before stretching a hand out to the pure silver armor enshrined on the pedestal to the right.

Before he even had the chance to realize that his fingertips were touching it, a purple system message scrolled through the center of his vision along with a light sound effect.

YOU ACQUIRED AN ENHANCED ARMAMENT: THE DESTINY.

The armor transformed into particles of light and dissolved while the blue light of the portal spread out and engulfed Chrome Falcon.

Blackout.

Spotlight.

In the center of the circle of white light, a comfortable although not particularly large room pops up out of the gloom.

The walls and the floor are well-polished wood. In one corner, a black cooking stove. Hazy steam rises up from the pot on top. On the wall on the opposite side is a large bed. And on top of the snow-white sheets, two human shapes are seated side by side.

But they are not flesh-and-blood people. The body of one is enveloped in a dark silver armor. And the other's entire form is a bright golden yellow, like the sun. The design of its short hair, shoulders, and hips is reminiscent of a flower that has just started to open.

Facing the silver figure hanging his head—a child being scolded—the golden yellow flower lightly raises an adorable fist.

"Honestly! Are you stupid?!"

She rapped his helmet sharply over and over. Pulling his neck in as far as it went, he made the same excuse he had already made repeatedly.

"Wh-which is why it was just supposed to be a test at first!"

"Then you should've come back the same way right away! Why would you just wander into the palace like that?!"

"B-because my HP was already pretty low...And I wasn't sure if I'd actually regenerate on the outside again if I Blinked from the inside of the valley and died halfway, okay...?"

"Even if you did regenerate on the inside, your HP gauge would be totally recovered, so you could've just jumped back to the out-side with Blink!"

"Unh...You're totally right, but..."

He had absolutely no hope of winning over his more logical partner in this sort of back-and-forth. As he dropped his shoul-ders dejectedly, Chrome Falcon heard a heavy sigh, followed by a slender hand stroking the top of his helmet slowly, instead of another punch.

"Well, I have to give you credit for being adventurous enough to try and get into the Castle, and for having the nerves to go so deep and come back alive. You really did good, Fal."

At this praise, he raised his head, feeling his chest tighten unconsciously. In front of him, a gentle smile spread across Saf-fron Blossom's sweet face mask.

"Th-thanks, Fron," he murmured, staring into her light blue eye lenses.

Blossom shrugged as if embarrassed, pulled her hand away from Chrome Falcon's head, and stood up.

"I'll put on some tea. Oh! And I'll cut some cake to celebrate your safe return. I bought a really tasty one from the food shop in the Ginza Area back then."

He watched his partner trot off to the other side of the room, where the kitchen was, and felt any number of emotions rise up in his chest once more, rendering him unable to speak.

After years—naturally, in Accelerated-World time—of hunting Enemies together, they had finally been able to buy the key to this small house in a corner of the Bay Area in the Unlimited Neutral Field, the reclaimed land called Odaiba in the real world. For Falcon, using those points to level up or buy an Enhanced Armament was indeed appealing, but seeing how moved Blossom was the first time he opened the door to their new residence instantly banished all such childish desires from his heart.

Since then, this room, with the household items they had brought in bit by bit over the course of nearly a year, was for Falcon now a more comfortable space than his own bedroom in the real world. Unlike the condo he lived in essentially alone, no brothers or sisters and parents working late every day, Blossom was always here in this room. Although sleeping in the bed together had unsurprisingly been fairly awkward for a while.

Why had she been so fixated on buying a house? She'd told him a month ago in real-world time.

Saffron Blossom had been born with an incurable disease that caused reduced performance of the mitochondria in her cells. Since it was genetic, the most cutting-edge micromachine treatment was ineffective. Although at present, her symptoms were on the level of tiring easily and getting headaches, she would eventually have attacks of seizure and paralysis, and at some point, lesions would spread to her heart. She had even been told by doctors that she most likely wouldn't reach adulthood. The reason she had been continuously wearing a Neurolinker since she was a newborn, a device that had only just come onto the market then, was to keep constant watch over her symptoms.

In the same bed they were sitting on now, Blossom had grinned brightly at Falcon, unable to do anything but listen with wide-open eyes.

"Don't make that face, Fal. Even if something does happen, we're

talking ten or fifteen years from now. And we have Brain Burst, don't we? In this Accelerated World, I can live a proper full life, like everyone else. I'll buy a cute and wonderful house and live there forever with the person I love, just the two of us…"

Blossom laughed, almost embarrassed, and when he accidentally asked, "Is that me?" she slapped at him.

He was happy. But at the same time, he felt a faint fear. *Am I really enough?*—that fear. *Is Chrome Falcon really qualified to share the rest of Blossom's life with her?* That fear, too. The fact that he had taken on the extremely reckless challenge of infiltrating the Castle by himself was also because of that fear, which sat in the depths of his heart.

Which was why now that he had come back alive from the place, he couldn't help but turn toward his partner in profile at the small table before him on which she had readied cake and tea and ask, "Hey, Fron? Why…Why me? I don't have any real abilities. And I'm basically half-baked even for a metal color. Why'd you choose me?"

For a moment, Blossom looked puzzled before she abruptly pursed her lips tightly. "Aah, you forgot! Look, Fal, you're the one who invited me to team up originally! You started talking to me in a superquiet voice in the Gallery, and I had to ask you to repeat yourself I don't know how many times."

"What…W-was that how it went?"

Flustered, he dug around in his memory, but that incident was already almost five years ago in experienced time. Even so, in the distant scene that drifted hazily back to life in the back of his head, it was indeed him speaking to Blossom first. *You really had some nerve, huh?* A virtual sweat broke out all over his avatar's body as Blossom set down the teapot and walked over to him, slapping her hand down on his shoulder.

"So then I'll ask you, Fal. Why'd you choose me? I didn't have any techniques at all back then, and I was being hunted by the high-firepower types. So why?"

How can I tell you? That I knew you were the one the moment I saw you?

But he apparently couldn't hide the strong emotions in his heart from his tag-team partner of so many years. Smiling gently, the sun-colored avatar wrapped slender arms around his helmet and hugged it to her chest.

"Me, too. I thought the same thing. There's no other reason or anything, and I've never once regretted it...Now let's have some tea. And then let's go look at the ocean. It's a Twilight stage outside right now, so I'm sure the sunset will be beautiful."

Blackout.

Spotlight.

In the center of the white ring of light, two human figures appear, standing huddled close together. Chrome silver and saffron yellow.

The light that follows highlights a broad vista. The gentle ocean, the sun sinking into the horizon. The reflected light of the setting sun glittering between the waves strongly resembles the colors enveloping the two who stand watching it.

The night view of Tokyo Bay seen from Akatsuki Futo Park in the southwest corner of Odaiba was so beautiful, it almost made him wonder if it was really a 3-D graphic reconstructed from social camera images.

However, he could see none of the airplanes that would have been taking off and landing nonstop at Haneda Airport on the opposite shore if this had been the real world; in their place, a large pterosaur Enemy danced lazily in the orange sky. Blowing salt water up high into the air along the coast of the bay was not a whale, but rather a plesiosaur.

Every time he looked out on the vast Unlimited Neutral Field like this with Blossom, he simply couldn't stop himself from thinking.

Just what exactly was this world created for? And what purpose is there in inviting only young children into it?

With his elementary school–student knowledge, he couldn't even imagine the total amount of money that would have to be spent on building and managing such an enormous system. And up to that point, the so-called BB players had not paid a single yen in fees. There were all kinds of rumors that it was maybe market research for a major game company or a PR company's new marketing method, but if that were the case, the program was distributed to far too few people to produce any real results.

About a year earlier, a hundred or so children had received client packages from an untraceable transmission source. Of these, a mere 30 percent had been able to make it to level two, where they could exercise the right to copy and install an unlimited number of times as a guardian—thirty people. From there, it had spread out again in the community of game-loving children as a medium, and although at present it had expanded to a total of five hundred people centered in the south of the twenty-three wards of Tokyo, this was still a scale so small as to make no sense for a business sales strategy.

Right from the start, the requirements to become a player of this Brain Burst game were too strict. There weren't that many children who had been constantly wearing a Neurolinker since immediately after birth, allowing them long hours of full-dive experience. At any rate, the Brain Burst program was equipped with an installation compatibility checker module, so players could secretly check whether or not someone met the requirements in the background before sending them a file through a wired or ad hoc connection. Falcon hadn't found a single person around him who qualified. And so, although he was already at level five, he had recently abandoned all efforts to become a "parent."

Why? This parallel universe containing infinities in terms of space and time, what was it for...

"Are you thinking about it again, Fal?" Saffron Blossom murmured suddenly, coming to stand beside him. He blinked rapidly beneath his silver mask and cut off his rambling thoughts.

"Oh…yeah…I don't really feel it in the general field, but looking out at the Unlimited Field like this, I can't help but wonder. About where I—where *we're* being taken."

"…I know. I get that feeling…I think. Lately, when I talk to my friends or my family in the real world, sometimes, they give me these weird looks. I don't mean for anything to change, but without even knowing it, I'm using these words and things I didn't used to use…"

Blossom leaned into him helplessly, and he put a hand on her shoulder to pull her closer.

"There's no way around it," he continued. "I mean, we've spent—no, *lived* five years in this world already. We've seen a lot of things in that time, talked about a lot of stuff, had a lot of thoughts. If we're just talking the age of our souls, then we're way past sixth grade already. But…it's not all bad, you know. The old me would have been too embarrassed to even be in the same place with a girl like you, much less talk to you."

"Ha-ha! From where I'm standing, you're still very much a kid, Mr. Peregrine." Blossom smiled slightly, but her cherubic face mask was soon colored with sorrow again. "Hey, Fal? You hear about…about what happens to players who lose all their points and have the BB program uninstalled?"

He froze instantly at these murmured words, but then quickly released that tension and took pains to make sure his voice was level as he replied, "I'm sure it's just a rumor. I mean, if you're talking about that thing where players who lose the program also lose all their memories of the Accelerated World…I mean, it's totally impossible. They can't just manipulate a person's memories like that."

"But if we're talking about that, the technology to accelerate your thoughts a thousand times, I mean, I couldn't believe it at first. To be honest, I don't fully understand the mechanism even now. Which is why I thought maybe deleting memories might be true, too…"

Given that his own grasp on the fundamental technology

behind Brain Burst was also fairly tenuous, Falcon could only sit in silence.

Both of them were first-generation BB players, players with no "parents," thought to number fewer than twenty already now, and neither had ever had a child of their own. So they hadn't had any opportunity to actually verify the rumor that players who lost the program also lost their memories.

Even if they did have such an opportunity, however, getting proof was likely difficult. Because according to the rumor, those who left the Accelerated World lost interest in and detailed knowledge of Brain Burst rather than completely losing all related memories. A manipulation of the mind with a buffer, as it were, that didn't create a blank spot in the player's memory or make too much of a strange impression on the people around them. This might have been a more terrifying measure than a complete erasure of the memories.

One day, a comrade from the same Legion or a partner bound by the strong bond of parent and child suddenly forgets themselves—or rather, they don't; they simply no longer show any interest in the whole thing. They treat all those other people as acquaintances they don't care one way or the other about. If that was how it ended, maybe it would have been better to be made into a complete stranger. At least then, there would still be the slim chance that you could meet and become friends once more…

These chilly thoughts suddenly shook his avatar. And then a whispered voice reached his ears:

"Fal. The thing is, I—in a little while, I think I might make a child."

"What…"

He stared down at his partner's face, her words completely unexpected. Blossom smiled for a moment as if embarrassed, but regained her composure soon enough and started speaking quietly.

"I never had the confidence that I could take care of a child, so I never managed to take the plunge, but lately, my win ratio in the general duels has stabilized, and I've collected a fair bit of know-how about fighting Enemies, right? So that means that even if my child's in danger points-wise, I should be able to support them to a certain extent. Still, that doesn't mean I'd spoil them and transfer them for free, y'know? Maybe like they could pay me back when they hit level four and can go hunting Enemies?"

"Uh…Uh-huh, right…"

He nodded as he thought about how Blossom would for sure be a strict, but kind and solid mom—or rather, "parent."

Turning her gaze away from Falcon and out toward the commanding view of the Pacific Ocean beyond Tokyo Bay, Saffron Blossom said something even more surprising. "And, like, this is way, way in the future, but I'm thinking of starting a Legion one day."

"Huh? You're gonna do the Territories?" he asked, flustered, and her short, golden yellow hair swung wildly from side to side.

"No, no. This area around Odaiba's been a blank zone all this time, so maybe I'll just make a territory announcement, but that's not my goal. I don't want to make a fighting Legion…I dunno, more like a cooperative Legion."

"Cooperative? Like everyone helping each other?"

"Yeah, like that. I said before that if my child was in trouble, I'd give them points and then they'd pay me back one day, right? I was kind of thinking I could maybe turn that into a larger-scale system."

His partner's words had at last gone beyond the realm of his comprehension, and he cocked his head deeply to one side. Blossom whirled around to face him and took both of his hands.

"Look, Fal," she said, the look on her face even more serious. "We've been a tag team since we were level one, right? Both of us lost ourselves in the fight, and we rose up to levels two, three, four. And before you know it, we're level five. But now I think we were incredibly lucky. I mean…it's not something I especially like to think about, but the flip side of us leveling up is who knows how many BB players losing all their points and leaving the Accelerated World…"

"……"

It was just like she said. He personally had only seen that instant when someone's points dropped to zero a few times, but it was a definite fact that a mere eleven months after the game started, four out of five of the first generation had already disappeared.

When he was unable to even nod at the weight of her words, the small hands gripping his wrists moved gently, as if to comfort him. At the same time came a soft murmur.

"Sorry, Fal. It's not like I especially regret anything. Brain Burst's a fighting game; someone has to win, someone has to lose. I'm not trying to deny that basic principle. But…But, you know, the idea of my points dropping to zero, of losing this program, my memories, everything, of never being able to come to this world again…It's just too harsh. I've seen so many people with only a few points left, and they didn't look like they were having fun at all. And if it's not fun anymore, it's not a game…"

Maybe that harshness is exactly what the mysterious game developer wanted. The thought flitted through his mind, but he didn't say it out loud. Instead, he asked gently, "So…you want to make a cooperative Legion?"

"…Yeah. We'll save up a lot of points and then lend them to people about to lose theirs. Once they're stabilized, they can participate in Enemy hunts to pay them back. These five years, I've learned all the tricks of hunting, so much so that I hate it. As long as we have this know-how, we should be able to seriously reduce the risk of accidents in Enemy fights."

"But…but, like." Trying desperately to understand this plan of hers, he very timidly asked, "If all the players joined this cooperative system, then there wouldn't be anyone losing all their points anymore, so the points players spend on acceleration and leveling up would just come from Enemy hunting? Is something like that possible?"

"It can be done. I'm sure we can do it…No, we *have* to do it," she said, a serious light he had never seen before shining in her pale blue eye lenses, so reminiscent of the spring sky. "I—The other day, I heard a terrible rumor. Some Legions are looking for kids with acceleration compatibility at arcades and amusement parks, and once they find one, they forward them the BB program."

"I-it's a bit crude, for sure, but wouldn't that work as a way to increase the number of players?"

"You don't get it. They're not taking those kids they make their children under their wings or anything. They don't tell them what Brain Burst is, they just fight duel after duel directing or on a local net, and steal every one of their child's initial hundred points. And then the child's forced into an uninstall…"

"Wh…" He swallowed hard. This wasn't canvassing. This was just hunting, wasn't it? Not Enemies, but players.

"If it's true," Blossom said tensely, staring at the speechless Falcon from extremely close up, "then it's just wrong. Even if the system lets it happen, it's absolutely wrong. I don't have any real power yet, but…But I have to do something. Bit by bit even, I have to do what I can. I don't know how long it'll take, but I'll make a child, try out a point loan structure, start up a Legion… so that someday, everyone in this world can laugh and have fun with this game."

Before he knew it, he was holding Blossom tightly. "I'll help," he murmured earnestly to the slender avatar in his arms. "Although I'm the one with no power, just a tiny metal color…For you, for this world, I'll do everything I can. Brain Burst is a fighting game, and games should be fun. I-I've had fun fighting alongside you up to now, Fron. Ever since I met you, I've looked forward to tomorrow coming. I want to share that with other players."

"Yeah. Yeah, me, too," Blossom replied in a shaky voice. "I've had fun with you, Fal. And we're going to keep having fun for a long time, I know it. Let's make it more fun together. I know the two of us can do it."

He hugged her tightly once more and then gently pushed her

shoulders back. He held up a finger to indicate she should wait a second, before touching his own health gauge in the top left of his field of view and opening a menu window. He ran his finger through his storage and turned a single item into an object.

A card that glittered silver like a mirror. Most items you could get in the Unlimited Neutral Field were in the shape of cards like this at first. Enhanced Armament was no exception; when you got some in dungeons or from Enemy drops, it was transferred to your storage sealed in a card. Ownership was set the first time someone equipped it.

He took the card from the window and held it out to Blossom.

Small letters were carved onto the surface—THE DESTINY. The silver armor he had obtained in the depths of the Castle, likely the world's best.

"Fron, I want you to have this. I'm sure it'll make your dreams come true."

Blossom raised timid hands and placed them gently on the card.

At that moment, they had no way of knowing yet that this incredible power would distort both of their destinies…

Blackout.

Spotlight.

In the circle of white light, a single slender figure appears.

Coloring its entire body is a saffron yellow reminiscent of sunlight in spring. However, a shade that did not previously adorn it can be spied here and there. A mirrorlike silver glitters on the forehead and chest, legs and arms.

The short hair, in the shape of a bud beginning to flower, hangs forward, toward the ground. Both arms are spread out to her sides, and the slim legs stretch out loosely, helplessly. She is able to remain unwaveringly upright in such an unstable position because something restrains her from behind.

Thin, something clipped from a large board, matte black—a

ENHANCED ARMAMENT
THE DESTINY

cross. Perhaps it emits some kind of magnetic force; the saffron-colored figure is stuck fast.

The illumination spreads gradually to finally light up her surroundings.

The ground, lustrous, greenish, metallic. Bizarre, similarly metallic insects rustle as they squirm along. The cross stands at the bottom of a large basin, an indent like a mortar without its pestle. Very close by, enormous pits open gaping black mouths, the sides wet with clear mucous.

The spotlight widens even farther outward.

At the edge of the basin, about thirty meters in diameter, several dozen human figures form a circle. Not moving nor speaking, they keep silent and stare at the cross at the bottom of the depression. Almost as if they know something is about to happen. They hold their breath, open their eyes wide, and fear this something—or eagerly await it.

From among these silhouettes, a single one falls to the ground.

A small body with a silver luster tinged black. Slim limbs, round helmet. Perhaps trying desperately to stand again, the sharp, tapered fingers dig deep into the metallic earth. However, the figure cannot move. He is restrained on both sides, pinched between two thin, matte-black panels, resembling the cross at the bottom of the basin.

The metallic insects crawling around sluggishly abruptly begin running in all directions. They crawl into the creases like the gills of a living creature that cover the ground and disappear instantly.

Zrr zrr zrr. Zrr zrr zrr. The low, weighty sound of vibration echoes from the enormous pit at the center of the depression.

"Stop...Stop! Stooooooooop!!"

He didn't know anymore if he had screamed the word dozens of times or hundreds, only to have it swallowed up in vain each time by the sky in the Unlimited Neutral Field.

Countless thin scratches were carved out of the ground in

front of him, where he clawed at it with his fingers. But no matter how much force he put into it, he could move only from the elbow. Although the jet-black panels squeezing his arms from the shoulders didn't have any thickness to speak of, they clamped tightly against the avatar of Chrome Falcon with an absolute pressure, like an enormous vise.

More incredibly, the player controlling these two panels had made the inky black cross appear, far away at the bottom of the depression, to restrain Saffron Blossom at the same time.

Blossom hung limply, no longer having the strength to move. And with good reason: The intensity of the agony she had tasted in this past hour or so far surpassed even the sum total of all the pain ever experienced in the Accelerated World up to that point.

And the fierce rage and despair that raced through Falcon's mind was also something he had never before in his life experienced.

"Stop...Stop, please stop..." He pushed a cracking voice out from between clenched teeth. At the same time, he dug out new parallel lines in the hard ground of the Purgatory stage with his avatar's fingers. But he couldn't move. This sense of helplessness further deepened his despair.

He felt the eerie vibration in his body. It was coming again.

That *something* was crawling out from a hole, more than two meters in diameter, at the center of the basin next to the cross holding Blossom up. A dozen tapered tentacles appeared first, waving back and forth. These were followed by two rows of red lights shining in the depths of the darkness. These lights—eyes—instantly made onlookers feel the creature's insatiable hunger. The countless eyes glittered fiercely the instant they detected Blossom, only steps away.

An utterly enormous worm-type monster then leapt out of the pit with a wet sound, scattering droplets of mucous. The hell snake Jormungand, a Legend-class Enemy, the strongest beings in the Accelerated World outside of the Four Gods that guarded the four gates of the Castle.

This type of Enemy appeared only in stages that were in part organic, such as Purgatory, Plague, or Corroded Forest, and if a player happened to stumble across one, their fate was essentially sealed. However, since its Territory as a Legend was only a small crater, thirty meters in diameter, even if you were killed by it once, it was possible to get away in the ten or so seconds before Jormungand appeared again after you were regenerated. As long as something—or someone—wasn't deliberately blocking your movement.

Jormungand approached the head of Saffron Blossom hung up on the black cross, completely unable to move. Beneath lens-like red eyes, neatly arranged in two rows for a total of sixteen, there was a circular mouth—a predation hole—surrounded by long tentacles. It was filled out by layers of sawlike teeth, and a viscous fluid dripped unceasingly from the bottomless hole as it shot out toward the slender avatar. Saffron's body shuddered momentarily; her head sagged even farther.

"Stop…Stooooooop!!" But there was no reason the inhuman Enemy would even hear the hoarse, unconscious cry from under Falcon's helmet.

The snake's meter-wide mouth stretched open above Blossom's head. The mucous it secreted continued to ooze out without pause, and white smoke puffed up from the golden yellow armor it fell upon. The fluid had the effect of temporarily and significantly reducing an avatar's physical defense power. The silver armor Blossom was clad in suddenly lost its sheen. As if waiting for this, Jormungand swallowed her torso wholesale with the cross.

Before his eyes, his view dyed a light red with the scorching heat of his emotions, the partner he had lived a lifetime with shrieked in endless agony.

The power of the Enhanced Armament Destiny far exceeded his expectations.

It rendered physical attacks essentially ineffective—slicing, hitting, piercing, shooting, exploding, all of it. When it came to energy attacks as well, it reflected laser types. Resistant against cold, heat, electricity. Only corrosion, the natural Enemy of metal armor, could not be repelled, but there were basically no duel avatars with that kind of attack anyway. Invincible, without exaggeration; its defensive power was almost frightening.

However, when he thought about it, in theory, only someone who had broken through the absolutely invulnerable superclass Enemies, the Four Gods, could obtain this armor, so it was probably the final item in this game Brain Burst. Aided by chance and luck, and some system flaws, he had managed to acquire it now, when the game was likely still in the opening stages. So it wasn't strange at all that it would exhibit such overwhelming power.

Even its owner herself, Saffron Blossom, was afraid of the power of the Destiny, so great that it could destroy the balance of the game itself. At any rate, the full-charge special attacks of red and blue types, which had up to that point taken essentially all of her health gauge in one blow, now carved away only the merest hint of damage, even with a direct hit. After she had appeared in just a few general duels, talk had raced around the Accelerated World, and Blossom had gotten a flood of offers to buy the armor and invitations to join powerful Legions. And of course, much cursing about how it was a fraud, she was a cheat, et cetera et cetera.

If this had been back when she had just been fighting tag-team duel after duel with Falcon, Blossom would probably have sealed the armor away or disposed of it.

But she now had an impossible dream. She wanted to start up a cooperative Legion to prevent total point loss, remove the brutal death game elements from the Accelerated World, so that everyone could have fun fighting—or, better yet, she wanted to make a place where they could *live*.

Given that Saffron had been sentenced to die before reaching adulthood and had accepted that destiny within herself, perhaps this was her own secret struggle. She wanted to scatter seeds over the desolate land of the Accelerated World and make flowers bloom. Maybe this had been her dream all this time, since the moment she'd become a BB player.

To actually make the burst point–lending system that was the heart of the cooperative Legion work, she first needed a sufficient points pool. And the fighting power to keep in check those participants of malicious intent planning to skip out on the bill who were sure to appear.

For Blossom, the Destiny and its overwhelming power, plenty even for Enemy hunting, never mind duels, was nothing other than a ticket to the realization of this dream. Although wearing the armor did cut back on the number of challenges from outside, Blossom and Falcon repulsed without exception the many warriors who did come at them.

On the day that they had managed to crush even one of the Pure Colors, said to be the strongest in that world—albeit two against one—Blossom finally announced her own plan to the broader Accelerated World. At the same time, she started widely recruiting people wishing to join the new Legion.

And then yesterday. More than thirty BB players had jointly signed and sent a message saying that they wanted to hear more of the details.

The pair was delighted, but they felt a hint of unease. Because those players had requested the Unlimited Neutral Field as a place to meet and talk. They wanted to confirm that it was really possible to safely hunt Enemies, and Blossom and Falcon basically agreed with their reasoning, but they couldn't know what would happen in that field. In the worst-case scenario, all thirty of the signatories would attack at once.

But even assuming they did, equipped with the Destiny, it was unthinkable that Blossom would be killed with one blow. So they gave themselves some insurance by specifying a meeting place near a leave point. If it was a trap, they could immediately leap into the portal.

Still, they couldn't say this plan was foolproof. Direct attacks weren't the only abilities duel avatars had. If anyone gathered at the meeting had some kind of obstruction attack like Blossom herself did, such as freezing legs or stealing vision, there was a possibility that they would be prevented from escaping through the portal. However, they dared to overlook this risk. Among the names in the message were more than a few old acquaintances. They couldn't really believe that all these people were conspiring together to set a malicious trap. They didn't want to believe it.

Just in case, they checked the place for the day's meeting—a portal in a building corresponding to the Shibaura parking area on the north side of the Rainbow Bridge in the real world—from afar first. Among the more than thirty avatars already gathered were indeed the faces noted in the message.

As Blossom and Falcon stepped out from under the elevated Shuto expressway and started walking, heaving sighs of relief, two thin black panels suddenly appeared from beneath their feet.

An incredible pressure held them categorically in place.

"Stop…Please stop! Why…Why would you…!!"

The screams poured out of him unawares as Chrome Falcon stared at the terrifying snake, worlds removed from the fabled image of the romantic concept of a legend, burying its countless fangs in his beloved partner.

The question was addressed to the dozens of BB players standing along the edge of the depression that was the snake's nest.

The majority were faces he knew, and there were several he was friendly enough with to make amiable conversation with if they happened to be in the Gallery together. Naturally, he had dueled them any number of times, but his wins and losses were about fifty–fifty. He couldn't remember doing anything that would cause anyone to hate him so much as to set up a trap this cruel.

But they maintained their silence, not even glancing in the direction of Falcon pinned to the ground. Their attention was focused completely on the tragedy unfolding at the bottom of the basin. A similar awe and shuddering fear colored all their face masks. But that wasn't the whole of it. Falcon felt strongly that the terror on their faces masked something very, very unpleasant underneath.

Suddenly, he heard a low, smooth voice from behind him to the right. "Sorry, Falcon. I at least will respond on their behalf."

The owner of the voice that so vividly reminded him of some schoolteacher somewhere was the very person controlling the two thin panels and the cross, restraining Falcon and Blossom. Falcon didn't know his name. He had never seen him before in the Accelerated World, not even once, this duel avatar and its bizarre form—pieces of a black sheet cut out and stood up in the shape of a person.

"The power of that Enhanced Armament is too far beyond the norms of this world, given that it is still in its dawn. You no doubt experienced this fact directly yourself via the duels you've fought these last few days?"

Even the oldest BB players could only be in second grade in the real world. Having worn a Neurolinker continuously from immediately after birth was a requirement for the installation of Brain Burst, and consumer Neurolinkers had gone on sale the year that Falcon and the others in the "first generation" had been born.

However, the tone of the jet-black layered avatar could hardly be thought to be that of a child. It sounded even older than the young man in his twenties who was Falcon's homeroom teacher in the real world. Fighting back against the pressure of the thin panels, Falcon focused on pushing his voice out.

"Then…we'll dispose of the armor in the shop. All the points we get for it, we distribute equally to everyone. That's gotta be good…There's no need to do all this. There isn't, right…!!"

"Unfortunately, with that method, the Enhanced Armament will remain in the shop. We very well might see someone come forward to obtain it and once again destroy the balance of the game. That armor must be returned to where it was originally. The only method of achieving that end, Falcon, is for a power other than that of a player to eliminate the owner."

At the same time as the infinitely calm voice related all this to him, Saffron Blossom's avatar crumbled into countless tiny pieces in Jormungand's mouth and was smashed to bits. A pillar of golden yellow light rose up high into the sky, drawing out a momentary grave marker before disappearing.

The hell snake, having butchered the intruder in a single bite, slithered back into its nest, waving its tentacles in a seemingly satisfied manner. The jet-black cross also sank soundlessly into a thin shadow on the ground.

And then all that was left was a small saffron yellow light. According to the rules of the Unlimited Neutral Field, Blossom would regenerate in that location after being placed in a ghost state for an hour. She should have, at least.

But to his left, from a place Falcon couldn't see, his view blocked by a black panel, a stealthy voice whispered, "Resurrect By Compassion."

Riding on a voice so pure and clean it almost couldn't belong to a human being, tiny particles of light flowed out into space and danced down to the bottom of the basin. The instant they touched the golden yellow "embers," a pillar of dazzling white light poured down from the sky, contracted and condensed to take shape as a lone avatar: Saffron Blossom. The cross appeared at the feet of the slender silhouette as she very nearly crumpled to the ground, to hold her in place once more and stand her up right next to the snake's nest.

They had already been through the same process countless times. The number of burst points a player lost in death in an Enemy fight was fixed at ten, so the points she had built up through successive wins this last little while weren't so easily exhausted. A never-ending cycle of cruel death and even crueler rebirth.

There were other instances before this of an avatar plunging deep into the territory of a Legend and being killed over and over, unable to escape, until they lost all their points. BB players fearfully called this phenomenon Unlimited Enemy Death. However, the layered black avatar and the others who had set this trap for Falcon and Blossom were deliberately bringing this phenomenon about with the black cross and the white light. As a result, it wasn't death, but rather a passive execution. Unlimited Enemy Kill.

…Please, just stop already. Having lost the power to even raise his voice in supplication, he simply prayed beneath his silver surface.

In the Unlimited Neutral Field, the sensation of pain from damage was increased, so that it was essentially the same as in the real world. Each time Blossom was killed by Jormungand, she would have experienced intense pain equivalent to her body actually being ripped apart. Even if there wasn't a scratch on her real body, the memory of the pain carved into her consciousness—her soul—would never disappear.

No…

Perhaps the source of the pain she actually felt was not the monster's fangs, but rather the stares of the dozens of players standing around the basin. These people who were once friends, who'd called Blossom out with a fake message, dropped her into this trap, and simply watched as she was killed over and over again by a horrific snake.

More than just terror and panic, Fal could definitely catch hints of a vague excitement in their face masks. Part of it was that childish element of *I saw something scary.* But an ugly emotion much more real hid behind that, the exact same thing that bled through when a group in elementary school tried to expel someone different from them.

And simultaneously, in the exact same position as the student who simply watches from a safe distance, unable to do anything for the person being expunged, was Chrome Falcon.

If only he hadn't snuck into the Castle; if only he hadn't brought out the Enhanced Armament Destiny. If he hadn't given it to Blossom, none of this would be happening. He had caused all of this, and yet he was simply staring at the suffering figure of the person he loved, not a scratch on him.

The snake, detecting the forcefully resurrected Blossom, came slithering out from the depths of its nest once again to approach her. The shuffling vibration shook the ground, but the golden yellow avatar no longer even flinched. She hung lifelessly from the black cross, waiting for death for the nth time. Or else the total loss of points, the loss of memory that came after these deaths, under the name "the end."

I...

I'm making the same mistake again.

I won't pretend not to see anymore. I'm never going to avert my eyes again from someone hurt and alienated and about to lose their place. I promised myself that. And yet I can't do anything. I'm just losing someone important like this again...

"...No." His mental energy almost entirely exhausted, he squeezed a voice out. "No more. I'm sick of being the one left behind."

The two thin plates that held his avatar communicated to his senses an absolute weight, as if the world itself were fixing them there. Falcon had already been made quite aware of the fact that, no matter how much strength he mustered up, he could not move them even a millimeter. But there was still just one possibility for escape.

Break his own metallic armor instead of the jet-black panels.

"Unh...Ah...Aaaaaah..." Focusing on his creaking groan, he mustered up the last of his strength and pushed at the panels on either side with both arms. Pushed.

The chrome silver armor shrieked, unable to withstand the pressure. Up to that point, this was where he had given up. But now he ignored the feeling that he would be crushed and pushed harder.

"Now stop that, Falcon," the layered avatar murmured, sounding genuinely concerned. "We have no intention of eliminating you. Once our plan is complete, we intend to properly release you. It'll likely only be one or two more times, so perhaps you could please sit quietly until then."

"Shut...up...!!" He turned his revolt at the selfish remarks into physical power and hit at the black panels. Thin cracks finally began to race along the armor of both arms. A pain resembling sparks. But this was not enough. It was most certainly not enough.

"...Ngh...!!"

With a soundless howl he released as much force as he could, and in an instant the armor of both arms crumbled away with a hard metallic sound. A damage effect resembling fresh blood gushed out from his dark-gray basic-construct body, and a pain so intense it stopped his breath raced along his nerves. And then, along with a serious drop in his HP gauge, his special-attack gauge was charged about 20 percent. He shouted hoarsely, "Flash Blink!"

The avatar of Chrome Falcon transformed into substanceless quanta and finally escaped the restraint of the thin panels. At a speed that was basically teleporting, he charged forward and materialized fifteen meters away.

Before his eyes was the crucified Saffron Blossom and the head of Jormungand ready to bite into that slim body.

With the last ounce of his strength, he beat at the enormous snake with the sharp toes of his right foot, smashing one of its many red eyes. The injured eye oozed a viscous fluid, and the two-tiered HP gauge of his Enemy dropped a depressingly minuscule amount. But, perhaps caught off guard and surprised, the snake released Blossom and shook its head wildly.

As they were bathed in the enraged thundering roar of the Enemy, a faint voice weakly disturbed the air.

"Petal Shelter."

Several massive green petals were generated from the base of the cross to create a round bud that enclosed them both—Saffron Blossom's level-five special attack. The tough flower petals protected the interior completely against any and all attacks. Effect time: thirty seconds.

Inside the sphere full of a peaceful light-green glow, Falcon caught Blossom as she fell from the now-vanished cross with his armorless arms.

He crouched down with her and stared intently at the face of his beloved partner. These thirty seconds were the final moments given to them.

Once the petals disappeared, the cross would reappear to restrain them both. And then there was no doubt that Jormungand would follow its instincts and continue to butcher its prey, now increased in number.

Naturally, he had no regrets at having leapt into the place of his own death. But Falcon couldn't find the words he should say in this precious time. So he clenched his teeth, suppressed a howl, and kept staring intently at Blossom's face mask. So that he would absolutely never forget the sky color of her eyes even after he disappeared from the Accelerated World.

"...I'm sorry." The words spilled out, her voice hoarse. "I'm sorry, Fal. I...I was spoiled by your kindness. I wanted to get back the future that was stolen from me in the real world...And because of that, I pushed you to pretend to be an adult, too. This end...my own impatience made this happen. I'm sorry..."

Particles of clear light fell from Blossom's eye lenses one after the other and melted into the air.

You didn't. Not at all.

He wanted to tell her this, but a hot lump blocked his throat, and he couldn't speak. He at least shook his head hard. She caressed his helmet with her slender index finger.

"But, y'know...Believe this at least. I loved you. I've loved you since the moment we first met. I mean, I knew it right away. That you wanted to protect weak me. While everyone else was thinking about how to steal someone else's points, you...you alone..."

Without giving voice to the rest of that sentence, Blossom smiled. And then she moved her hand from his cheek to clasp his hand and guide it. To the center of her own chest, gruesomely torn up by Jormungand's teeth.

"A last request. Fal, make me disappear."

"...What..." He finally managed to utter just that, and Blossom smiled.

"I only have seven points left," she announced. "If I'm going to be killed by that Enemy and disappear from this world, then I want you to be the one to send me off. That way, Brain Burst might force an uninstall, but I'm sure I'll still be able to remember you. Even if all my memories are erased, at least you, forever."

Here, the effect time of the technique finally ended, and the green flower bud slowly began to melt away from the top. The howl of rage of the snake shattered the silence that had filled the sphere.

"...Fron." The time they had left was much too short for him to put into words all the thoughts that filled him. Pulling the destroyed, sunlight-colored avatar tightly to him with his left arm, Falcon whispered, with all the emotion in his heart, "Thanks."

Thanks. Thanks for taking the hand I offered. Thanks for teaching me so many things. Thanks for expanding my tiny world.

He stretched out the fingers of the hand she held. His sharply tapered fingertips, patterned after a bird of prey, touched down in the center of Saffron Blossom's chest, immediately above the critical point of her heart.

"...I love you."

As Falcon made this declaration, words he had never once been able to get out before, he thrust his sharp right hand downward.

His flat hand pierced deeper and deeper into the Destiny armor, rendered ineffective by Jormungand's fangs and digestive fluids.

Good-bye, Fal. I love you, you know.

Her voice became the faintest hint of a gentle breeze, flowing through his consciousness and disappearing.

Rather than breaking into a thousand fragments and scattering explosively, Saffron Blossom's avatar gently unraveled. Bathed in light the color of the warm spring sun, the slender silhouette split into countless ribbons and danced up into the sky. Those ribbons were reduced to even smaller threads of code, and then melted into the air before finally vanishing.

The final extinction phenomenon. The complete retreat from the Accelerated World of those who lost all their points.

When he came back to himself, his heart was empty.

Almost as if he himself had vanished, a sense of loss overcame the crouching Chrome Falcon as the countless fangs of Jormungand bit into his back with a screech.

In the Enemy's mouth, he was raised up high. Orange sparks scattered from his silver armor. *Kree, kreee.* His avatar's entire body squealed and groaned, and the health gauge in his field of view dropped before his eyes. At the same time, he was assaulted with a dizzying pain.

But he did not scream. Blossom had experienced this pain a practically infinite number of times. He gritted his teeth; he desperately endured it. In the distance in his hazy, warped vision, he could see the figures of the players standing in a circle.

In their eyes was a uniform surprise—and a hint of contempt. They were laughing scornfully at a fool who would senselessly throw his own life away.

It wasn't actually impossible for him to escape from this situation. All he had to do was use his special-attack gauge and do his Blink once again.

But he wasn't going to run anymore. Was there even any meaning in living?

Saffron Blossom was gone. He was alone again. Even if he did escape and live on, what would be the point in going back to his solo player life and fighting purposeless duels? If that was how it was going to be, he was better off devoured here by the snake like Blossom. Over and over and over again. Have his points run out like she did and be expelled from this world. Until that moment—

Abruptly, he noticed a small light flashing beneath the HP gauge being carved away and the special-attack gauge being filled up. The light followed precisely when he turned his head. It was a system message. The square cursor was trying to tell him something.

The instant he focused his hazy vision on that point, a row of text flowed soundlessly out from it.

YOU ACQUIRED AN ENHANCED ARMAMENT: THE DESTINY.

For a minute, he couldn't understand what this meant.

The message was telling him he had acquired an Enhanced Armament. And it didn't say GOT like it did for Enhanced Armament obtained in sealed card form, but ACQUIRED to indicate that he had become the owner of it. The subject was armor. The Disaster, which should have disappeared together with Saffron Blossom.

But why? The only methods of transferring an Enhanced Armament were to sell and rebuy it in the shop or hand it over in a direct duel.

Or wait. He'd heard vague rumors of one other way. When the player who owned the Enhanced Armament was eliminated from the Accelerated World, in a very small percentage of cases, the Enhanced Armament was transferred to the storage of the player who delivered the final blow.

He had no way of knowing now if Blossom had asked him to strike the final blow for her because she had been hoping for this result.

However, to Falcon, it felt like a final message from her.

Live. Live and fight.

Unconsciously, he murmured under his silver surface the default voice command to equip an Enhanced Armament.

"Equip...the Destiny."

An intense light like a small star was born, and the world was dyed platinum.

Thick silver armor covered his limbs and torso with a sharp metallic sound. The design was very different from when Blossom had been wearing the armor. By nature, Enhanced Armament would automatically adjust in size according to the stature of the duel avatar putting it on, but the way this armor changed went far beyond the realm of adjustment. It lost its former elegance and delicacy and took on the appearance of plate armor, all sharp edges.

The last piece, covering his head, was an samurai-style helmet rather than the original crown. Enclosing more than 80 percent of Falcon's body, the thick armor repelled with a fierce *clang* Jormungand's fangs as they were about to dig into his avatar.

The enormous Legend-ranked Enemy let out a cry of fury as it tried to devour Falcon once more, while at the same time, excreting a large quantity of transparent, viscous fluid from the glands between its fangs. This dripped down onto the silver armor and tried to steal its strength with a corrosion effect.

But the gleaming, mirrored silver clouded over for an instant before changing to a blackish chrome silver, as if a thin film had been peeled off and then resisted the corrosion. The new color matched that of Falcon's original armor perfectly.

Chrome fell basically in the middle of the metal color chart, between precious and base metals. It had only mediocre resistance to physical and special attacks. Its lone special characteristic was that it essentially completely repelled corrosion-type attacks.

The armor, a supposedly volitionless Enhanced Armament, was resisting the monster's mucous by absorbing the characteristics of the avatar wearing it—that was the only explanation for this phenomenon. Although Falcon couldn't have cared less about suppositions of this sort on the logical side of things.

As if guided by something, he raised both hands and seized the enormous fangs trying to pierce his chest, sending sparks flying everywhere.

Fwoosh! In the depths of his heart, something began to burn.

It was a feeling he had never had in the eleven months since landing in the Accelerated World, a subjective time of more than five years. Molded by and born from his deep affection for Saffron Blossom and his despair at her death: rage.

"Unh…Unnaaaah…" A husky groan spilled out from deep in his throat.

In the real world, too, Chrome Falcon was a child who did not get angry. He did what grown-ups told him to, he was careful to watch the faces of those around him, he lived with his own self on the back burner.

So when the class started bullying his best friend from kindergarten the instant they started at the same elementary school, he did nothing; he simply distanced himself from the other boy. He shut his eyes, plugged his ears, and waited for someone else to do something. But before that someone could appear, the boy who had been his good friend was gone.

He really should have gotten angry at least. At the children who instigated the bullying. At the teacher who was oblivious to it. At himself pretending not to have seen anything. But, unable to do even that, he pushed and shoved until all his memories and feelings were the size of a pebble and then buried that in a deep place.

"Unh…ah…aaaaaah…" Falcon's cry continued, his voice warped. He felt like now the pebble had fine cracks in it, and something incandescent was gushing out.

All ten of his fingers transformed into massive talons with a *chang*. The sharp tips creaked as they dug into Jormungand's fangs. The edges of the armor from his arms to his shoulders became even more tapered and increased in volume.

Now he understood why the thirty people who had sent the fake Legion entry message had betrayed him and Blossom and set this trap. Wasn't it because they wanted to get this Enhanced Armament, maybe thinking they could cheat with it?

Saffron Blossom's not like us. She had the strength to protect her ideals and make them a reality.

"But…you…"

All of you, you're BB players; you had to have been treated more or less like aliens in the real world. You had to have been shunned by some group and come to this Accelerated World with that hurt carved into your soul. And yet you still shun someone else? You make a circle around someone different from you and throw rocks at them?

"For people like you...Fron was...trying to make...a place to belong..." As he squeezed this rage out from his depths, his avatar's hands took on a weak light. Not energy to illuminate anything. A negative fluctuation to steal heat, light.

An aura of darkness.

This kind of continuous effect was supposed to cloak a duel avatar only when it was using its gauge and activating its special attack. And yet Falcon's special-attack gauge stayed at essentially full charge; it didn't drop a single pixel.

But he continued to spit out his strangled speech, unaware of this abnormality.

"Fron was...just trying...to make this world a place...where you could always...play, where you didn't have to...be scared of losing all your points...that's all..."

Before he even knew it, Falcon had buried his ten talons deep into Jormungand's fangs and pulled them completely free of his body. The monster blinked two rows of eyes and twisted itself up and writhed violently, but the avatar's arms didn't budge beneath their aura of darkness.

"That's all...she wanted!!"

A roar like vomiting blood.

Deep in his mind, Falcon heard the sound of the pebble of frozen feelings being smashed to bits.

Rage. Any- and everything he had suppressed all this time—from before he could remember until this very moment today—exploded and ran wild within his avatar before becoming a shadowy aura and being released to the outside world.

Pulsations of darkness shook and cracked the snake's thick skin, as though they were an actual physical phenomenon, splitting the top edge of the Enemy's round mouth as it screeched.

"Ah...aaah...*aaaaaaaaaaah*!!" The yell was distorted, metallic, as Falcon thrust the arms clutching the fangs out to both sides.

Jormungand's head was ripped in half with a curious sound. The majority of its eyes ruptured from the inside, and massive quantities of fluid jetted out of the deep fissure. Ignoring this, he plunged his hands into the crack, grabbed on to the soft matter inside, and pulled the monster even farther apart. Split it.

When his feet hit the ground, the hell snake was in two parts down to its midsection. As the right half writhed and tried to disappear into its nest, he caught it in the talons of both hands and similarly held the left side fast with the pointed ends of his feet. Mustering up every ounce of power in his body, he ripped the beast in half in one pull, right down to its tail.

The body of the Enemy, finally completely divided, stopped in an unnatural shape for a moment before turning into thousands of fragments and scattering.

From the center of an explosion effect so grand it blanketed the entire basin, something long and slender materialized and stood before Falcon. A long sword with a cool, clear crystal-white blade. An Enemy drop Enhanced Armament. Without hesitating, he reached out and grabbed onto the hilt, which glittered like it held a star within it.

Instantly, the longsword became a small card and disappeared. In the top of his field of view was a small system message: You acquired an Enhanced Armament: Star Caster.

"Equip Star Caster," he muttered in a creaking voice.

The divine design of the longsword reappeared in his right hand. However, the dark aura immediately blanketed the sword, distorting the color and the shape. The transparent crystal became a dazzling chrome silver. The straight lines of the hilt twisted ominously. The blade itself doubled in width and thickness, fangs popping up in several places.

He gripped the large sword in its new form with both hands and held it in front of his body. The blackish-silver blade reflected a single duel avatar. It was no longer the simple, slender Chrome Falcon and his round helmet. The silhouette was the epitome of brutal, the will to destroy itself made into an object.

Only his original smooth mask was exposed beneath the open helm. But the aura of darkness cohered on the forehead of the helmet, creating a visor large enough to cover his entire face.

Once he lowered it, he would never be able to go back to what he had been. He knew this instinctively.

If I changed, Fron'd definitely be sad.

But she's not in this world anymore.

Taking this as his last moment, he abandoned the name Chrome Falcon. He buried it in this ground with Saffron Blossom. Her ideals, her kindness, her compassion, he would bury it all here.

Because the ones who had rejected those ideals were the players standing stock-still around the basin. Rather than harmony, they chose war. Instead of joining hands, they preferred to steal life from one another. More than love, they desired anger and hatred. In which case...

He would give it to them.

Brandishing the sword high with both hands, indignation and rage still jetting up from the depths of his body, he howled once more.

"Ngah...*Aaaaaah...*!!"

The aura of darkness gushing from all parts of his body gave rise to jet-black lightning, striking the metallic earth one bolt after another. Cracks raced out in circles from beneath his feet; the ground rippled and shook. He screamed again, almost in resonance with the cries of the earth.

"Rrraa...aaaaaaah!!"

He felt the bottomless rage welling up inside him become a kind of medium and interfere with the system itself. As proof that this was no mere hallucination, even the font in the system colors still displayed in the top of his vision flickered repeatedly. The two lines of text, THE DESTINY and STAR CASTER, twisted, crumbled, and melted into each other. They became one line to form a new word.

THE DISASTER.

"Grrr...raaaaaaah!!"

The scream was already not that of a person. It was the howl of a starved, enraged beast.

Kasshk. The visor on his forehead came down by itself with a violent sound.

A light-gray filter covered his field of view. However, the resolution doubled, and he could clearly make out the expressions on the faces of the duel avatars in a circle around him. They were blurred with confusion and surprise and unease. But what they were feeling, what they were thinking, no longer held any meaning for Falcon. They were nothing more than targets for the slaughter. He narrowed his eyes beneath his visor and sought out the body he should hunt first.

When he turned his attention to any particular spot in the circle, the murmured conversation of the several avatars standing there was amplified and delivered to his sense of hearing as if a high-powered directional microphone had been turned on them.

"...ge full recovery confirmed. No depletion of special-attack gauge. No doubt about it, it's Main Visualizer overwrite through Imagination circuit."

The voice belonged to a tiny avatar with four excessively large, shining eye lenses. Responding to it was the layered black avatar that had restrained Falcon and Blossom with its strange technique.

"It seems that an explosion of sentiment through deepening of concentration can indeed bring about the phenomenon overwhelmingly fast. Although whether it can be controlled or not is a different issue."

The four-eyed avatar nodded. "True, true. And it's basically for sure that peeps with a mental-scar shell strength that goes beyond a certain level turn into metal colors. But whether that fusion's a power inherent to the Seven Stars or just 'cause he's a metal color, I can't tell with my Analyze."

"Hmm. If possible, I'd want you to take your time and do a thorough analysis, but—"

At that moment, there came a different voice from behind them. "Can you secure him, Vise?"

Brimming with a clear sweetness almost like the water of a snowmelt, with no hint of bitterness, without a doubt, this was the voice of the player who had continuously forced Blossom to resurrect. Fal sharpened his eyes even further beneath his visor, but a mysterious light blocked his view, and he couldn't see the avatar on the other side.

"I suppose I'll give it a go." The layered avatar nodded a head that was nothing more than an arrangement of thin panels and raised a left hand of the same design.

The several panels comprising that arm slid off and disappeared into the ground one after another. Immediately after this, the black cross appeared soundlessly behind Falcon and pulled at his body with its bizarre magnetism.

But.

"Gr...aaaah!"

With a short roar, he sliced the sword in his right hand to the rear, and the cross was quickly destroyed, producing a sound and feel like glass shattering. The bright light of a damage effect gushed out from the left shoulder of the wielder of the panels.

"Whoops. Quite incredible. I very much cannot hold him with a normal technique."

Falcon focused more intently on the layered avatar muttering this. There were too many words in this conversation that were impossible to understand, but one thing at least was clear, and that was that they had planned the whole thing. That, in line with some kind of scheme or another, they had called Saffron Blossom out and tortured her to death with Unlimited Enemy Kill.

In which case, they should be the first ones he hunted.

Gripping the big sword with both hands, he brandished it high above his head in a solemn motion. He completely ignored the dozen or so confused and panicking players on the outer edge of the crater, turned toward the jet-black layered avatar, and took a single step. He soundlessly uttered the name of his technique.

Flash Blink!

He brought down his blade at the same time as he teleported at super-high speed and severed the layered avatar's remaining arm at the base. However, his opponent, who lacked a face-like face, showed not the slightest air of being disturbed; he took a single step back and disassembled the body that had suddenly lost both arms.

These pieces transformed into two enormous panels, which then closed around the four-eyed avatar standing next to him and also the avatar enveloped in light from behind. By some logic, the massive panels closed into one single, thin panel.

Falcon sliced horizontally with his sword at the enormous ink-black panel sinking into the shadows on the ground. But the swing managed only to slice off a diagonal piece of the top edge and send it flying. The panel produced a gentle ripple in the shadow and sank into it completely; the aura of the three mysterious players vanished from the field.

"Gr...raaah..."

A groan of rage slipped out at having his Enemies steal away on him. A few seconds later, *skrrinnk!* An ear-splitting metallic sound accompanied a light blow to his left shoulder.

He turned around languidly. Standing there was a midsize blue duel avatar. In both hands, it held a large, close-range weapon that was like a cross between a wooden sword and a traditional longsword. His opponent was someone whose face he knew well, who he could have been said to be close with. One of the few first generation, a direct attack from that long spear had even shattered the armor of the former Chrome Falcon. But a glance at his right shoulder showed that there wasn't a crack or even the tiniest dent now.

His opponent looked as though he couldn't believe what he was seeing, and without even trying to remember his name, Falcon casually brought down the sword enveloped in the dark aura.

Whud. The heavy noise shook the cool air. The weapon the blue avatar held fell apart in the middle, and then the top half of its owner's body also slid off and tumbled onto the ground. The lower half was a little late to tilt backward, only to stop halfway into its fall and explode, scattering at the same time as the upper half. Now all that remained was a small light the color of its armor.

A violent and distinct shiver ran through the thirty or so people still left at the sight of a high-tier player being slaughtered with a single blow. Trembling voices—*What's happening, this isn't what I signed up for*—gradually increased in volume.

"Crap...R-run!!"

The instant someone shouted this, they all began to race in a single direction, like a dam had broken. They were no doubt intending to flee to the real world through the leave point in the Shibaura parking area some dozen or so meters ahead. However...

Flash Blink.

As he sent up this silent prayer, his blackish silver armor disappeared and reappeared immediately in front of the fleeing players. Another slicing attack. Three heads fell simultaneously.

"Unh...ungah...ungaaaaaah!"

Shrieks. Screams. Some players still tried to run, others tried to hide in the surrounding buildings, and still others tried counterattacks, but the sword of darkness swept down on all of them without exception and stole their gauges from them in one blow.

Propelling Falcon forward now was no longer simple rage. A sublime determination that went beyond resentment or revenge—a curse.

That this world would be destroyed.

If a Burst Linker from later years saw Chrome Falcon at this time through some hidden logic of Brain Burst, they would have made this judgment: that this dark overlay was a manifestation of a purely negative will. That this was the dark side of the Incarnate System itself, smashing everything in existence through an absolute desire for negation.

When the slaughter—barely seconds long—was over, only the countless embers flickered silently around the basin. The blackish-silver destroyer plunged the great sword into the earth, now that it had absorbed plenty of blood, and grew still.

To wait for them to regenerate in an hour.

*   *   *

That day, more than thirty players were exterminated from the Accelerated World all at once.

The lone survivor who had the good luck to make it to the portal alive gave an account to freeze the blood in anyone's veins, shaking with terror all the while. The story—that Chrome Falcon clad in an evil armor had slaughtered all of her companions—was initially met with raised eyebrows.

But those who challenged Falcon to a general duel in an attempt to confirm her story were, without exception, decimated in a single blow from that great sword, and everyone was forced to accept that it was true. That a terrifying catastrophe had been born into the Accelerated World that had grown up over this last year or so.

At some point, the players stopped called this destroyer by the original avatar name. Crowning him with the name of the Enhanced Armament, they called him thus:

Chrome Disaster.

Blackout.

Spotlight.

In the circle of white light, a knight appears, body wrapped in dark metallic armor, holding a sinister sword. The crouching figure is tattered and wounded, cracked; the sword is also severely chipped and scratched.

To back him up against this wall, the strongest players in the Accelerated World challenged him to endless battles and exhausted him, sometimes in the one-against-many Battle Royale mode.

But the destroyer did not refuse a single duel; in fact, he even took off the intrusion limit of once per day and accepted any and all fighting conditions. Despite the fact that normally, after ten successive battles, even in a normal duel, a player couldn't really move very well due to mental exhaustion, he easily fought his way through more than a hundred duels in a day, wearing down his soul itself.

At some point, the dark aura blanketing the sword grew weaker, and the armor lost its shine, but even still, the destroyer continued to fight. His win ratio dropped, and his points were eaten away bit by bit, until they finally drove him into this corner on the verge of losing all his points in this final, greatest battle in the Unlimited Neutral Field.

Several duel avatars steadily close in on the crouching knight. All of them are masters, said to currently be the strongest in the world. Among them are even a few of the Pure Colors, the leaders of the major Legions.

On the verge of death, the destroyer clings to his sword and staggers to his feet. One part of the brutal design of the visor has fallen away, allowing the merest glimpse of the smooth helmet and its single, curved line, held inside.

That mask looks up at the sky of the Accelerated World.

I—the BB player formerly known as Chrome Falcon—disappear here today.

If the rumor that your memories disappear or there's some manipulation of your thoughts is true, then I will forget everything about the Accelerated World, even Saffron Blossom, whom I loved so much, and return to being a regular second-grade student who doesn't even know a single big word.

But this rage of mine—this sadness—and this despair will remain.

Neither I nor Saffron Blossom wanted power. The thought of establishing a hegemony over the Accelerated World with the power of the armor never even occurred to us. All we wanted was to be able to stay in this world with everyone, forever.

Those who saw domination and destruction and pillage in the mirrored surface of the armor saw nothing more than the reflection of their own desires.

They were the ones who longed for power. The ones who killed Saffron Blossom over and over again in the cruelest manner.

So then I'll give it to them.

I'll leave my rage and Blossom's suffering to this armor, to the Disaster. The next time someone craves power and puts this armor on, they will become something that attacks all Burst Linkers, destroys them, devours them. They will eat them and steal their powers and become infinitely strong. Until they are the last one. Until the end when only one remains in the wasteland of the infinitely vast Accelerated World.

Because that is the true nature of your desire.

I curse this world. I defile it. Even if I disappear temporarily here, my rage and hatred will come back to life any number of times.

Blackout.

2

At the sensation of slender fingertips caressing his cheek, Haruyuki Arita opened his eyes a crack.

The blurry world slowly came into focus. A small hand encased in pure white armor. Arms in the shape of short sleeves of the same color. Charming face mask and round, adorable scarlet eye lenses.

Haruyuki stared for a while at Ardor Maiden—level-seven Burst Linker with the power of purification, one of the Four Elements of the former Nega Nebulus—standing on her knees, hand outstretched.

A single transparent drop glittered at the tip of her slender finger. He cocked his head at the worried look on her face before realizing that the droplet had been flowing down his own face.

"Huh...oh...," he muttered hoarsely, and hurriedly rubbed at his face with his right hand before closing his half-open helmet all the way. He turned the face of Silver Crow, the duel avatar wrapped in the half-mirrored surface, and made his excuses.

"Uh, sorry. I'm okay. I was sleeping and I had this...this super-long dream." Here he stopped and furrowed his brow.

He had been dreaming. And in that long, long dream, Haruyuki hadn't been Silver Crow. He had been a metal color that looked a lot like him; the shade was just a little different. But that's all he could remember. Where he went, what he did, and what happened was blocked by a soft white wall like silk floss, and he couldn't recall any of it.

All that was left was a faint feeling like a hole had opened up deep in his chest. And a prickling, sharp pain racing through that emptiness…a sense of loss?

…I love you, you know…

A voice he had never heard before passed through his ears, and he managed somehow to fiercely blink back the tears that threatened to spring up once more. He shook his head hard and inhaled deeply of the cool air while he was at it, pushing back the bizarre sadness before checking their surroundings again.

At some point, it had gotten dark. Above his head, clusters of stars twinkling crisply, a sight not seen in the Tokyo of the real world, even in dreams. He could see the sky because they were not inside a building, but rather a courtyard-type space. Supporting his back as he sat, legs stretched out, was a thick pillar, about a meter or so in diameter. Immediately to his right, a high wall rose up very nearly to the sky.

Nothing had changed; this was the same terrain he had seen before falling asleep. But when he at last looked down between his own legs, he realized that the thick ice that should have been there had been transformed into gravel, and he cocked his head to one side. Hurriedly looking over his shoulder, he saw that the pillar behind him was also not pale-blue ice, but rather vermilion wood.

"Huh…Did the Change happen while I was asleep?" he asked Ardor Maiden in a hushed voice, and the white-and-scarlet shrine maiden avatar nodded sharply.

"It would appear so." Her reply was also whispered, her voice echoing with a crisp youth. "But I was asleep next to you, C, and so I didn't notice it myself."

The Change was the phenomenon in which the attributes of the world—the "stage" of the Unlimited Neutral Field created by the Brain Burst program—were switched periodically. When Silver Crow and Ardor Maiden had begun their nap, this place had been an Ice stage where everything was frozen solid, but he could see no sign of snow or ice now.

Almost as if the season had rolled back, the trees were brilliantly colored in fall plumage, and the pillars were wooden, the walls painted white. He very much wanted to call these attributes pure Japanese style.

"This is the Heian stage," Ardor Maiden murmured as she spread out her scarlet armor skirt and sat neatly on her knees, matching their surroundings so perfectly she could have been part of a painting. At his unconscious staring, the small shrine maiden hung her head, seemingly embarrassed, so he hurriedly averted his eyes.

Controlling this adorable yet severe duel avatar was a girl four years younger than eighth-grade student Haruyuki, a girl named Utai Shinomiya. In fourth grade at Matsunogi Academy, a girls' school affiliated with Umesato Junior High, she was basically a real-life sheltered princess. She had, no doubt, almost no experience with an older boy staring at her, and so he shifted his eyes away from her and around the scene once more.

Vermilion-painted pillars standing in a row from north to south. A large cobblestone street stretching out between them. The flickering orange light of countless watch fires. And the stately silhouette of the enormous palace he could see in the distance in the north.

The attributes for the Japanese-style Heian stage were essentially the ultimate match for this place. That was because they were inside the address of 1 Chiyoda, Chiyoda Ward, Tokyo, in the real world and also the center of the Accelerated World: the Imperial Palace of this side, the absolutely impenetrable Castle.

Haruyuki and everyone belonging to the Legion Nega Nebulus had that day—Tuesday, June 18, 2047—at just after 7:20 PM, undertaken without a doubt their greatest mission since assembling their current regiment.

The exceedingly difficult operation to rescue Ardor Maiden from where she was sealed upon the altar of Suzaku was, in terms of process, actually extremely simple.

Their leader, Kuroyukihime/Black Lotus, with the support of Chiyuri/Lime Bell and her pseudo–healing powers, was to fire a long-distance attack on Suzaku and make herself a target. Haruyuki/Silver Crow would fly at top speed assisted by Fuko/Sky Raker's booster over Suzaku, charging down the large bridge stretching out from the south gate. He would recover Utai/Ardor Maiden at the moment she appeared once she had been given the signal to dive by Takumu/Cyan Pile before turning up into the sky at 180 degrees and escaping from the bridge.

He had believed the strategy would go well.

However, at the last of last moments, something entirely unexpected happened. Despite the fact that Haruyuki had not so much as breathed on it, Suzaku shifted its target from Black Lotus to Silver Crow and launched an extremely powerful fire-breath attack from behind him.

With the hot flames roasting his back, he had been unable to turn after grabbing Ardor Maiden from the ground, and so he had simply kept charging forward. Since the palace's southern gates were said to open only when Suzaku was defeated, he steeled himself to slam into them when, for some reason, the gates opened the merest hint of a crack for just an instant. Long out of other options, Haruyuki and Utai plunged through it.

Haruyuki then crashed as he heard the sound of the gates closing behind him. After temporarily losing consciousness, he asked Utai, who was holding him tightly, *"Um, are we maybe alive...?"*

The shock of her response to that question still reverberated in his mind.

"We are alive. But...aah, but..."

"Here...This place is inside the Castle."

"I still can't believe it. I mean, us inside *that* Castle," Haruyuki muttered, leaning up against the pillar.

Utai, kneeling neatly before him, nodded. "I was surprised when we entered the Castle, but I'm even further surprised that we live on like this after more than six hours."

"What...D-did I sleep that long? So then this darkness isn't a characteristic of the stage, it's just nighttime already?" he asked hurriedly.

Although you could see your total dive time in the Unlimited Neutral Field if you opened a menu window, there were very few methods of learning the precise internal time—what time it was in the hours and minutes of this world. Somewhere in the field, there was apparently a large clock that had been marking the passage of all the time that had passed since the start of this world, but he felt like that would be a terrifying thing to see. That clock would have to be displaying a date and time greater than one thousand times seven years; i.e., seven thousand years.

"You can see the stars in the Heian stage." Utai pointed with her small hand at the night sky above their heads. "From the position of the stars, it appears to be already very nearly midnight."

"Uh, uh-huh. Makes sense." Haruyuki threw his head back up at the star-filled sky.

Having dropped down in a corner of the courtyard adjacent to the Castle's south gate approximately six hours earlier—although this was naturally in accelerated time—they had huddled together and reflected upon their own shock and feelings for a while, but they couldn't just sit tight there forever. At every spot along the main road that stretched out due north from the south gate to the main building of the palace enshrined on the far side, they could see slow-moving groups of human-shaped Enemies.

The Enemies were about three meters tall, and thus far smaller than the Four Gods, but they were clad in thick armor and wore longswords on their hips, reminiscent of warriors from the Warring States era; they radiated an impressive force that was more than enough to set Haruyuki shivering. And on top of that, they strutted around in groups of at least three.

Moreover, they could see the shadows of warrior Enemies

in the hallway outside, running along the inside of the castle wall, and when these warriors approached, armor clanging, the trapped Burst Linkers needed to take immediate action. But fighting was simply too foolhardy. Haruyuki's HP gauge had been cut basically in half by Suzaku's flames, and Utai wasn't unharmed, either.

Thus, they had avoided the main road and the halls and fled to the maze of the courtyard, securing a resting place in the shadow of a pillar that seemed safe for the time being. The sun set then, and despite the fact that he was fully aware of how worried Kuroyukihime and the others outside the castle gates must have been, he had fallen asleep sitting at the base of the pillar, perhaps exhausted mentally from all the action. And now they were here.

When they had slipped into this safe zone, the setting sun had dyed the cloudy sky of the Ice stage purple, but that color was completely gone now; the stars twinkled brightly in raven heavens.

Just as Utai said, those stars seemed to perfectly reproduce the array of constellations he had learned in a full-dive lesson a long time ago. Leaning back against the pillar, he looked to the east, and his eyes stopped on a remarkably bright star glittering pure white. He was pretty sure that was…

"Lyra…So Vega?" He was talking to himself, but Utai nodded, still kneeling and looking up at the sky.

"That is correct. In Japan, we also call it Orihime."

Haruyuki had considered all that knowledge drilled into him in class at school to be a total waste of time. He'd never expected that any of it would come in handy in a place like this, and he was suddenly delighted.

"So then below that to the right is…Aquila's Altair." He pointed at the starry sky. "And to the lower left is Cygnus's Deneb, right? Umm…so which one's Hikoboshi again?"

Giggling, Utai raised her arm, so like the sleeve of a shrine maiden's costume. "It's Altair. These three together are called the Summer Triangle. Although it's June right now, so their positions are still a little low."

"Huh. So that means the stars in the sky in the Accelerated World are based on the actual seasons…" Forgetting for a fleeting moment that they might not get out of this alive, Haruyuki was struck by a strange emotion and stared single-mindedly up at the sky.

The point of reproducing real terrain from images from the social cameras might have been to increase the number of strategic and tactical elements of the game. That made sense. But no matter which way he looked at it, the night sky was just scenery. No player would complain if the game had simply stuck up a single image made up of random points of light.

But there had to be some kind of intent or statement being made in going so far as to place the stars in the same positions as in the real world and reproduce even the movements of the constellations with the seasons; most likely the assertion that this wasn't just a game, it wasn't just an imaginary world.

"The early Burst Linkers—apparently, they used to use the expression 'BB players,'" Utai began to relate quietly, abruptly bringing both hands back down to her knees. "They, too, when they realized that the night sky in the Accelerated World was exactly the same as reality's—albeit the beautiful stars shone brightly with a clarity you could never dream of in Tokyo where the artificial lights are simply too bright—felt something uniformly. That's the reason that the prominent Legions were given names evocative of space."

"What? Are there really that many space names?" Haruyuki twisted his head around, and the childlike shrine maiden allowed a faint, bitter smile to rise up on her trim mask.

"All of the Legions of the Seven Kings have one. Our Nega Nebulus as well, a dark interstellar cloud…Although strictly speaking, it's apparently a 'dark nebula' in English, but the name is from that concept. And the Red Legion's 'Prominence' is the jet shooting up from the surface of the sun. The Blue Legion's 'Leonids' is a meteor shower in the constellation Leo."

"W-wow. So that's why…"

I just know Chiyu and Taku both realized this right from the start and felt like it went without saying. I'm so glad Utai's telling me before I have to hear them all shout, You didn't know?!

Whispering all kinds of reassuring thoughts to himself, Haruyuki asked, "So that means the White Legion's, um, 'Oscillatory Universe' isn't because the Legion Master's a white Shiratori bird or anything, but because it's actually a name related to space?"

At this, another smile with the slightest element of exasperation bled onto Utai's face, but she quickly recomposed her expression. "Yes," she said, in a whisper that was slightly tense for some reason, as she lowered her eyes. "'Oscillatory universe' means…a vibrating universe. But I haven't learned about that in school yet, so I don't understand the precise meaning."

"V-vibrating universe…"

I mean, the universe doesn't actually shake or vibrate or anything.

He shook his head from side to side, but eighth-grade student Haruyuki couldn't remember ever having heard those words in his science classes. To begin with, he wasn't sure if this level of concept would even show up in the compulsory education curriculum. He decided to look it up later if he remembered and turned his eyes up once more to the starry heavens.

Above the Summer Triangle, at precisely the pinnacle, several fairly weak stars were huddled together. He was pretty sure that was Hercules. To the left, Draco, the hundred-headed dragon Ladon defeated, rose up into the sky nearby the hero. And then farther to the left was a group of stars so bright they approached the brightness of the large triangle.

Ursa Major. The tail shone especially brightly. He learned in class that because of this brightness, the tail had been a constellation all by itself in ancient China.

The dipper shape with the long handle.

The seven stars of the Big Dipper.

Thmmp. He felt his heart jump abruptly. In the back of his mind, he felt small sparks firing, and his eyes were drawn to the center of the three stars that made up the dipper handle. He felt like this star alone, the name of which he didn't know, was pulsing in sync with those sparks in him.

A pulsating throb descended slowly from the center of his brain into his central nervous system. It flowed through his neck, past his shoulders, down the center of his back, and reached the space between his shoulder blades. *Thmmp.* It hurt. *Thmmp. Thmmp.* The sensation was both as though his own body itself were in pain and also as if some foreign body had embedded itself in—

"...C. C!"

At his shoulders being shaken gently, Haruyuki lifted his face with a gasp. Immediately before him, Ardor Maiden looked on, a worried light shining in her scarlet eyes.

Hurriedly, he shook his head and mumbled an answer. "S-sorry. I just sort of spaced out..."

"Is...that so? Then...I must have seen wrong. My apologies. Your body—For a moment, it seemed as though something shadowlike was covering it..."

"......"

He felt like he had heard her words somewhere else. And not that long ago. In the middle of the Hermes' Cord race a week before, when the shuttle was racing through warp space, Sky Raker had made a similar remark...

"I-it's just your imagination. I'm not doing anything." His response was essentially the same as it had been with Sky Raker, and then, unconsciously glossing over a nebulous unease, he added, "More important, we should get to thinking about what we're going to do now. It's not like we can just sit in this safe zone forever."

"Yes. That's...You're right." Utai nodded largely, as if to shake away her concerns, and then whirled her head around.

At that moment, they were hiding in the Castle's plaza, about fifty meters to the northeast of the southern gate. On the other side of the vermilion pillars, directly to the west, was the cobblestone main road stretching from north to south. Spreading out to the east was the complicated Japanese garden–style maze they had stepped into. The corridor along the circular castle walls was south of them.

Since fearsome Enemies patrolled a fixed course on the large main road and the corridor, it would be difficult to slip through either of those. And from the garden to the east, he could hear loud splashing noises and the heavy slithering of something massive crawling around from time to time; he was very much not interested in going that way.

The one place where they might be able to move was the narrow space between the rows of pillars and the maze of the garden, a course toward the north hiding behind pillars as they went, but there was no exit to the north—only the palace, which was the main building of the Castle. Inside there would be what was called the Inner Sanctuary, if it kept with the design of the Heian stage. The place was all so reminiscent of an enormous shrine, Haru had no doubt that monsters even fiercer than the current warrior-type Enemies would be parading around.

Given that their goal wasn't to storm the Castle, it was to return alive with Utai—Ardor Maiden—to a portal, they needed to avoid carelessly approaching the inner sanctuary at least, where they could get caught in an even worse Unlimited EK situation.

"Most likely…" Returning her gaze to Haruyuki after taking in their surroundings again, Utai opened her mouth as if thinking out loud, still seated neatly on her knees. "Lotus, Raker, and Bell should have already returned to the real world through the portal at the police station. When you're separated from your comrades during a battle in the Unlimited Neutral Field, the general idea is that rather than continuing to risk the danger, those who can escape, escape."

"Yeah, makes sense."

The younger girl continued in a childlike, yet clear tone. "Then in that case, if a safety's been set, those who left first would activate it, and then an assessment of the situation would take place in the real world. Thus, if we continue to wait here like this, there will soon be a discussion, and in the meantime, we will be able to return to your house. Or we *should* be able to."

A safety was when, instead of connecting Neurolinkers wire-lessly to the global net, Burst Linkers connected using a wired connection through a home server or mobile router. Doing so allowed their comrades who managed to escape before them to cut the circuit of this stepping-stone and log them out for the moment even if they couldn't reach a portal in the Unlimited Neutral Field.

Currently, Haruyuki, Utai, Kuroyukihime, Fuko, Takumu, and Chiyuri were gathered in Haruyuki's living room, their Neurolinkers connected in a daisy chain. If, having made it alive to the portal at the police station at the base of the southern bridge of the Castle, Kuroyukihime and the others pulled out the XSB cable connecting Haruyuki's Neurolinker to the Arita home server, in that instant, Haruyuki and Utai would automatically burst out.

However, Utai moved her avatar's mouth again, as if lost in fur-ther thought. "But, the situation being what it is, Lotus and the others are no doubt unsure. Because regardless of anything else, it was a one-in-a-million miracle that you and I slipped through the watch of Suzaku. We will likely never have another chance to investigate the interior of the Castle."

"Never?......I dunno. If we charge at the gate with the same strategy again, maybe we could..." Naturally, he had no desire to do this again, but he gave voice to the idea as a possibility at the very least.

"C, please look over there." Utai raised her right hand to point across Haruyuki's shoulder to the southwest. "That's the inside of the south gate."

"O-okay." He turned around and carefully poked his face out from the shadow of the pillar behind him to see an enormous castle gate soaring up fifty meters ahead.

The gate doors, made up of two large panels side by side, sep-arated the inside and the outside of the Castle absolutely, with an impressive mass and density. He could hardly believe that six hours earlier, the seam between those panels had opened up barely half a meter and allowed them to pass through.

Utai was pointing at the very center of the doors. Straining his eyes to see the spot, a place where the light of the watch fires on the ground just barely reached, he realized he did indeed see something large there.

Maybe a bas-relief? A square metal plate, about three or so meters on each side, connected the doors. Some kind of detailed engraving appeared to be carved into its surface, but it had a gravity that made it seem like more than simply a decorative object.

"…Oh…"

Squinting harder, the design of the relief suddenly snapped into clarity before his eyes. An enormous bird, wings spread wide to both sides, sharp beak open at the end of a long head. The God Suzaku itself.

"A seal…for the gate?" Haruyuki murmured unconsciously, and felt Utai nodding next to him.

"I think so, too. C, I believe you likely haven't noticed this, but in fact, at the point in time when we charged through those gates, that seal had been destroyed by someone."

"Wh-whaaaat?!" Unthinkingly, he cried out in surprise and hurried to clamp his hands over his mouth. Lowering his voice, he asked urgently, "D-destroyed?! So the seal's not actually supposed to split in the middle? It was broken?"

"That is how it looked to me. Rather than the center being vertically divided in a straight line, it was cut into a diagonal cross, as though an enormous sword had sliced into it twice."

To reproduce the situation for him, Ardor Maiden stretched out five fingers and drew an X in the air with her right hand. As she lowered it, she continued in an even quieter voice.

"However, a few seconds after we charged in and the gates closed, the seal was completely restored, as you can see there.

In this world, any kind of lock or seal is a metaphor for a system lock. If that seal had been functioning properly, the main gate most certainly would not have opened without the defeat of Suzaku. In other words, it was precisely because something—or some*one*—cut that seal from the inside with a sword that the gate opened for us when we approached it, even if only for a moment. That is what I believe."

Still staring at the metal bas-relief reflecting the light of the torches in the distance, Haruyuki opened and closed his mouth beneath his silver surface any number of times. He sorted through his thoughts and finally put the first of them into words. "So that means a Burst Linker got into this Castle before us…and deliberately destroyed that seal for someone coming along later?"

"…Yes, I think so."

"B-but, like, Suzaku's going strong out there. So then, how on earth did that Burst Linker get into the Castle? If that seal automatically restores itself after the gates open and close, like you saw it do, Mei—I mean, it can't have been broken since the birth of the Accelerated World. And there's no way for this whoever to break through the gate other than…defeating Suzaku…"

Hands on her knees once more, Utai gently shook her head.

"That I don't know. To obtain any further information, it's likely necessary to enter the inner sanctuary of the Castle." Her words dropped to a whisper toward the end, and Haruyuki turned his gaze north, toward the silhouette of the inner sanctuary cutting a black sheet out of the starry sky.

Go in there? The very center of the center of the Accelerated World…?

We can't. We totally can't do something that outrageous. First of all, the entrance to the inner sanctuary's obviously gonna be guarded by Enemies even more incredible than those terrifying warriors. How are we supposed to break through something like that…

He pulled his shoulders in tightly with a shudder, his pessimistic thoughts taking charge in his brain. And then Haruyuki got the feeling that he was watching a mysterious scene dimly projected on a screen somewhere deep in his brain.

Although his own avatar was definitely still seated on the gravel, another self stood up and advanced to the north. Hiding behind the pillars from the gazes of the warrior Enemies patrolling the main road, he approached the inner sanctuary, cautiously but at a steady pace. Rather than aiming for the strictly guarded main entrance, he had his sights set on a single window on the white wall a few dozen meters east of it…

"—setting aside the matter of the seal, I believe that at any rate, we do have to move."

Utai's voice in his ears shattered the bizarre vision. He opened his eyes with a gasp and blinked repeatedly. Seemingly paying this no mind, Utai kept her eyes on the inner sanctuary in the distance and continued speaking quietly.

"If we wait here like this, at some point, Lotus and the others will force us to Burst Out. But if, for instance, we do manage to return to the real world for a time, the next time we use the "unlimited burst" command, we will appear here in the inner garden of the Castle again. There's not such a difference between that and Unlimited EK."

"Oh…y-yeah, right." Haruyuki simply agreed as he tried to get his head together somehow. "So then this mission isn't over until me and you, Shino—Mei—leave properly through a portal somewhere. To do that, we have to open that gate again, get outside, dodge Suzaku's attack, and reach the police station on the other side of the bridge…or find a new portal inside the Castle…"

"Yes, that's exactly right." Ardor Maiden nodded crisply, and Haruyuki stared into her scarlet eyes before deliberately opening his mouth again.

"Mei. I have a proposal. I don't have any real reason or confidence, but…I want to try heading for the inner sanctuary. I don't know why, but…I think we can make it." As he stared at the child shrine maiden cocking her head slightly, his own avatar, which had been sitting cross-legged on the gravel, shifted to sit properly on its knees without his being aware of it. He clenched his hands lightly on his knees, straightened his back, and continued speaking.

"Naturally, I get that the worst-case scenario is we're killed by some Enemy stronger than those warriors and get stuck in an Unlimited EK in the Castle. I know we shouldn't risk that danger on a gut feeling. But, still, I want to go...I kinda feel like...we maybe...have to go..."

It was a fair bit of work for Haruyuki to get all this out, and toward the end, his voice turned into his usual mumble, and his shoulders started to drop. There was no way he'd be able to persuade a very veteran Burst Linker two levels higher than he was.

"Understood." Utai nodded.

"What?!" he cried out in surprise.

The shrine maiden let a little laugh out and, while still kneeling, deftly moved to bring her knees right up alongside his. From this position, she reached out with her right hand and gently placed it on top of his clenched fist.

"C. Back there, you ignored Lotus's order to retreat, and you rescued me when I appeared on the altar, all while being chased by Suzaku's flames. In that instant, I understood that you are a person I can trust—someone I *should* trust. No, actually, perhaps I knew it from the time we first met, from the time I saw you all alone in the yard at Umesato Junior High School, so earnestly cleaning out the animal hutch."

"Th-that's—I mean, I, like, totally, it's just..." Haruyuki hung his head deeply, his usual stammering reaching new levels. "I never think—I always mess up. I mean, that time cleaning, I totally sprayed you with water."

Perhaps remembering it, Utai let a giggle slip out and held Haruyuki's hand even more tightly. "I believe I told you: that true strength is moving forward without giving up, even if you lose or fall down or fail. If we are killed by Enemies aiming for the depths of the inner sanctuary, I have faith that you will manage something there."

They were kind yet harsh words. But Haruyuki lifted his face and firmly met Utai's eyes, glittering brightly before nodding deeply.

"Yeah. I'll work something out. We're going home alive...to everyone waiting for us in the real world."

3

The cobblestone main road continuing from the south gate of the Castle—which was named Suzakumon—to the main entrance of the inner sanctuary was approximately three hundred meters long. Standing on both sides every eight meters was a vermilion pillar. Since the pillars themselves had a diameter of two meters, the gap between each pair of pillars was six meters. The warrior Enemies patrolling the main road didn't appear to notice the existence of the intruders when they were hiding quietly behind a pillar, but it wasn't hard to imagine that the instant the warriors saw them moving or heard the sound of footsteps on gravel, they would swoop down upon them.

Thus, to make it to the inner sanctuary of the Castle, the only choice Haruyuki and Utai had was to cross from the shadow of one pillar to the next of thirty-five pillars while avoiding the warriors' reaction range. Naturally, Haruyuki's first inclination was to consider using his wings for an aerial approach, but the falcon-like birds dancing slowly in the night sky concerned him. If they were some of the harmless critter objects, simply one part of the stage's terrain, it would be fine, but he and his partner would be in serious trouble if they turned out to be some kind of lookout Enemies.

Nevertheless, his wings weren't entirely useless. Crouching in the shadow of the umpteenth pillar, holding the small body of Ardor Maiden in his arms, Haruyuki listened hard and waited for his moment.

Warriors marched south along the main road five or so meters to their left, armor clanging. Those weighty footfalls came up directly beside the pillar, passed by, and receded farther.

Utai, in his arms, nodded her tiny head. At the same time, the metal fins on Haruyuki's back fluttered with the minimum output, and lightly, soundlessly, the pair flew—or rather, jumped. They landed gently on tiptoe behind the pillar eight meters ahead. The warriors behind them continued to walk away at the same pace, not seeming to notice anything out of place.

"Phe…" He suppressed the sigh that started to slip out, and Utai turned worried eyes on him. He looked back into those ruby-like lenses and nodded that he was okay.

He had a certain amount of experience fighting Enemies in the Unlimited Neutral Field, but this was the first time he had been forced to engage in covert action that used so much mental energy. In more than twenty minutes, the distance they had covered was at most a hundred meters. However, they couldn't rush this. He had to concentrate and make a perfect jump each time.

It was a difficult situation, but luck was also on their side. To begin with, there was the fact that Haruyuki's flight was not a special attack that required him to utter the name of the technique in order to activate it, but rather a normally activated ability. Thus, they didn't have to worry about the warriors hearing his voice.

And one more piece of luck was that holding his breath and hiding himself was real-world Haruyuki Arita's big signature move. Of the three hundred and sixty people at Umesato Junior High, no one had polished their Inconspicuous skill to the extent that Haruyuki had. The seemingly paradoxical trick to this was to sneak out in the open. Because Haruyuki had been excessively bothered by the eyes of the students around him back in seventh grade, he had provoked the sadism of some delinquents. Nothing was ever good in excess.

Right: careful guard, but without fear; join the natural flow—complete the next jump.

His precious special-attack gauge, filled up when he was scorched with Suzaku's flames, had about 60 percent left. If he used it well, that would be plenty. If he flew steadily between one pillar and the next without rushing, he'd reach the finish line at some point. A lesson he'd learned cleaning out that animal hutch.

A new group of warriors approached and passed by on the other side of the pillar. Utai nodded. Haru nodded back and gently vibrated his wings. *Jump.*

Forty minutes later, when they had finally reached the base of the last of the pillars, Haruyuki let out a long, heavy sigh of relief this time.

The patrolling warriors apparently didn't come up to the side of this pillar. After checking that there was no sign of any Enemy around them, Ardor Maiden, in his arms, whispered at minimum volume, "Very nice work, C."

"Yeah. You, too, Mei." He let the slender avatar down gently onto the gravel. Huddled together, crouching, they cautiously peeked out from the shadow of the pillar.

The inner sanctuary of the Castle, the very center of the center of the Unlimited Neutral Field—the true Accelerated World—rose up a mere five meters ahead of them. Given that this was the Japanese-style Heian stage, the design of the building also closely resembled the reproduction model of the Council Hall of the Imperial Palace in ancient Kyoto, which he had done a full dive into in his Japanese history class. It was just much, much bigger.

The roof was black tiles. The walls were painted white, and the pillars and latticed windows were vermilion. To their right was the main entrance, leading off from the center of the main road. But going in through there was probably—no, definitely—impossible. On either side of the gate stood Enemies far more massive than the courtyard's warriors; they were fearsome, imposing, and perhaps best described as two guardian Deva kings.

"C, I have to ask at least. Are you planning to challenge those people?"

At Utai's whispered question, Haruyuki moved his head at high speeds, horizontally, back and forth. "N-n-n-n-n-no way, y-y-y-y-y-you gotta be kidding! I don't want to get another centimeter closer to them."

"...Neither do I. But...then what exactly are you planning to do? I do believe that we won't find a portal without going into that inner sanctuary."

"...Um, okay." Beneath his helmet, he bit his lip for a moment. He didn't know if she'd believe him if he told her what they were going to do and the basis for that action. However, Haruyuki didn't want to tell any kind of lie to this girl, Utai Shinomiya, still so childlike and innocent despite having borne a massive weight on her shoulders for more than two years. Which is why he simply told the truth.

"When I was dozing back there under the pillar at the southern edge, I had a dream. Someone who looked a lot like me but who wasn't me took the exact same route as us and got into the inner sanctuary." He still couldn't fully remember all the details of that dream. But when he saw that vision of the silver avatar moving forward across the gravel, the part that came after that returned hazily to life in his mind.

Ardor Maiden stared at him curiously as he put a hand on her right hip and stood her up with him. Holding her gently, he raced his eyes around to the left and right to check it was safe. He used the tiny bit left in his gauge for the final long jump.

He was aiming for not the main entrance to their right but the latticed windows along the white wall—specifically, the one fifth from the left.

When he landed immediately in front of the window, which itself was a careful hatching of vermilion crosspieces, Utai took a step forward and then turned around, shaking her small head.

"It won't open, I think. And it's almost certainly impossible to break it—this type of window is almost always an unbreakable object, locked by the system."

She was absolutely correct. Unlike the Normal Duel Field, which was a straightforward fighting-game stage, the Unlimited Neutral Field that the Brain Burst program generated was more role-playing game, good for strategizing and adventuring. Pretty much any building in the Normal Field could be destroyed, but that was not necessarily the case in the Unlimited Field. Just like a locked door wouldn't open unless you had the key that fit it, if you didn't have a reason to go inside places closed off in this world, the system would most certainly not let you.

But Haruyuki simply half nodded at Utai and looked up at the latticed window. He reached up and grabbed a thin vermilion crosspiece. *Please*, he prayed as he gently pulled it forward.

Sure enough, the latticed window rotated soundlessly with the central crosspiece as the axis.

Utai took a sharp breath. Her scarlet eye lenses opened wide as though she couldn't believe what she was seeing.

It was only natural she'd be surprised. On the inside of the latticed window, on the bottom, a hefty lock glittered gold. But the bolt had been completely opened, showing that this window was in an unlocked state, according to the system.

Ardor Maiden took a few steps, still saying nothing, and reached up to the next latticed window. She tried to pull it open in the same way, but the vermilion crosspiece stayed firmly fixed to the window frame, not even bending. Clearly, only the fifth window had been unlocked from the inside by someone.

"Did you also dream that this window would be open?" Utai asked him hoarsely, having returned to his side.

"Yeah." Haruyuki nodded slightly. "In my dream, someone got in through this window, like they slipped through it and opened the lock."

"Was that someone the same person who broke the seal on the south gate?"

"I...don't know. But I feel like there wasn't a bit like that in my dream. And the person I saw maybe didn't have anything sword-like," he replied, almost absently, as he searched his memory intently. But they were talking about a dream he'd had while napping. All that came to mind were confused fragments of images; he couldn't even put them in chronological order. Maybe if he had had the dream recorder app that all the Neurolinker companies were working on, it would have been a different story, but even still, that would have only worked in the Basic Accelerated Field, where you could launch external programs.

But, more important, had it really been just a dream?

Dreams were essentially something produced from your own memories. So he shouldn't have been able to see anything in a dream that he didn't actually know. This was obviously the first time Haruyuki had entered the Castle. In which case, where did the memory that this window was unlocked come from...?

Haruyuki had gotten this far when a faint sound reached him from the east, and he turned his gaze with a gasp. The clanging drew nearer on the narrow path between the courtyard of trees in autumn brilliance and the endless white wall. There was no doubt it was a group of warrior Enemies. Apparently, this path was also a patrol course, albeit an infrequent one. They had to move right away.

After meeting each other's eyes for half a second, Haruyuki and Utai nodded together. They couldn't go back now, not when they'd come so far. Haruyuki first poked his head in through the unlocked window and checked that there were no Enemies inside the wide hallway. He slid gently inside before reaching out to pull Ardor Maiden up with both hands. Without a moment's delay, he closed the lattice, and they crouched below it, side by side.

The heavy footfalls on the gravel of the lane outside passed by, turned near the main gate, and passed by once more before disappearing back into the east.

"Phew..." At the same time as he let out yet another sigh, they looked at each other again, gently bumped fists, and grinned.

Finally.

They had at last succeeded in entering the inner sanctuary of the Castle itself, famed as being impenetrable. They were drawing infinitely closer to the center of the Accelerated World. Unfortunately, however, it was almost certainly a fact that another Burst Linker had made it this far before them. And if the person who destroyed the Suzaku seal on the south gate and the person who unlocked the latticed window here were not one and the same, there had actually been two intruders before them.

If they wanted to know who those other Burst Linkers were, their only choice was to head even farther into the inner sanctuary. The fearsomeness and number of the guardian Enemies here was likely an order of magnitude higher than outside, but all they could do was keep moving forward.

"Umm." Haruyuki blinked hard once before quietly asking, "How much real time has passed since we dove here?"

"I'd estimate that it's been about seven hours of inside time, so twenty-five thousand, two hundred seconds divided by a thousand…about twenty-five seconds."

"Okay, then it's probably been about twenty seconds since Kuroyukihime and the others got back. How long you think they'll wait before pulling our cables out?"

"At the earliest, I think they will force a disconnect at thirty seconds. Another ten seconds in real time…Here, we have two hours and forty-five minutes left." Utai's prompt response was just what he'd expect from a veteran Burst Linker; Haru was still not that great at mentally calculating accelerated time.

He bobbed his head up and down. "We either make it all the way in alive, or we die along the way. Either way, that much time's plenty. Let's go, Mei. Going to the right is probably safe." He sat with one knee raised and stretched out his left hand.

Utai stared at him for a moment, scarlet eye lenses glittering in her snow-white face mask. When he cocked his head to one side, she spoke in a voice colored with a smile. "It's just that since we got here, I've steadily felt more and more like I could rely on you, C. Almost like…my older brother."

Having something like this sprung on him sent his awkward meter shooting through the roof in the blink of an eye. "Wh-what? Mei, you have an older brother? What grade's he in?" he asked shrilly, eyes frozen in place.

But Utai grabbed his hand and stood up without responding to this question. Once more, a thin smile crossed her face, this time lonely somehow. "Well then, shall we go? Whether we live or die...I leave my life in your hands, C."

"...Yeah." Pushing aside his confusion, Haruyuki nodded firmly.

He was the one who had insisted on aiming for the inner sanctuary. So he had to give his all to keep Utai safe now. As a Burst Linker, Utai was overwhelmingly the stronger one, but this was a different sort of problem. Even if he had to sacrifice himself, he wanted to make sure Utai at least avoided falling into an Unlimited EK state again.

Secretly resolving this to himself, he started walking along the wooden floor of the silent, cool hallway, when a tiny voice came back to life in his ears.

Look, big brother Haruyuki. If one of us—or maybe both of us—lose Brain Burst, we'll probably forget everything, everything about each other, you know...

This wasn't a fragment of that strange dream. These were the words of Yuniko Kozuki—the second-generation Red King, Scarlet Rain—when she suddenly showed up at his house after the Meeting of the Seven Kings. It had been held in the east gardens of the Imperial Palace in the Normal Field two days earlier in real time, on Sunday, June 16. She had looked scared somehow. Or, given that she was saying things like *lose Brain Burst*, maybe she actually had been afraid of something.

But what? Did anything actually exist that Niko—a top-level Burst Linker at level nine and one of the Seven Kings of Pure Color ruling over the Accelerated World—would have to be afraid of? Considering the fact that in addition to the terrifying firepower of her Enhanced Armament, she had also mastered the Incarnate techniques of Range Expansion and Movement

Expansion, she should have been able to escape from even the territory of Suzaku under her own power.

Still, she might have been a king, but Niko was a sixth-grade girl in the real world, so it was no wonder if she got anxious about things sometimes. And in the Armor of Catastrophe incident six months earlier, she had herself condemned to exile Cherry Rook, a Linker close to her who had become the fifth Chrome Disaster. Rook had apparently been one of the few friends she had at her real-world boarding school, and now he had lost his memories of Brain Burst and transferred to a school far away. It would have been strange if she wasn't a little lonely.

"Hey, Mei?" Haruyuki unconsciously opened his mouth as they walked down the long hallway.

"Yes?"

After fumbling for the right words for a minute, he started talking again to the young shrine maiden looking up at him. "If we find a portal and get out of here...if we get through all this, I have a friend I want to introduce you to."

"A friend? Do you mean in the real world?"

"Yeah. She's two years older than you. She's in grade six right now. Kinda sassy, kinda rough, but...but she's really great. If it's all right with you—if you're okay with it, I mean, maybe you could be friends—"

Suddenly, a sensation like pain pushed up from the center of his chest. Haruyuki stopped breathing, and his eyes flew open. Was this...a premonition? That what he had just said would probably not come true? That some terrible...sad catastrophe would befall them before it could...

As if there's any such thing!

I'll keep my world safe. I won't make anyone unhappy anymore. I won't let anyone be sad. Kuroyukihime, my teacher, Chiyu, Taku, and Shinomiya, too...and Pard and, of course, Niko. I'll protect this warm circle, these bonds we have, modest and yet bigger than anything else. I will keep this safe.

"C." A tense voice called to him, and Haruyuki opened his eyes with a gasp. When he turned his gaze to his side, the young shrine maiden was focused intently on the path ahead of them in the hallway. Drawn in, Haruyuki looked ahead and noticed several massive auras. Soon, a heavy sound of creaking movement reached his ears.

"It appears that there are indeed Enemies inside as well."

He nodded quickly and looked to both sides. On the wall to the right, the line of vermilion latticed windows. They could probably unlock one and get outside, but there was the possibility of the warrior Enemies there, too. On the left, rather than a wall, a row of brilliantly painted sliding *fusuma* doors. He couldn't see anything resembling a lock, so he expected they would open if he pulled on them, but which of the *fusuma* should they slide open?...

He then had another strange vision: A pale, human-shaped silhouette pulled open the *fusuma* two meters or so ahead and slipped inside.

"Over there." Rather than doubting his eyes, Haruyuki followed the phantom avatar. Without hesitating, he pulled the *fusuma* open and found another hallway with a polished hardwood floor. Another line of *fusuma* both ways. They slipped into the space stretching out to the north and closed the room dividers behind them with a *thump*.

They didn't even get the chance to breathe for a second before movement somewhere along the hall made the floorboards creak loudly. The shadow before his eyes that looked so much like himself glided forward, opened a *fusuma* to the right, and disappeared.

Just what was that shadow? And why was he the only one who could see it? There were a lot of things he didn't understand, but at this stage, all he could do was trust and follow where it led. Swallowing the echoes of the pain lingering in his heart, he forcefully called up all his focus and opened the next *fusuma*, pulling Utai along by the hand.

If they had tried to advance on their own and avoid the herds of warriors and Shinto-priest guardians that crowded the map of the interior of the Castle's inner sanctuary, even a full day would not have been anywhere near enough time.

Although the hallways were wide and they didn't lack for objects like pillars and sculptures to hide behind, the Enemy patrol patterns were complicated, definitely not readable with a few moments' observation. The building was also made up of a series of *fusuma* and hallways that looked almost exactly like one another, making it very easy to get lost, and, of course, there was no auto-mapping function, so before they knew it, they had lost all sense of north and south. The fact that they had been able to make any headway at all in a labyrinth of this level of difficulty was because they had help from the strange silhouette that floated up in Haruyuki's field of view.

The small nameless duel avatar found the blind spots of patrolling Enemies with a timing like passing through the eye of a needle and opened one unremarkable *fusuma* door after another, guiding Haruyuki and Utai forward. It was already quite evident that this was no mere dream or hallucination.

It was probably a "memory." The logic of it was unclear, but the memories of a Burst Linker who had once snuck into this Castle were replaying in Haruyuki's consciousness. He couldn't come up with any other explanation for this phenomenon. But if that was the case, then that meant whoever this was had succeeded in reaching the most central depths of the Castle, and then left their memories in some kind of media after they made it home alive. Which meant there had to be a portal connected with the real world in the final site this hazy silhouette arrived at.

Haruyuki believed there was and chased after the memory shadow with undivided attention, pulling Ardor Maiden along by the hand. They had a few close calls, but after more than an hour had passed and they hadn't been targeted by a single Enemy, the pair finally reached the entrance to a large hall that seemed to be very close to their goal.

"This is...," Utai murmured, and squeezed his hand in hers tightly.

It was an enormous space, one better described as a massive temple than a hall. Vermilion pillars supported the high ceiling, and the walls on all four sides were adorned with dazzling color prints. It had a very "last boss room" look to it, but there was no sign of any Enemy. Regardless, a concentrated *something* hung in the air that made them hold their breath. Haruyuki squeezed Utai's hand back and strained his eyes intently beneath his silver mask.

The silhouette of memory that had guided them here was stepping slowly into the hall and heading toward the gloomy depths. Steeling himself, Haruyuki followed it. The shadow glided in between the row of pillars and—

The moment it had advanced to a certain point, it vanished without a sound.

"Ah!" A quiet cry slipped out of Haruyuki, and he quickened his pace. If the memory shadow had disappeared, then the portal had to be in there. But only darkness and cool air filled the depths of the hall; he definitely didn't see any flickering blue light. But that...to come all this way and have there be no exit, it couldn't be...

Half running, he crossed the last ten meters and was forced to acknowledge that his fears had been realized. There was indeed something there. But it was very clearly not a portal.

Square stone pillars blackly lustrous side by side, a distance of about two meters between them, standing as high as Silver Crow's chest perhaps. When he saw the thin, disparately colored panels on them, he figured these were no ordinary pillars, but rather pedestals to place something on.

But both were empty. If anything had sat on them at some point in the past, those items had already been carried off. The gray shadow who had guided them here had probably taken at least one of them. So then a onetime portal that—as the name suggested—activated only once.

"I...We came all this way..." Enormously discouraged, Haruyuki started to drop his shoulders.

Utai suddenly squeezed his left hand so hard it creaked.

"...?!" Hurriedly looking to his side, he saw the young shrine maiden, who he had never once seen lose her cool composure, staring at the pedestal on the right as if she were trying to devour it, scarlet light spilling from her eye lenses.

"A Seven Stars plate."

"Huh...huh...?" Bewildered by the words, which he'd never heard before, Haruyuki looked at the pedestal once more...and realized that a small silver plate was indeed embedded in the front, which he hadn't noticed before. He took a step toward it and stared hard. Several characters were carved into it, along with a curious diagram.

Seven dots, and six lines connecting them. He had seen this before. There was no mistaking it; it was the shape in the night sky he had looked up at from the Castle garden two hours earlier. The tail of Ursa Major. The seven stars of the Big Dipper.

Thmm.

The point on his back throbbed sharply again. It seemed like this pain had a bit more presence to it than it had before. He shook his head lightly and pushed it out of his mind. "Seven Stars?" he asked in a low voice. "Do you mean the Big Dipper stars carved into this plate? Is there something going on with this pedestal?"

Utai finally lifted her face. "What sat on this pedestal was an Enhanced Armament," she told him in the quietest voice possible. "However, it is no normal weapon or armor. A group of legendary armaments, said to be the most powerful in the Accelerated World, the Arms of the Seven Stars, also known as the Seven Arcs."

"Seven...Arcs..."

There's no way he would have forgotten that term. Haruyuki's teacher, Sky Raker, had explained it to him at the Meeting of the Seven Kings the day before yesterday. The Tempest, the staff owned by Purple Thorn, the Purple King. The Impulse, the great-sword worn on the hip of the Blue King, Blue Knight. The Strife, the large shield carried by the Green King, Green Grandé. All of these together were called the Seven Arcs.

At that time, Raker had told him that the prevailing hypothesis was that there were a total of seven Arcs existing in the Accelerated World, but the existence of no more than four had been confirmed. The basis for this hypothesis was probably the plate embedded in this pedestal. When he looked very closely, the sixth star from the left in the relief of the seven stars of the Big Dipper carved into the plate was bigger than the others. He supposed that meant that particular star corresponded with this particular Arc.

"So then, the Arcs that the Blue King and the others have, they were on pedestals like these?" Haruyuki's question omitted the thought process that preceded it, but Utai still nodded.

"Yes. The Arcs that the Vanquisher and the others have obtained were enshrined in the deepest parts of the four great dungeons of the Accelerated World: Shibakoen, Tokyo Dome, Tokyo Station, and the Shinjuku government building. I subsequently saw only the pedestal for the Impulse, but it was exactly the same design as this. C, please take a look here." Utai pointed to a spot on the plate.

Two characters were carved out beneath the seven stars relief in a severe typeface. They could be read as *kaiyou*, but he had no idea what that was supposed to mean.

"This *kaiyou* is the Chinese name for the zeta star of the Big Dipper. The pedestal for the greatsword Impulse that I saw had the characters *tensuu* cut into it, the Chinese name for the alpha star. Similarly, the Chinese name for the beta star—*tensen*—was on the pedestal for the staff Tempest, while the pedestal for the shield Strife was imprinted with the Chinese name for the gamma star, *tenki*."

"...I get it." Haruyuki nodded deeply, intently etching the string of peculiar nouns into his brain.

Four great dungeons set to the north, east, south, and west of the Castle in the Unlimited Neutral Field. Four Enhanced Armaments sealed away deep within them. And carved into those pedestals, the Chinese names for the four stars that made up the bowl of the Big Dipper. Given that, it was only natural that the veteran Burst Linkers who found them judged that they were four of likely seven powerful armaments.

Aah, seriously, why didn't I get to be a Burst Linker sooner?! Exploring the four great dungeons, capturing the bosses inside—probably super huge, too—getting the most powerful equipment... All the fun's already over.

After letting these regrets race around his mind, Haruyuki quickly rethought things. Hadn't his teacher, Sky Raker, said that everything was starting now? And if he had become a Burst Linker in the early days, there was a possibility that right about now, he might belong to a side against Nega Nebulus—against Kuroyukihime. And he had no greater fortune in this world than that of having been able to become her child.

He covered his face lightly and reflected deeply on his own thoughts. "That reminds me," he said to Utai in a low voice. "I didn't see it at the Meeting of the Seven Kings, but what's the last of the four Arcs presently confirmed? I'm assuming someone's already got it, like the other three hidden in the four great dungeons?"

"That...It's been confirmed that the delta *tenken* pedestal in the lowest level of the large Shibakoen maze was already empty..." Utai broke off momentarily, and a look like she was thinking it over herself rose up on her face as she continued. "It's unknown to the present day who obtained the Luminary, the Arc that should have been there. At the very least, as far as I'm aware, there is no record of it ever having been used in a duel."

"What?!"

That was unexpected. Having expended the effort to obtain one of the most powerful Enhanced Armaments in the world, was it even possible to not use it? Perhaps whoever had it was worried about standing out and becoming the target of concentrated attacks, but if they had the actual strength to break through an enormous dungeon, then they were probably safe to stand up proudly and call themselves the owner of an Arc.

And there was something else that didn't quite click. Puzzling over this, he asked Utai, "But I'm sure Master Raker said there were just four Arcs confirmed. So if they only found the pedestal, does the Luminary count as one of the confirmed Arcs?"

"No." Utai shook her head, and the hair parts of her shrine maiden avatar swung back and forth. She lowered hesitant eyes before murmuring at minimum volume, "Luminary is treated as unconfirmed. The last of the four Arcs that have appeared up until now in the Accelerated World should have sat on this *kai-you* pedestal, the Destiny."

"Des...tiny..." Repeating the name, Haruyuki looked at the plate on the front of the pedestal as if drawn in by it. Beneath the relief of the Big Dipper with the single larger star and the two characters that spelled out the Chinese name for the zeta star, he did in fact spy several roman letters: THE DESTINY.

It was a name he had never heard before. Or it should have been. And yet Haruyuki felt that strange piercing sensation in the center of his body once more. *Thmm, thmm.* It throbbed somewhere deep in his soul. The pulsing reached his central nervous system and gave rise to a small spark at a single point on his back. Abruptly, the world before his eyes shook. Or no, not the world—only the roman letters on the plate he had his eyes focused on were losing shape. The seven letters of DESTINY shuddered, twisted, and transformed into another row of letters, similar and yet different...

"C."

Haruyuki's eyes flew open at the firm squeeze of his left hand.

The vision disappeared, and the letters on the metal plate returned to their original arrangement. At some point, the throbbing in his back had also vanished. He blinked several times before remembering what they had been talking about immediately before the vision.

"Oh! S-sorry." Haruyuki apologized to a worried-looking Utai in a voice that was still slightly hoarse. "I just…spaced out. Umm, so then that means that some Burst Linker did come here before us and got the Disaster from this pedestal and used it in a duel, right? Who was it? Probably one of the kings or something?"

But Ardor Maiden only shook her head in tiny increments at this question. "You'll have to excuse me. I haven't seen it directly, either. I heard that it was a long, long time before I became a Burst Linker."

"It was?" Haruyuki pushed back his frustration. If it was something even a serious veteran like Utai didn't know, then Haru would definitely have no point of contact with it, given that he had been a Burst Linker for only eight months. Which was why this uneasiness smoldering in the back of his brain had to be a misapprehension. This itchy, annoying feeling practically insisted he knew the answer, but he just couldn't remember.

Almost as if he were unconsciously trying to avert his eyes from the name Destiny, Haruyuki moved another few steps to the left, still holding Utai's hand, and examined the neighboring pedestal. This one had a similar metal plate embedded in it. The carving of the Big Dipper was also the same. But the larger star was fifth from the left. The characters inscribed there were *gyokusho*.

"*Gyoku…sho*, maybe?"

"Yes. The Chinese name for the epsilon star. The Arc inscription is…"

He brought his face in closer at the same time as Utai did and found the English letters there. Together they murmured, " 'The Infinity.' "

"This is also the first time I've heard this name. Since this pedestal is as empty as its neighbor, someone—perhaps the same person—has already carried it off. If that's the case, then like the Luminary, it would be an unconfirmed Arc, never once used."

"I…I guess so." Haruyuki let out a small, secret sigh.

Immediately before the Meeting of the Seven Kings the day before yesterday, where he had seen the Castle rising up in the distance in Chiyoda Area, Kuroyukihime had said there was a rumor about some incredible Enhanced Armament being hidden in the very innermost room of the Castle's inner sanctuary. And that had evidently been true. And that Enhanced Armament was likely higher in status than the Arcs the Blue, Green, and Purple kings had.

And yet what they found were only the pedestals; the essential items had been carried off by someone long ago. As not just a Burst Linker but also a hardcore gamer, there was no way he was not going to be utterly and crushingly disappointed.

"Infinity, huh…It was prob'ly an amazing piece of equipment. I wish I could have at least seen it," he muttered in frustration, and then jerked his head up in sudden realization.

Four Arcs in the four great dungeons scattered about the Unlimited Neutral Field. And two Arcs in the innermost room of the inner sanctuary of the Castle in the center of the Accelerated World. All together, six. But there were seven stars etched into the pedestal. Hadn't Utai said that was why they were called the Arms of the Seven Stars? In other words, that meant…

"There's one…missing…" His mouth opened of its own accord.

Ardor Maiden, next to him, nodded firmly. "I—I was also thinking that myself. In this hall, meant to be the very center of the Accelerated World, there are only two Arc pedestals. Then Alkaid, the eta star of the Big Dipper, which would be 'Hagun' in Chinese readings…Where on earth is it?"

Exchanging a glance, the silent pair heard—

"Allow me to answer that question."

—the clear, bright voice, like the wind blowing across the autumn sky, of a young boy.

4

Hearing this voice, Haruyuki was simply surprised and merely turned his head in the direction of the source—farther toward the north side of the two pedestals.

However, Utai Shinomiya's reaction was different. She had no sooner released the hand she had been holding than she was pushing Haruyuki back with her palm. Stepping forward, she dropped into a stance with one leg in front and the other behind, raised her left hand slightly, and turned toward the gloom filling the depths of the hall.

An orange veil of light added a thin layer to the entire body of the slender shrine maiden avatar. Overlay—proof that she had activated the Incarnate System. But Utai had been one of the Four Elements of the former Nega Nebulus; there was no way she didn't know the number one rule of the Incarnate System: that it must not be used unless you yourself have been attacked with Incarnate.

Utai manifesting the ultimate power of a Burst Linker at the stage when they couldn't even see their opponent was perhaps to signal her firm intention to protect Haruyuki, even if she had to violate taboos. And the pressure being emitted by Ardor Maiden, which threatened to scorch even the air, made overwhelmingly clear the difference in actual power between her and Haruyuki.

If, hypothetically, it did turn into a fight on this level, he was only going to be in the way. Even as he acknowledged this, Haruyuki also raised his hands and focused his imagination, albeit belatedly. A silver overlay took up residence in fingers stretched out into the shape of a sword, and he somehow managed to make it cover the lower half or so of his arm.

As they braced themselves, completely prepared for battle, the voice came at them again. "I apologize for my rudeness. But please believe me. I haven't the slightest intention of fighting you."

He felt like there wasn't any malice in the voice—somehow more refreshing now—just as it proclaimed. However, Utai didn't drop her guard even slightly.

"Then you should first show yourself," she responded firmly, and enhanced her overlay as if trying to push aside the darkness beyond. Remembering that this light flickering in the red spectrum became, with the shrine maiden's dance, a conflagration raging through the field, Haruyuki held his breath.

"Understood. I'm coming toward you now," the owner of the voice replied, and they heard the high-pitched sound of footfalls.

From the depths of the hall, a stride that seemed to deliberately sound against the floorboards drew nearer. The flames of the candles lined up along the walls on either side flickered in unison, despite the lack of wind.

Tak, tak. The approaching steps couldn't have been more than fifteen meters away from them. Completely within range for a long-distance or a nimble-type duel avatar. Yet the other person stepped forward at a steady pace, the atmosphere around him tense.

Finally, his figure appeared in the light of the candles.

Blue. A perfectly clear azure, the depths of a lake, the heavens seen from above the clouds. Just like the boy Haruyuki had imagined from the voice, the duel avatar was fairly small, perhaps a little taller than Ardor Maiden. But there was no hint of her delicacy.

Limbs covered in a thick armor reminiscent of kimono sleeves and *hakama* pants, long, bound hair parts stretching out from the back of his head to below his waist. The face mask peeking out from beneath a front fringe was immature and imposing. The overall impression was Japanese; if Ardor Maiden was a shrine maiden, then he was a young samurai.

As if to own that particular description, a short-range Enhanced Armament hung from his left hip. It had an elliptical guard and a slender hilt. While you would call it more katana than sword, there was essentially no curvature to the blade itself. The whole thing was silver like a mirror, and the way countless lights flickered in the reflection of the blue of the avatar made it seem like the infinite starry sky had been compressed into the shape of a katana.

The young samurai stopped about ten meters from them and placed his left hand on the katana's scabbard. Utai's readied hands did twitch, but the next instant, he removed the Enhanced Armament, complete with scabbard, with a light metallic *clink*. Placing the katana at his feet on the floor, the unarmed samurai spread out both hands in the air and indicated Haruyuki and Utai.

"As you can see, I do not intend to fight." A quiet voice.

If the boy who lived inside that duel avatar was equipped with the personality of the swordsman he appeared to be, then laying the katana—his soul—down on the ground was a definite display of his nonhostile intentions.

At basically the same time Haruyuki had this thought, Utai slowly lowered her hand. The overlay blanketing her body abruptly melted away into the air.

"We shall trust that," Utai responded, so readily that Haru almost cried out in surprise behind her. Haruyuki hurried to similarly release his readied hands. He had felt it when they were up against Bush Utan as well, but this girl was apparently fairly quick to decide whether or not she trusted someone.

The young samurai avatar softened clear eye lenses brimming with blue light and let out a small sigh. A voice that was even calmer flowed out from him. "Thank goodness. The truth is, I was incredibly nervous about what I should do if you intended to fight."

"What?" This time, Haruyuki couldn't keep a cry of surprise from slipping out and continued with an impression that was the slightest bit rude. "S-someone who could make it all the way to a place like this...even now, acting like a newbie..."

The young samurai grinned before offering new surprises. "No, I am a complete newbie. I mean, from the time I became a Burst Linker until now, I've never once fought a normal duel."

The navy samurai, having picked up his katana from the floor and attached it to his waist once more, led Utai and Haruyuki to one of the candle stands lining the wall to the left.

On both sides of the flickering candles, thick wooden bars protruded from the wall in the shape of benches. The samurai sat on one, while Haruyuki and Utai sat on one across from him, and a brief silence fell upon them.

Haruyuki muttered, "Excuse me," and touched on his own HP gauge to call up the main window. The continuous dive time was more than seven hours. An hour and a half had already passed since they infiltrated the inner sanctuary of the Castle, and if Kuroyukihime and the others in the real world were in fact waiting thirty seconds before they cut Haruyuki's and Utai's global connection, then they probably had about an hour left.

At the same time as he closed the window, the samurai-like boy avatar seated before him shook his head slightly. "To be honest, I feel like I still can't believe it. That the time would actually come when I would meet someone in this palace..."

Haruyuki was just as surprised. But there were too many things he wanted explained, and he didn't know where exactly he should start asking questions. *Who are you, where did you enter the Castle, how did you get to this hall, and what do you mean you've never dueled even though you had the power to make it this far...*

While an infinity of words whirled around in his mind, Utai next to him lowered her head in a bow. "My name is Ardor Maiden. I belong to the Legion Nega Nebulus."

R-right, first introductions! Haruyuki hurriedly bowed. "Also a member of Nega Nebulus, Silver Crow."

"Nega Nebulus..." The young samurai blinked exaggeratedly

as though it were the first time he was hearing the name, before abruptly snapping to attention. He seemed to fumble for words for a moment. Before Haruyuki had the chance to frown in puzzlement, the other avatar bowed awkwardly and offered his own name. "Oh, excuse me. I should have introduced myself sooner. I'm Trilead Tetroxide. Please call me Lead."

"Trilead..." Rolling the name around in his mouth, Haruyuki mentally cocked his head. According to the rules of duel avatar naming, that should have been a word describing the armor color, but was that actually a way of saying navy or indigo? He glanced at Utai next to him.

She appeared to be considering the name as well, but she soon nodded crisply. "Well then, we will call you Lead." A beat later: "Lead. You were the one who broke the Suzaku seal on the south gate from the inside of the Castle, weren't you?"

Haruyuki threw his head back in surprise after the extremely heavy question slipped smoothly from the shrine maiden's mouth.

The young samurai Trilead was equally surprised. His deep blue eye lenses flickered several times before he looked up, abashed for some reason, and quietly asked, "Why would you think that?"

"To destroy an object with such a high level of endurance as that in a mere two blows, even more than the technique of the person who did it, an appropriately high level Enhanced Armament would be necessary. Such as, for instance, the Seven Arc that you have on your hip right now, Lead."

"Whaaat?!" This time, a fairly loud yelp of surprise snuck out of him, and as he hurriedly snapped his mouth shut, Haruyuki stared intently at the mirror-silver straightsword shining on the boy's left hip. When he first saw it, he had figured it was no ordinary weapon, but he never dreamed it was one of the most powerful arms in the world. "Th-that's an Arc? So then, the one that was on that pedestal over there, you—?" Haruyuki blurted, looking at the straight sword and each of the empty pedestals a dozen meters to the right in turn.

The young samurai turned his face to the ground, seemingly

even more embarrassed. "Y-yes," he replied in a small voice. "Please excuse me. Someone like me truly isn't qualified to have this sword, but…

"The first time I saw it, I couldn't restrain myself. I reached a hand out toward it…"

The boy, who was probably younger than Haruyuki, turned his entire body into an expression of apology, and Haruyuki, turning toward him, hurriedly waved his right hand back and forth as he shook his head.

"Oh! No! You totally don't need to apologize. It's only natural that the first person to find it would take it. Sorry. That came out all weird." Haruyuki bowed his head neatly as he finished, and Lead timidly raised his face again to meet his eyes. The instant Haruyuki saw something like a shy smile rise up on that crisp face mask, a type of emotion that was extremely rare for him welled up in his heart.

He's a good guy, this one.

The only other people he had felt this kind of sincere affection for upon first meeting were his childhood friends Takumu Mayuzumi and Chiyuri Kurashima. And despite the fact that this young samurai, Trilead, was, at the moment, an unknown Burst Linker encountering an unusual situation, Haruyuki got the feeling that if their selves in the real world were exposed, they'd definitely be good friends.

Abruptly feeling eyes on him, Haruyuki turned his gaze and met that of Ardor Maiden, also smiling faintly, and was suddenly embarrassed. He quickly gave voice to a very unassuming question. "Oh, um, Trilead…Which pedestal was that sword on? I think the one on the left was the fifth star of the Big Dipper, and the one on the right was the sixth."

"Please, Lead is fine, Silver Crow."

Lead grinned before replying, and Haruyuki hurried to add, "Th-then just call me Crow."

But Lead bowed his head, noting that he was too much younger than Haruyuki to use a nickname. And before the silver avatar could protest, he began to explain. "This sword rested on the

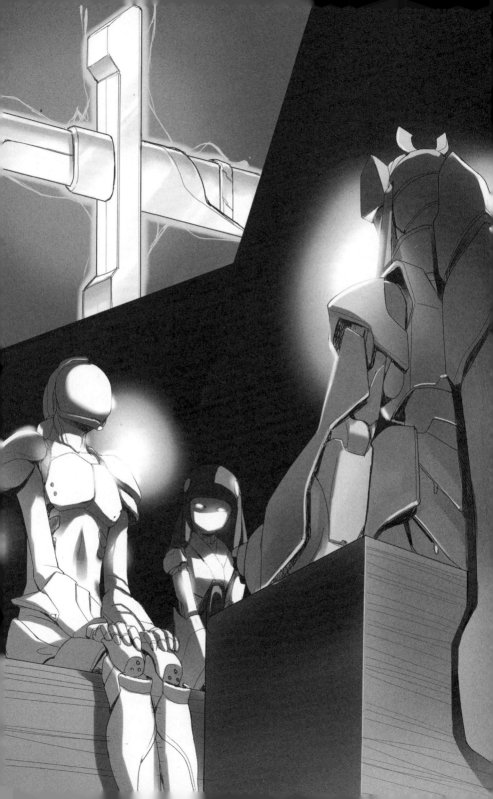

pedestal to the left, the epsilon star, *gyokusho*. It bears the inscription THE INFINITY." Haruyuki and Utai shifted their eyes toward the center of the great hall, and Trilead continued, looking in the same direction. "Further, when I found this sword, the neighboring zeta *kaiyou* pedestal was already empty."

"Huh." Haruyuki nodded.

Utai spoke up. "I heard that the Arc Destiny appeared in the Accelerated World in the very beginning, before a full year had passed since Brain Burst was distributed to the first-generation Burst Linkers."

"Huh? That long ago? So then I guess that means...the Burst Linker who got Destiny was the first person to enter the Castle? And Lead's the second?" Unaware that he had unself-consciously used the younger Linker's nickname, Haruyuki bent the fingers of his right hand. "Mei and me, we're third and fourth? I dunno. For how impenetrable it's supposed to be, that's a lot of people getting in."

The three exchanged glances and grinned at the same time.

But Lead's face quickly became serious once more, and he shrank into himself apologetically. "It's an honor to be counted among their number. But I'm sorry, I didn't come in through the four gates like everyone else."

"What? That's...So then, that means you came over the moat or the cliff or...?" Haruyuki cocked his head to one side, but before he could ask what Lead actually meant, Utai opened her mouth.

"If that is so, then C and I were able to come inside precisely because you cut the seal for us, Trilead. That seal was likely set so that in the event that four squads assaulted the Four Gods simultaneously, as the former Nega Nebulus did, as long as the group could break through one of the gates, they could let the other squads in from inside the Castle. That is to say, if the seal had been intact, the door would not have opened, and we would definitely have been roasted alive by Suzaku."

"Oh, I get it. So that's it, huh?" He nodded deeply as his body shuddered at the memory of the molten flames pressing in on his back. He forgot his previous question and lobbed a new one at the young samurai. "So then, you broke the seal because you were going to escape from the Castle through it?"

"No, that is not…the case." He denied Haruyuki's suggestion in a voice tinged with a faint loneliness and answered with a shy smile. "In fact, just the opposite. I thought that perhaps if I broke the seal, then someday, someone might come in through it for me…"

"Come in? For you?" Lead was supposedly an intruder, and yet it was almost as though he had completely given up on escape; it was a slightly curious turn of phrase. Haruyuki blinked furiously beneath his silver mask and pressed the question. "But, Lead, you're here in the inner sanctuary of the Castle, so you have to be stuck in a pseudo–Unlimited EK like we are. I mean, you're locked up in here, right? Ah, no, wait…"

Without noticing the expression flitting across Trilead's face—as if he were trying to conceal something—Haruyuki dropped his gaze to the silver straight sword glittering on the young samurai's hip. "Infinity. When you got that Arc, wasn't there a portal that activates just one time? When you took the sword, you should've been able to get out normally."

It was a simple question, with nothing especially behind it. But Lead lowered his face as if abashed once more. As Haruyuki stared dumbfounded, Utai placed a small hand gently on his left knee.

"Even if there is a portal, that doesn't necessarily always translate into a smooth escape, C."

Instantly, he realized that his own question might have sounded like he was reproaching Lead for his actions, and he reflexively bowed his head deeply. "Oh! S-sorry, Lead, I wasn't trying to blame you or anything. I mean, the same kind of thing's happened to me tons. The reason we're even here now is that we couldn't follow the strategy, so…"

The young samurai finally lifted his face. "Excuse me, Crow, Maiden." He placed his hands on his *hakama*-like legs and bowed again. "I will tell you that story when the time comes—how I came to be in this place."

There was a nobility to Lead's voice and expression, in his

entire being, that almost took Haruyuki's breath away. On behalf of the speechless Haruyuki and not to be outdone when it came to proper manners, Utai bowed lightly in return.

"I understand, Lead. Then we will tell our story. Of why we stepped into the territory of Suzaku, one of the Four Gods, and how we came to break through the south gate into the Castle."

For the following five minutes, Haruyuki and Utai went over it briefly. The challenge and destruction of the Legion Nega Nebulus two and a half years earlier. Ardor Maiden sealed away immediately before the south gate in order to secure the escape of the others. The plan for rescue by the current Legion members to bring that avatar out alive, and the result.

Taking it all in with wide eyes, Trilead let out a long sigh when the pair closed their mouths. "Such things happened," he murmured finally. "That there would be such people who attempted to challenge those Four Gods and crush them..."

Haruyuki got the sense that he heard a faint note of longing somewhere deep in that voice and opened both eyes wide. Something in a place deep within his own self resonated with it, and that vibration turned to sound and attempted to crawl up his throat.

You are one, too.

On the verge of saying this, nonetheless, he closed his mouth. Because he couldn't find the words that should come after that.

Perhaps noticing the movement, or perhaps not, Lead allowed a faint smile to cross his face before speaking in his calm voice again. "Given that that is the situation, I would be delighted if you would allow me to aid you in your escape from the palace."

"Huh?...Th-thanks." Haruyuki dipped his head before leaning forward to ask with some urgency, "Do you know a way to get out normally?! Is there a portal somewhere we can still use or something?!"

"I personally use an automatic disconnection via a timer to leave, but I have confirmed the existence of just one portal. However..." Although Lead nodded, he interrupted himself as though dropping into thought for a moment. He soon raised his face again and opened his mouth, looking at Haruyuki and Utai in turn. "It would perhaps be best if you were to see it yourselves. At the same time, I will be able to accomplish the matter I first promised."

"Umm, wh-what was that again?" Haruyuki twisted his head to the side.

"The agreement to reply with the location of the seventh star, the last of the Arcs of which you spoke," the boy clad in azure replied smoothly.

Standing up from the crosspiece-turned-bench, Trilead led Haruyuki and Utai into the darkness where he had first appeared on the north side of the hall.

The wall at the end, where the light from the candles basically did not reach, was made up of vermilion pillars and white wall as the walls to the sides were, but there was something in the center of it that he hadn't noticed before.

An entrance, a gate. Pillars put together in the shape of a small *torii* shrine gate, the opening between them heavily spilling out black, cool air.

Unconsciously pulling into himself, Haruyuki murmured, "So this hall...isn't the deepest part of the Castle..."

"No. This is the last of the court's gates. Once we slip through it, we will find the Shrine of the Eight Divines. Shall we go?" Trilead said, and stepped with his *hakama*-clad leg into the dense darkness. Without appearing to hesitate in the slightest, Utai followed him, and Haruyuki steeled himself to join them.

Once they had gone through the *torii*, he saw there was just a tiny bit of light in what he had thought was the completely dark interior. The hallway soon turned into stairs leading underground, where the faint light seemed to originate. With an assured step, Lead started to descend, and the other two Burst Linkers followed him.

As they advanced, Haruyuki felt a pressure pushing on his avatar of a type he had never encountered before. It wasn't the sense of power the God Suzaku or the armored warrior Enemies emitted, but rather a sensation that the air itself was tinged with some kind of spiritual energy.

But the word *spiritual* didn't really fit with the Accelerated World. This was a VR world generated by the Brain Burst program, and all the information received by the five senses was digital data that could be replaced with code. Niko had used the phrase *information pressure* for the pressure received from other Burst Linkers. Taking that analogy, did that mean that even the air in this place was included in some kind of data set? Not surface information like temperature and smell and wind direction, but a series of existences equal to infinity that expressed time, or rather history…

When they had gone down thirty or more of the ebony stairs, the steps wrapped around 180 degrees and continued on. Right around the time he was starting to lose track of exactly how far they had crept underground, the stairs ahead of them finally ended, leading into a fairly large room with a wooden floor. But it was a mere fraction of the size of the great hall on the top floor where the two pedestals sat.

"Huh? Is that the last room of the Castle? It's surprisingly small. And I mean, it looks like there's nothing in it," Haruyuki unconsciously let slip.

Ahead of him on the stairs, Trilead looked over his shoulder, a faint smile on his face. "No, you'll be able to see when we get to the bottom."

Haruyuki wondered what exactly he was going to see and quickened his pace. A few steps behind Lead he entered the room, only to find a second and much, much larger *torii* gate jumping up into his field of view.

The vermilion gate soared to such a height at the front of the room that almost touched the walls on both sides and the ceiling above. However, an object that hadn't been on the gate upstairs connected the two pillars: an impressively thick snow-white rope. A *shimenawa*, used to bind sacred spaces. An address border dividing the world of the living from the holy.

Swallowing hard, Haruyuki took a few steps toward the gate and its display of absolute separation and tried to look into the gloom beyond.

"...It's huge...," he murmured like a gasp.

Two rows of small watch fires flickered from the sides of the *torii* toward the interior, but he couldn't see the third wall at all. The latticed ceiling was also just barely visible. The floor was polished stonework, but the area of the room far surpassed that of the gym at Umesato; he had absolutely no idea exactly how many meters it was in any direction.

Big, chilly, and silent, and yet definitely not futile—he knew this sensation. He thought about it for a minute, and it hit him: that enormously pregnant tranquility that had filled the space before Suzaku appeared on the large bridge stretching out from the south gate of the Castle.

Unable to say anything more, Haruyuki simply stood there, and Trilead stepped soundlessly forward from between himself and the similarly silent Utai. He raised his right arm and indicated the line of watch fires in the distance.

"Over there."

Straining his eyes as told, Haruyuki could see a light up ahead that was a different wavelength from the flickering flames. He held his breath and focused more intently on looking at it. The darkness receded slightly to reveal what it had hidden.

A pedestal cut out of black stone.

It was the same as the two in the hall above, metal plate embedded on the front. But it was just too far away; he couldn't make out the characters on it. And then on the pedestal itself, a warm, golden yellow light pulsed slowly, as if it held the blue light of a portal. As if it were whispering. As if it were calling out.

Unconsciously, Haruyuki went to take a step forward toward the *shimenawa*, and Lead gently held him back with his right hand on Haruyuki's shoulder. "You mustn't. It's too dangerous up ahead."

"B-but..." Haruyuki was unable to make much in the way of

a response, so filled was he with an emotion resembling impatience or perhaps even...*craving*.

"Trilead, that is the last Arc, the eta star of the Big Dipper, yes?" Utai asked softly.

"Yes, that's exactly right." Lead nodded, hand still on Haruyuki's left shoulder, and continued in a sweetly ringing voice. "To even draw near enough to be able to read the inscription carved on that pedestal required an amount of time that was essentially infinite. The name of that light is—"

"—*Youkou*. The Fluctuating Light."

"Fluctuating...light..." Without being aware of it, Haruyuki repeated the name.

It was a phrase he had absolutely no memory of hearing. To begin with, Haruyuki hadn't even known about the existence of the Arcs until he took part in the Meeting of the Seven Kings the day before yesterday. But despite this, the word that most closely described the emotion that brimmed up from his heart and filled his chest was a kind of fond remembrance.

"I—I—" Still without his awareness, Haruyuki's mouth began to move. "I've seen that light before..."

Both of the small avatars to his left gasped sharply.

Their questioning eyes on him, Haruyuki fumbled intently for the right words. "It's—Right, that's—Of course, in the Unlimited Neutral Field—It was when I was first training in the Incarnate System. Master Raker pushed me off the top of the old Tokyo Tower and told me that I had to climb back up with my own hands..."

The moment she heard this, Utai let out a small sigh. Given that Sky Raker had similarly made her do all kinds of things, she had to be thinking that this was only too plausible, but he had no mental leeway then for conjecturing about her emotional state.

"At first," he continued in a hoarse voice, "I couldn't even make a scratch in the wall. But I kept shooting my hand at it day after day after day, and I gradually managed to get so my fingertips would dig into it. And then I got so that my fingers would pierce it all the way to the knuckles. After a week, I started to climb the tower. I totally lost myself in it. I just climbed the wall for hours, stabbing my right hand in, then my left, back and forth…Sometimes…that light…But I feel like it wasn't an object…that golden light…"

Here, Haruyuki finally turned his gaze on Lead and Utai. He announced his final words to the pair—listening with wide eyes—in a trembling voice.

"It was a *person*. It was *calling me*."

For a while, silence filled the space.

Breaking this was not anyone speaking, but rather the crimson characters that filled Haruyuki's view. DISCONNECTION WARNING. Kuroyukihime and the others had burst out thirty real-world seconds earlier, and they were now about to pull out Haruyuki's direct cable.

The direct connectors on Neurolinkers were water-resistant, noncontact-type ports. Thus, even if the cable was pulled out, the signal would continue, albeit for a very brief time. Naturally, this was a matter of units in the point-zero-second range, but even so, in the Accelerated World, this allowed an extension of dozens of seconds from the time the warning appeared.

"Ah! Um!" Abruptly dragged back from the reaches of his memory, all he could do was flap his mouth open and shut.

It was Utai who explained in a calm voice, "Trilead, our comrades have activated the disconnection safety in the real world. I do apologize, but we will soon burst out temporarily."

"Y-yes, I understand." The young samurai nodded.

"It is a forced disconnect from outside," the shrine maiden further added, albeit at a slightly quickened pace. "So the next time we dive into the Unlimited Neutral Field, we will appear once more at these coordinates. Therefore, although I do realize this is rather impudent of me to ask, if possible, I'd like to meet you here once more. When would be the next time you would be able to dive in real-world time?"

"Yes, let me think…" Considering it for a mere instant, Lead soon responded, "Well then, two days from now. How is precisely seven PM, Thursday, June twentieth?"

"Understood. We truly appreciate your assistance. Thank you so much."

Following Utai's lead as she bowed her head, Haruyuki bowed himself before finally managing to get some words out.

"Uh, um, Lead, I want to thank you, too. You taught us a bunch of stuff. But there's still a ton I want to talk to you about, a ton of things I want to ask you. So I'm excited about seeing you again."

The disconnection warning in his field of view began to blink at top speed. In the real world, the XSB cable was likely almost completely pulled out of his Neurolinker.

At Haruyuki's rushed yet earnest words, the azure samurai avatar blinked once before a smile colored with a complex set of emotions rose up faintly on his face. "I also very much enjoyed speaking with you both. I promise, the day after tomorrow, I will definitely be here. I would also like to talk with you both much, much more."

And then the boy with the strange avatar name Trilead Tetroxide took a step back and looked at Utai and Haruyuki in turn. The crisp figure standing there, reminiscent of an autumn wind, was finally blanketed by the oncoming darkness and disappeared.

5

The very first thing Haruyuki was aware of upon his return to the real world was not the weight of his physical body sinking into the sofa nor the cool of the air-conditioning, but rather supple fingertips touching his cheek.

His eyes flew open. And stared into the beautiful starry sky he had looked up at in the Castle garden only moments earlier. Except, wait—that wasn't it. Jet-black eyes filled with particles of light like stardust?

When those eyes blinked once, slowly, the tiniest droplet of water bounced off long eyelashes and disappeared into the air. At the same time came the whisper of a voice. "So you're back, Haruyuki."

After staring for a bit at the clear, crisp beauty of Kuroyukihime—swordmaster, leader of the Legion Nega Nebulus, Black King, Black Lotus—who he respected and adored more than any other, Haruyuki replied hoarsely, "Yes, Kuroyukihime. I just got back now."

The place where Haruyuki awakened was number 2305 on the twenty-third floor of the mixed-use skyscraper condo in northern Koenji, Suginami Ward, in the real world—in other words, the living room of the Arita home. He sat in the center of the sofa set near the southern windows, and directly before him, Kuroyukihime was leaning forward, left hand pushing up against the backrest of the sofa, the fingertips of her right hand gently resting on his cheek. In her palm, she held the plug for the XSB cable, the silver cord that stretched out to the connector panel on the wall.

The panel was for wired connections to the Arita family home server. For this dive, Haruyuki and his friends had connected globally via a wired connection to his home server, rather than wirelessly. Haruyuki and Utai had returned to the real world without using a portal because Kuroyukihime had pulled this cable out of Haruyuki's Neurolinker.

"That was a long thirty seconds, you know," Kuroyukihime murmured, fingers still touching his cheek. "While we sat here like this, you and Utai were perhaps being chased by Enemies inside the Castle. Or maybe regenerating and dying over and over and over. I could hardly stand it."

The instant he became aware that this voice contained the slightest hint of a tremor, something burst open in Haruyuki's heart. He sat up straight, took a deep breath, and opened his mouth. "Kuroyukihime...That time—When Suzaku shifted its target to me, I'm sorry for disobeying the order to retreat. But—But I had to..." Even though he had so firmly decided that he would apologize properly when he got back to the real world, when it came right down to it, his faculty with words lagged far behind the intent in his heart.

He bit his lip, opened his mouth, and then bit down again. Over and over.

Kuroyukihime took her left hand off the sofa and dropped the cable in her right hand to wrap now-empty hands gently around his shoulders. A smile like the bud of a water lily bled onto her pale, glossy lips. "It's fine, Haruyuki. It's precisely because you do such things that I believe I can entrust myself and the future of the Legion to you. You shook off even Suzaku's flames and simply flew forward. There's no way I could fault that kind of bravery."

"...Kuro...yukihime..." Choking back all the things welling up inside him, Haruyuki simply stared wholeheartedly

into her eyes. He clenched both hands tightly and tried to turn the emotions overflowing within him into words. "Kuroyuki-hime. Th-the reason I could fly was because you told me to fly—*han-huh-hee-hoo-ha!*"

Ruining the tail end of his so carefully crafted speech were two hands stretching out from either side of him to pinch his cheeks and yank hard.

"Okay, look! Exactly how long—" Chiyuri yelled, pinching his left cheek.

Fuko, yanking on his right, picked up where she left off. "—are you two going to keep this up?!"

Three minutes later.

Once they had switched locations from the sofa to the dining room, with Haruyuki and Utai settled into the chairs on the south side, Takumu and Chiyuri across from them, Kuroyuki-hime to the left and Fuko to the right, they all checked the current time.

7:35 PM.

Not even ten full minutes in real-world time had passed since the start of Operation Rescue Ardor Maiden. However, in Haruyuki's actual perception, it seemed like yesterday already when they had called out the "unlimited burst" command to dive into the Unlimited Neutral Field. And actually, given that he had napped for six hours inside the Castle, it was only natural he'd feel that way. Not to mention that during that nap, he'd had a very long dream, vicariously lived through memories that spanned no mere six hours but several days—and really, several years of experience.

"First of all, nice work, everyone." Kuroyukihime's voice interrupted Haruyuki's thoughts. He hurriedly added his voice to the chorus of "nice work!"

After taking a sip of the café au lait Chiyuri had made for her, Kuroyukihime looked around at them and continued. "The second phase of the plan to purify the Armor of Catastrophe,

Operation Rescue Ardor Maiden, was unfortunately not a total success on all fronts. All the fault for that lays squarely with me and the fact that I could not keep the god Suzaku focused on me and me alone. I'm sorry."

At their Legion Master's contrite words and deeply bowed head, her five subordinates cried out together, "That's not true!"

"Sacchi." The Legion's second in command, Fuko Kurasaki—Sky Raker—quickly spoke out for all of them. "Suzaku changed its target despite the fact that Corvus had not attacked in any way. No one could have predicted that behavior. Most likely, it's set to add more Hate for people intruding deep into its territory than people causing it the most damage."

Kuroyukihime raised her head briefly, then lowered her eyes as though she were deep in thought again.

Haruyuki timidly raised his right hand and broke the short silence. "Um, Master? About the Hate-adding just now..."

Hate was, put simply, a word to explain numerically the logic by which Enemies selected their attack targets. Naturally, Hate increased for Burst Linkers directly attacking them, but also for Burst Linkers who were only supporting other Burst Linkers with their abilities, such as with indirect interference attacks. The Enemy attacked whichever opponent had the maximum Hate value at that moment. Or so it was generally assumed. Suzaku may have been a top-level inhuman Enemy, one of the Four Gods, but it still should have selected its targets based on the Hate principle. The fact that it had turned from Kuroyukihime to Haruyuki on the big bridge meant that Suzaku was set so that people approaching the Castle's south gate earned more Hate than people attacking it directly—that was the general gist of Fuko's remark.

"What is it, Corvus?" Fuko cocked her head to one side, setting her long, airy hair swinging.

"So, Suzaku." Haruyuki pushed his question out with some difficulty. "No, the Four Gods, including Suzaku, don't actually have AI more advanced than any of the other Enemies, right?

Wait, maybe not AI, I dunno…Umm…" Vexed at being unable to clearly put what he wanted to say into words, he flapped his mouth open and shut.

Utai Shinomiya, seated to his right, was the only one among them holding a mug of hot milk, and she set this down on the table before making her hands dance through the air. Cherry-pink font scrolled by shockingly fast in the semitransparent window displayed in the lower half of Haruyuki's field of view.

UI> ARITA IS LIKELY TRYING TO SAY THAT PERHAPS THE FOUR GODS HAVE A TRUE INTENT OF THEIR OWN THAT GOES BEYOND THE REALM OF AI.

"R-right! That's exactly it!" Bobbing his head up and down, Haruyuki was suddenly and belatedly self-conscious about the absurdity of this idea, and he flinched in preparation for the beams of eye-rolling power sure to snap into laser focus on him at any second.

Unexpectedly, however, not a single one of his comrades gathered around the table laughed or sighed or did anything else to indicate exasperation. Even Takumu, who hadn't actually seen Suzaku directly, narrowed his eyes behind frameless glasses, as if he was thinking hard.

In the silence came once again the light sound of Utai's fingers tapping on her keyboard. UI> AT THE VERY LEAST, IT'S CERTAIN THAT THERE HAS BEEN A CHANGE IN SUZAKU'S BEHAVIOR ALGORITHM SINCE THE FOUR GODS OPERATION THAT LED TO THE DOWNFALL OF THE FIRST NEGA NEBULUS. THERE IS NO DOUBT THAT TWO AND A HALF YEARS AGO, SUZAKU GAVE PRIORITY TO TARGETING THE PERSON DOING THE GREATEST DAMAGE TO IT. HOW WAS IT WITH BYAKKO AT THE WEST GATE WHERE YOU FOUGHT, SACCHI, FU?

"Just as you say, Uiui," Fuko murmured, nodding. "I recall that in the previous battle, Byakko also seemed to set its sights on the main attack squad alone, regardless of the position of the attack subject."

"Mmm. I'm certain of it. That's exactly why I was able to act as bait to allow the other members to retreat in the end," Kuroyuki-hime affirmed from the opposite end of the table, narrowing her eyes sharply before continuing. "But this time, there was indeed a part of Suzaku's behavior that I can't believe was the Enemy simply obeying increases and decreases in Hate. That said, there was no sign of remote operation by a third party or a simple algorithm anomaly."

Takumu, seated directly across from Haruyuki, brought his right hand to his chin and opened his mouth. "But, Master, it's almost as if Suzaku saw that our objective this time was not to defeat it, but rather to rescue Shinomiya. In which case, that's no longer within the realm of AI. It's as Haru said: It has powers of insight, perhaps intelligence."

Again, silence fell for several seconds. Finally, Kuroyukihime smiled softly. "We're not going to be able to get an answer to that now. But I will add just one more piece of information. When Suzaku was responding to my Incarnate Attack and advancing, immediately before targeting Haruyuki, I think I saw that bird open its beak as though it was sneering at me."

Yes.

Haruyuki was sure he'd heard it. Suzaku, on the verge of releasing its flame breath, in a voice that was not a voice. *Small one, become ash.*

"But, like!" The very first of their downturned faces to pop up was Chiyuri, speaking forcefully. "Whether that bird's got a will or intelligence, or if maybe it's actually a real god, it only half got us, right? The operation wasn't a total success, but it wasn't a total failure, either, Kuroyukihime. I mean, like, Haru and Ui are alive, aren't they? They're alive, and on top of that, they flew right through those gates. Right, Haru?" she shouted, catlike eyes glittering as she leaned across the table, hands clenched. "I seriously can't take it anymore! What's it like in the Castle?! Did anything happen?! Hurry up and tell us everything, start to finish!"

Haruyuki darted his eyes about, flustered and bewildered at the abrupt interrogation.

To his left, Kuroyukihime raised her voice in laughter. "Ha-ha-ha! Hard-hitting as ever, Chiyuri. I'm sure that many Burst Linkers would pay ten, no, a hundred points if they could hear that story. I was even restraining myself here."

"Hee-hee, it's true. Just thinking that Burst Linkers who have set foot in that impenetrable Castle and succeeded in returning with information about the inside are sitting before my eyes has had my heart pounding this whole time." Fuko made a show of pressing a hand to her chest.

The right side of Haruyuki's face turned upward in a somewhat complicated smile, and he exchanged looks with Utai. The fourth grader and one corner of the Four Elements of the former Nega Nebulus tilted her head to the side as if to say, *I'll leave this to you.*

And when he thought about it, if she tried to explain everything that happened in the Castle via chat, she'd have to type out so many characters her hands would cramp up. *I'll just have to do what I can here!* Stepping up to the plate, Haruyuki looked at his clock once more before giving a bit of an introduction.

"Umm, I think it'll take a relatively long time if I tell you everything from start to finish. Is everyone okay for curfew?"

The time was just shy of eight o'clock on a Tuesday night, but there wasn't a single person who shook their head, including elementary student Utai.

The main cobblestone road stretching out straight to the north from the south gate of the Castle and the groups of terrifying Enemies patrolling it. The massive inner sanctuary with its successive layers of connected *fusuma* doors adorned with brilliant paintings. The great hall at the center and the two pedestals placed there. The names DESTINY and INFINITY carved in plates with the Big Dipper.

When Haruyuki got to this point in the story, Kuroyukihime and Fuko seemed to suddenly exchange a look with each other. However, neither of them tried to interject, and since the real center of the story was from this point, Haruyuki didn't dwell on it and continued speaking.

The young azure samurai avatar that suddenly called out to them in the hall. The enormous underground space at the bottom of the stairs he guided them to. And the golden light flickering off in the distance. The seventh Arc, the Fluctuating Light.

By the time he had finally managed to finish telling the story—with occasional comments from Utai—up to the point where they left the Unlimited Neutral Field because their companions cut the connection, a full thirty minutes had passed.

While Haruyuki expelled a long breath and drank the rest of his second café au lait, no one made a move to speak. A few seconds after he placed his mug on the table, Kuroyukihime finally said, almost muttering, "The owner of the fifth Arc, Infinity. Trilead Tetroxide...Fuko, have you ever heard that name before?"

Fuko, the most senior Burst Linker there alongside Kuroyukihime, quickly shook her head. "No. This is the first I'm hearing of the Enhanced Armament *and* the Burst Linker. I don't even know these English words *trilead* and *tetroxide*. Although it has the sound of a molecular formula..."

If the sole high schooler among them didn't know the words, then the other five—still in junior high and elementary—could hardly be expected to.

"Shall we look them up?" Takumu said, pushing up the bridge of his glasses and running a finger along his virtual desktop. Naturally, his search skills were impressive, and in less than ten seconds, he had found the terms. He lifted his head and nodded once. "Raker is correct. It is a molecular formula. Three lead, four oxygen."

Even with this information, it was hard to suddenly picture what exactly it was. Haruyuki furrowed his brow. "Taku, so, lead, that's a metal...right?" he asked in a small voice.

"That's right." A ridiculously kind smile spread across his good friend's face.

Haruyuki cleared his throat to hide his embarrassment at having apparently asked a dumb question and put a serious look on his face. "But he—Trilead didn't look like a metal color at all. He was this clear, pretty indigo, or maybe navy. Even his weapon—all of him was a solid blue type." Haruyuki cocked his head to one side, remembering the crisp presence of the young samurai.

Kuroyukihime, to his left, folded her hands together on the table. "At any rate, at present, our urgent business is not to solve the mysteries of the Castle but to get Utai and Haruyuki out. If we can't purify the element of the Armor of Catastrophe parasitizing Silver Crow before next Sunday, Haruyuki will become the second-biggest bounty in the Accelerated World." Here, she glanced at him, and a momentary smile slipped across her lips. "Although, naturally, if that were to happen, I wouldn't allow you to be hunted so easily as that."

"...Kuroyukihime..."

"Okay, cut! Cut!" Chiyuri slapped the table with both hands as they were about to slip back into stare-at-each-other mode. "That reminds me, Kuroyukihime, there's something I've been wondering about ever since I heard about this bounty thing."

"Wh-what is it, Chiyuri?" Kuroyukihime cleared her throat.

"How are the Seven Kings going to check whether or not the Armor of Catastrophe parasitizing Haru has actually been purified in the first place?" Chiyuri asked, spreading out both hands. "You can't see another person's item list, and doesn't the armor not show up in the item list anyway?"

"Oh! N-now that you mention it." The words slipped out of Haruyuki. Even though this was about his own self, he had never once even entertained this most basic of questions. He couldn't actually be more careless.

Seeing him like this, Kuroyukihime grinned wryly, but soon regained her serious expression. "Most likely, a Burst Linker with the ability to see other people's statuses will show up at the assembly on Sunday. The kings probably intend to have this person examine Silver Crow's purification."

"I suppose so." Fuko nodded slowly on the other side of the table. Her normally gentle, smiling eyes were cut by a hard, sharp light. "The quad-eyes analyst. I expect we'll be seeing her appear for the first time in a long time."

The instant he heard this name—a nickname rather than the Burst Linker's particular name—something inside him clicked. It was definitely new to him. He knew he had never heard it before; he hadn't even known there was an ability to see a person's status in the first place. And yet something deep in his memory itched and throbbed. This sensation spilled out to his central nervous system, ran up his spine, and arrived at a single point on his back.

Thmm. Thmm. In sync with the sharp pain, distantly— someone's voice.

...Destroy...

Destroy them, devour them...Release...this rage of ours...

At some point, he had clenched his right hand so tightly his nails were digging into his palm. But then something soft touched it abruptly. He looked and found Utai gently pressing his fist under the table. In the large eyes she sent glancing at him, there was a hazy note of apprehension. He hurriedly spread his hands out and nodded his head to say he was okay. Fortunately, the others were talking about the purification verification and didn't seem to have noticed anything unusual about him.

"In the worst case, perhaps we can have Ardor Maiden purify Silver Crow inside the Castle and make it in time for the meeting on Sunday?" Takumu suggested.

Utai pulled her hand back and tapped at her keyboard with both of them. UI> I wouldn't say it's definitely impossible, but if possible, I'd prefer not to use a large-scale Incarnate technique within the Castle. There is a risk of the waves of a strong overlay calling high-level Enemies.

"Mmm. And the higher the level of the Enemy, such as Beasts or Legends, the less impact Incarnate attacks have, while at the same time, the more aggressive they become to Incarnate users. Most likely, the abnormal local load due to the Incarnate System causes their Hate to increase irregularly. We should also assume that this reaction is only stronger when it comes to the Enemies guarding the Castle," Kuroyukihime remarked, and snapped to attention in her chair, looking around once before continuing. "Well then, Silver Crow, Ardor Maiden, we'll have to have you leave the Castle before Sunday. To that end, although he is an unknown, I believe the best route is to petition this Burst Linker Trilead Tetroxide for his aid. Utai, Haruyuki, when you meet him again on Thursday, in the name of the Black King and Nega Nebulus, tell him that you will pay him an appropriate price for his assistance."

By this time, it was ten to nine in the evening, so Kuroyukihime finished by adding, "Today's mission is over for the time being."

Fuko had come by car after going home briefly, so it was decided she would take Utai and Kuroyukihime, and the three of them got into the elevator first for the parking lot. Then Chiyuri and the plate that had been so full of sandwiches returned to her home two floors down, leaving Haruyuki and Takumu in the hallway on the twenty-third floor.

"Okay, Haru. See you at school tomorrow." Takumu started walking toward the passageway that connected the separate wing of the condo.

"Taku, you still got some time?" Haruyuki stopped him in a small voice. His old friend turned around, head cocked to one side, and Haruyuki asked, falteringly, "So, like, how many times have you dueled since the beginning of this week?"

"Huh? Two, three times on my way home from school every day. No more than ten times, I think," he replied, before blinking as if guessing at something. He lowered his voice and continued. "Ohh. If that bit about me and Chii giving you points if you do end up with a bounty like we said yesterday is still bugging you, don't worry about it. My win rate's the same as ever, but Chii's getting some serious skill lately. If we're not careful, she's gonna jump right past us to the next level." A self-deprecating grin slid onto Takumu's face as he spoke.

"Th-that's not it." Haruyuki hurriedly shook his head from side to side. "That's not what I'm talking about. Umm, during those ten duels, did you notice anything weird?"

At this vague question, Takumu got a doubtful look on his face before smiling a little wryly. "That question's already weird. I mean, 'something'? I don't know what I should be remembering."

"O-oh, yeah, I guess so." Haruyuki scratched his head, and an embarrassed smile popped onto his face. What he was trying to ask was if any of Takumu's opponents had used a technique with a power that went beyond the framework of a normal duel; more specifically, if there had been any close- or long-range Incarnate attacks clad in a black aura.

After school the previous day, a Monday, Haruyuki and Utai Shinomiya had fought a tag-team duel together in Suginami Area No. 2, their opponents Bush Utan and Olive Grab from the Green Legion. Haruyuki had been left to take Utan and had gained an advantage in the fight after using the "way of the flexible"—a guard reversal technique Kuroyukihime had shown him.

However, in the middle of the battle, the moment Utan summoned a bizarre Enhanced Armament, the nature of the fight was flipped upside down. With two types of Incarnate attack—Dark Blow, an attack with a fist covered in a dark aura, and Dark Shot, which shot a beam of darkness from his palm—Utan had Haruyuki up against the wall, completely at wits' end. It wasn't hard to imagine that that would have been the end for him if it hadn't been a tag-team match with Utai.

Utan called the black eye-shaped Enhanced Armament affixed to his chest an ISS kit—in other words, an Incarnate System study kit—and said that someone had given it to him. And if Utan was able to instantly use the Incarnate System, which should have required long hours of training, by simply wearing it, then this was a situation that threatened to shake the very foundations of the Accelerated World.

With this in mind, Haruyuki had asked Ash Roller, Utan's motorcycle-riding big brother figure, for a closed duel on his way to school that morning and explained the situation. Ash Roller had then noted in an unprecedentedly serious tone that if this ISS kit could be copied infinitely, then it was probably already too late. It might have been handed out any number of times and proliferated beyond a number it was possible to deal with.

Which was why, in a certain sense, the ISS kit could be said to be a much more serious issue than the element of the Armor of Catastrophe that was parasitizing Haruyuki. He should have tabled the appearance of the ISS kit for discussion at the meeting that day before the start of Operation Rescue Ardor Maiden. Or he could have raised his hand and said something when Kuroyukihime announced the end of that meeting only a few minutes earlier.

However, Haruyuki had done neither. First of all, he thought everyone should concentrate on the rescue mission. But he felt that wasn't the only reason. He could see that somewhere inside, he didn't want to tell his friends about the ISS kit. He couldn't say what he should. Maybe his guilty conscience had prompted him to call out to Takumu.

Takumu. His best friend, the person he had gone up against for real, who he had exchanged real blows with, who had pulled through a truly difficult battle with him in the whole Dusk Taker thing. He was sure that Takumu of all people would undoubtedly share this burden he had picked up at some point. But...

In a corner of the dim hall, he looked up at the face of his tall childhood friend, and the moment he went to explain everything, Haruyuki felt the brakes put on his own mouth once more.

Why? Why am I hesitating?

This is Taku. A friend above all others, my partner at the front line of the Legion. The best partner, always cool and collected and helping me out when I don't think. There's no one better than Taku to talk to first about the ISS kits.

So why am I so freaked out about it?

Still staring at Takumu, who was looking more and more

doubtful, Haruyuki took a deep breath and pushed back the mysterious clamor in his heart.

"The truth is…" Even after he started to speak, his tongue froze and his throat ached. Working to ignore this feeling, Haruyuki continued. "The truth is, Taku, something weird's happening in the Accelerated World right now…maybe. It'll take a while. How about we talk inside a bit more?"

The pair returned to Haruyuki's living room, and as he spoke absorbedly, wetting his lips with the remaining coffee, the strange uneasiness in his heart finally disappeared.

Bush Utan. The ISS kit. The Incarnate attacks cloaked in a dark fluctuation.

Once Takumu had heard it all, he clasped his hands and pressed them to his forehead, elbows on the table. He was silent for a while, his face turned downward. Just when Haruyuki was starting to become uneasy with the fairly long silence, he finally lifted his face back up. The usual intellectual light shone behind his glasses.

"So what do you think?" Haruyuki asked, heaving a sigh of relief for no reason he could understand.

"Hmm." Takumu took a sip of cold coffee. "To be honest, it's hard to really process this all of a sudden. I'm only too aware of how hard it is to learn the Incarnate System after my training with the Red King. I don't know how many times I ripped an enormous hole in my left hand trying to learn to stop my own Pile."

In Cyan Plate, the Incarnate attack of Takumu's avatar, Cyan Pile, he caught with his left hand the iron spike that shot out of the Enhanced Armament Pile Driver equipped in his right hand and pulled it out, transforming it into a longsword. Rather than simple repetitive training, he had to confront painful memories in order to catch the spike, a symbol of his own mental trauma.

"Yeah. I trained until I nearly passed out before I learned

how to pierce the wall of the old Tokyo Tower. I was just totally focused on speed, speed, speed."

Their eyes grew distant. For a variety of reasons, the head of the Legion Prominence—the Red King, Scarlet Rain—had been the one to initiate Takumu into the Incarnate System, but her Spartan style was basically on par with Haruyuki's Incarnate instructor, Sky Raker. Yet they had suffered through it and somehow managed to learn a basic Incarnate technique: Haruyuki, range expansion; Takumu, power expansion.

"But just by equipping this ISS kit, you're able to use both the power expansion technique Dark Blow and the range expansion technique Dark Shot. Is that it?" Takumu said hoarsely, and dropped his gaze to his own left hand, a smile with a color Haruyuki couldn't remember seeing too much bleeding onto the corners of his mouth. "It doesn't matter how hard you try—if something's out of reach, you'll never be able to grab on to it. That's the basic principle of Brain Burst. That's what I've always thought. Your duel avatar is almost cruel in how it unequivocally teaches you the limits of your own physical self. Which is exactly why this game gains another reality, right?"

"Taku?" Haruyuki cocked his head to one side, slightly bewildered by this small outburst.

Takumu lifted his face with a gasp. All that was on his lips now was his usual faint intellectual smile. "Oh, sorry. Don't worry about it. You're right. If someone's distributing Enhanced Armament like that, this situation is pretty serious. The balance between duel and Territories will crumble."

"Yeah, you're right." Haruyuki nodded and brushed aside an irrational sense that something was out of place. "Although it's bad enough that Incarnate techniques are being used in normal duels, that power is just too great. To be honest, beginner Incarnate users like us can't fight that. Like, in the Meeting of the Seven Kings the day before yesterday, some people thought that depending on the situation, the existence of the Incarnate System should be disclosed to all Burst Linkers, but…if the ISS kits are on the market everywhere, is there any point in training now from the first steps in Incarnate techniques? It's almost like..."

"Someone's beat them to the punch?" Takumu hit the nail on the head while Haruyuki was searching for the words. He pushed up his glasses, an even more complicated look on his face. "But, Haru, if that's the case, that means that the guys who showed off the power of the Incarnate System to all those people in the Gallery at the Hermes' Cord race last week are the masterminds behind disseminating the ISS kits now."

"Ah!" Not having even considered the possibility up to that point, Haruyuki threw himself back so hard that his chair clattered. Both eyes open wide, he murmured the name of the organization Takumu was hinting at. "The Acceleration Research Society?"

"Let's think about it from the beginning. The first time they showed themselves was in April of this year. Dusk Taker skillfully made use of an illegal brain implant chip to attack the Umesato Junior High local net, while Rust Jigsaw did the same at Akihabara battleground. Maybe there were other closed nets they ran wild in using the same methods."

Haruyuki remembered Twilight Marauder's menacing power, so great that it had forced Haruyuki and his friends to surrender, however temporarily, and shuddered all over, nodding. But recollecting the whole incident now, a question he hadn't noticed at the time popped into his head.

"But, Taku, when I think about it, it's weird. At the time, in April, neither of them actively went to use Incarnate techniques themselves. Dusk Taker only started using that purple fluctuation when you pushed him into a corner in a duel. And I feel like Rust Jigsaw actually didn't end up using it at all. But for those guys, it wouldn't have been weird at all if they attacked with Incarnate at full throttle right from the start."

"We should think of it like they were limited. But I don't think the reason is that abuse of Incarnate risks calling the dark side, like the Red King and Raker warned us."

Haruyuki nodded deeply at Takumu's words.

In the power that the Incarnate System revealed, there were four quadrants, like the xy plane in mathematics. The x-axis was the breadth of the imagination—in other words, moving toward the individual or toward the world—while the y-axis was the lightness of the imagination—whether it took hope as its source or despair. The first quadrant, in the upper right, was positive will with range as its target; the second quadrant, to the upper left, was positive will with the individual as its target; the third, to the bottom left, was negative will with the individual as its target; and the fourth, to the bottom right, was negative will with range as its target.

Attack-type Incarnate techniques like Haruyuki's Laser Sword, Takumu's Cyan Blade, and Kuroyukihime's incomparably more powerful Vorpal Strike were categorized in the second quadrant because they used as their source the hope inside themselves. The universal wellspring of Incarnate was mental scars, but whether they would pump hope from that deep hole or fall into the darkness of despair was left to the choice of the person themselves.

And although they were rare, there were some Burst Linkers who had mastered Incarnate of the first quadrant. Fuko's Wind Veil, which protected herself and companions around her, was the most conspicuous example. Haruyuki didn't know its name, but Utai's Incarnate technique, which burned a wide range with crimson flames, was probably also in the first quadrant because Bush Utan, burned up by those flames, hadn't felt the slightest suffering. Those were flames of purification to exorcise pain.

However, it wasn't the case that all Incarnates showed this kind of positive power. For instance, Dusk Taker's "purple fluctuation," which had no fixed name. That technique shaved off whatever it touched and swallowed the object up into nothingness; it was a third-quadrant, dark-side attack power that used internal despair for energy. And Rust Jigsaw's Rust Order. That power to summon a storm of red rust a hundred meters in diameter to corrode and destroy all things within its range had to be a power of the fourth quadrant. The imagination of the end, born from a despair against the world.

In short, these two from the Acceleration Research Society had probably learned negative Incarnate right from the start. At this late stage, there would be no reason why their teacher would caution them about falling into the dark side.

"So then that means they had a specific reason for limiting their Incarnate, I guess," Haruyuki muttered.

Takumu nodded slowly. "Yeah, I guess so. But last week, when he stormed into the Hermes' Cord race, basically the moment Rust Jigsaw appeared, he was using Incarnate. Except that wasn't on the level of just *using* it. Dragging not just the other teams, but however many hundreds were in the Gallery into it, that was to make us feel in our bones just how tremendous Incarnate attacks can be. And that guy calling himself the vice president of the Acceleration Research Society, Black Vise, he was even there. So I think we have to assume that large-scale attack was exactly what that organization wanted."

"B-but if that's true, isn't that like a huge policy flip in just two months? In April, they were trying to lie low, but June rolls around and they're showing off?" Haruyuki said, waving both hands around on the table.

Takumu paused for a moment before responding quietly, "It means that in those two months, they finished their preparations."

"P-preparations? For what?"

"Preparations to distribute the ISS kits."

"Hng!!" Once again, Haruyuki made his chair clatter against the floor.

The two of them looked at each other wordlessly for several seconds. Takumu's cheeks had lost their color and were paler than usual, and Haruyuki was pretty sure his own face was even whiter than that.

Eventually, after drinking the last sip of his cold coffee, Takumu moved his lips. "If that assumption is true, then all I can say is they're meticulous. It's like they're always one step ahead, planning their next move. They make a show of the absurd power of the Incarnate System to many members of the Gallery with a large-scale attack at Hermes' Cord, and then immediately after that, they start distributing the ISS kits as a device to easily learn Incarnate. Honestly, after that display, even veteran Burst Linkers, who should hesitate at wearing that sort of dodgy Enhanced Armament, would give in to their impatience and reach out for it."

In the back of Haruyuki's mind, Bush Utan's cracked voice from the previous day came back to life.

IS mode has that kind of incredible power. The ultimate power, skipping over all the rules of Brain Burst even. And there's some jerks who knew about it and kept it quiet all this time.

There hadn't been only fear and impatience in Utan's monologue; it had also contained a strong animosity toward the people who had kept the existence of the Incarnate System hidden until then—and that naturally included Haruyuki. That kind of emotional energy alone was plenty motivation to accept the black eyeball and its eerie appearance.

"So then, Taku, is their ultimate goal to spread the ISS kit throughout the Accelerated World? Or...?" Haruyuki timidly asked his best friend, pursing his lips.

"Is there another 'next move'?" Takumu stared at his empty coffee cup and nodded slightly. "We don't have enough information to determine that. I haven't even seen this ISS kit with my own eyes." Before Haruyuki could say anything, Takumu glanced at the clock display in the bottom right of his field of view and stood up. "Haru, isn't your mom going to be home soon? Let's leave it here for today."

"Yeah."

Now that Takumu mentioned it, it was almost ten already, in what seemed like the blink of an eye. Haruyuki's mother worked at a foreign investment bank and in exchange for a late start to her workday, she also came home late, but even so, at this hour, she could basically come home any second. And although his mother wasn't the type to get angry at Takumu being here at this time of day, they couldn't exactly continue openly chatting about Brain Burst.

"Hey, Taku?" Haruyuki asked one final question in a small voice as he followed Takumu out of the living room. "This—we should probably talk to Kuroyukihime and the others about it... right?"

"...Well, of course." On Takumu's face as he replied, waving a hand in the entryway, was the same intellectual expression as always.

So Haruyuki forgot about the slightly long silence that preceded that reply and bobbed his head up and down. "Right? Okay. I'll talk to Kuroyukihime tomorrow. Fortunately, it's Thursday when we're diving back into the Castle so we don't have to do a bunch of stuff tomorrow."

Once again, Takumu was silent, narrowing his eyes as though something had dazzled them. When Haruyuki raised an eyebrow, he laughed it off. "It's just the way you're all casual, 'diving into the Castle.' I was just thinking you jump in with both feet like always."

"N-no, I mean, it's not such a big—"

"Ha-ha-ha! It wasn't a compliment." Takumu reached out with his right hand and jabbed Haruyuki's shoulder lightly before slipping his shoes on. Looking serious once more, he added, "I'll try some tricks of my own to get information on the ISS kit thing."

"Y-yeah. Good idea. But don't do anything too reckless," Haruyuki said, finding it a little weird himself that he would say something like that. For many years, doing reckless things had been Haruyuki's job, and Takumu's role had been to stop him.

Perhaps feeling the same way, Takumu grinned again and nodded. "Yeah, I know. Okay, see you at school tomorrow."

"Yeah, see you tomorrow." Haruyuki raised his hand lightly, and his best friend opened the door and slid out into the dim hallway.

Listening to the sound of the automatic lock as the door shut once more, Haruyuki was aware of that sensation returning to his chest. That he didn't want to talk about it. That he shouldn't have talked about it.

A delusion. It was good that he talked about it. After all, it was precisely because he and Takumu discussed it that he realized the possibility that the source of the ISS kits was the Acceleration Research Society. And when he told Kuroyukihime about the situation the next day after school, she was sure to show him the right way to proceed, just like she always did.

Clenching his hands tightly, he forced his own thoughts to this conclusion before tracing his steps back through the living room into the kitchen to wash the coffee mugs.

6

The next day was Wednesday, June 19.

He opened the door to his mother's bedroom a crack to tell her he was leaving for the day, and to his Neurolinker came a five-hundred-yen lunch allowance. Afterward, he took the elevator to the ground floor and stepped out onto the sidewalk of the ring road, Kannana Street.

In social studies class the other day, he had gotten the chance to watch a video from a long, long time ago, recorded on the streets of Suginami where Haruyuki and his friends lived. It had been taken at the beginning of the century, around the year 2010, with a video camera, so it wasn't a 3-D video you could do a full dive in, but rather a flat image. However, the images of the town in such disarray had made a serious impression on the students. It was different from the electrical chaos of the current Akihabara, half of which was really just for show. This was everyday life laid bare, steeped in years of history and the work of its citizens. Even along Kannana, supposedly the main thoroughfare in the city, small individual-owned shops and even regular homes could be seen everywhere.

Of course, if you went down a little into one of the back streets, there were any number of stand-alone homes and old apartment buildings even now. But the main thoroughfares of Kannana and

Oume had been nearly doubled forty years earlier, and only strings of large-scale commercial institutions, housing complexes, or tidy green spaces lined them now. At and around Koenji Station as well, the unorganized bustle of the past was gone; the area had been completely transformed into a multistoried combination building linking the facilities around the pedestrian deck.

And there was one more thing. Haruyuki noticed an inconspicuous change that nonetheless held major significance. Something he couldn't go a day without seeing, everywhere, inside and out. No one paid them any mind precisely because there were so many. Black half or full spheres, about five centimeters in diameter. In the old video, there wasn't a single one of these so-called social cameras anywhere.

In class, they also learned that this entirely automatic monitoring camera net began to be set up in the mid-2030s. After that, occurrence of crime in public spaces dropped dramatically. Considering the formidable performance of the cameras, this was only natural. After all, when the system caught any illegal activity within its field of view, it automatically identified and tracked it, while reporting it to the local police at the same time. Naturally, this was not to say that every little crime without exception ended up in arrest and indictment, but, for instance, if you tossed a cigarette butt or an empty juice container on the ground within view of a camera, a warning mail would arrive from the authorities the next day, and a fine would be automatically withdrawn from your bank account at the end of the month.

Exactly where this extremely advanced and complicated image processing was carried out and by what system was a state secret of the highest order, and not a single detail was disclosed to the citizens of the country. The sole fact made public was the name "Social Security Surveillance Center," or the SSSC for short. Even *the* Kuroyukihime said she could only guess at where the center was. Obviously, Haruyuki couldn't even do that.

Immediately before the raised platform of the Chuo Line, he turned right off of Kannana and arrived at the road to school, bathed in the ceaseless roar of cars racing along. As he walked, he started wondering and whirled his head around; he knew the social cameras were looking down with a bird's-eye view from everywhere: power poles and street lamps, traffic signs, signals, all of it. To be honest, he could see how it would be creepy, but for Haruyuki, the system held a significance greater than maintaining public order.

It went without saying that this significance was Brain Burst. The BB program easily infiltrated the social camera net, supposedly guarded by top-level walls, and generated 3-D fields from those super-high-precision images to produce a reality that rivaled that of the real world. The fact that Burst Linkers were able to gain another self in their duel avatars and another reality in the Accelerated World was first and foremost because of the overwhelming amount of information in the duel field.

However, this system, utopia though it may have been for gamers, had just one negative side.

In seventh grade, Haruyuki had been subjected to horrible bullying by three students in his class. On an almost daily basis, they'd forced him to buy them bread and juice with the five hundred yen he got for lunch and bring it up to the corner of the roof where they hung out. If he refused—and even when the bread they had specified was sold out and he couldn't buy it—they had punched and kicked him mercilessly, and forced him to grovel on his hands and knees, scraping his face against the concrete of the roof.

Those three had been able to continue with this sort of behavior, clearly against the rules of the school and wandering into the criminal, for more than six months partly because Haruyuki was too timid to tell his homeroom teacher or the school authorities about what was going on, but the fact that their hangout behind the air conditioner at the west edge of the roof of the second school building was one of the few places on campus outside the reach of the social cameras also played a large part. It seemed that a map or something of places outside the view of the social cameras was passed around among this kind of outlaw student, so they could carefully select "safe zones" and continue their bullying. This sort of thinking was shared not just among delinquent students, but among adult criminals as well.

Naturally, however, the cameras weren't in the same locations permanently. The update speed in a semipublic place like a school was a bit lenient, but in places like shopping districts or back alleys, cameras were added and moved with incredible frequency, making it nearly impossible for professional criminals to always be aware of their range of view.

But there were people who could perfectly identify random places outside the view of the cameras in a mere second. Burst Linkers. All a Burst Linker had to do was shout, "Burst Link," and do a full dive into the clear blue, Basic Accelerated Field. In that world, things existing within view of the social cameras were reproduced as they were in reality, but for those items outside their view, the system "conjectured and complemented." These items were basically reproduced as smooth objects with few details, so a Linker could tell at a glance whether something was within view of the cameras or not.

This "privilege," unattainable even to the leader of a large-scale criminal syndicate, had sent a small portion of Burst Linkers running toward a certain type of criminality. They were the ones called Physical Knockers, or PK for short. Several of them would target Burst Linkers outed in the real and attack them outside the view of the cameras. Initially, it was in the shadows, but in recent years, they would lock hapless Burst Linkers in cars and things, and in both cases, threaten them with violence and force them into direct duels. Unlike normal global net duels, there was no once-a-day limit in a direct duel, so the person being attacked was doomed to face loss after loss. In mere seconds of real-world time, the attackers stole a massive amount of points, and in the blink of an eye, the victim had lost everything, ending up in a forced uninstall of Brain Burst. It was a "death" for Burst Linkers that was even crueler than Unlimited EK in the Unlimited Neutral Field.

Thus, Kuroyukihime had told Haruyuki to at least pay mind to the view of the cameras on the road. It might have been a little creepy, but the fact that he was able to see those black spheres around him meant he was safe. Although he didn't expect to be attacked in the real when streams of students and office workers were flowing all around him. Yawning deeply, he called up the schedule for that day on his virtual desktop and went to check that he hadn't forgotten some homework or report.

At that moment, a hand stretched out from the gloom beneath the overhead train tracks immediately to the left of the sidewalk and grabbed on to the collar of Haruyuki's shirt from behind.

"Hinhk...?!"

No way! PK?! A flat-out real attack when there are this many people, and in full view of the social cameras?! He began to freak out and very nearly started to wave and kick his arms and legs, but just as he was on the verge of doing so, a familiar voice whispered in his ear.

"Hi."

A single word, a single syllable, likely the shortest of all possible greetings. He stopped flailing and nervously looked over his shoulder to find the face of a slightly older girl, with an adult look that somehow managed to provoke a sense that she was no ordinary person.

"P-Pard?" he said, dumbfounded, but his attacker did not reply. It was self-evident, and there was no point in her replying. As usual, she was sticking to her style of finishing up anything conversation-related in the barest minimum time. At any rate, he left out the question of what she was even doing here and returned her greeting, collar still in her hand. "G-good morning."

She nodded lightly as she released him, and his floating heels hit the ground. Sighing, he turned around and took in the presence of his attacker once more.

Her understated hairstyle was the same as always—black, parted in the middle, and bound in a single braid on her back. But she wasn't wearing the maid's uniform from the first time they had met, at a cake shop in Sakuradai in Nerima Ward, or the rough T-shirt and jeans look from when they met later at Tokyo Skytree. Instead, a white collar on a navy top, with a triangle scarf and a thin-pleated skirt of the same color—the typical sailor school uniform, in other words.

It wasn't a particularly unusual look. Looking around, he could see any number of uniforms like it among the students headed for the station. However, when the wearer was leaning up against the seat of a large electric motorcycle with a low, ferocious form like a large carnivore, it was a different story. The combination was just too out of place, and earned one gawking stare after another from the sidewalk.

The bike was parked at the entrance to a narrow alley that passed under the overhead line and broke off to the south from the road Haruyuki took to school. To avoid the inquiring eyes, Haruyuki took a step into the dim alley and fumbled for what he was supposed to say. He didn't know the real name of the uniformed rider who had suddenly appeared before him. The nickname "Pard" had slipped out but was normally not something to be used around regular people, because it was a contraction of her avatar name.

Blood Leopard. The deputy of the Red Legion, Prominence, which ruled over the area from northern Nakano to Nerima, a level-six Burst Linker, nicknamed Bloody Kitty. A warrior among warriors, who had destroyed Rust Jigsaw of the Acceleration Research Society before Haruyuki's eyes with a single bite.

Now that he thought about it, she always appeared before him out of the blue and surprised him, but even still, this was just too sudden. Unable to decide on what to ask first, he flapped his mouth for about two and a half seconds. Then it was apparently the end of Haruyuki's turn, and Pard leaned forward off the motorcycle, her left hand shooting out. In her fingertips was a small plug dangling from a red shielded cord—a direct XSB cable.

He let out a mental cry, but since she'd end up jabbing it into

his Neurolinker if he just stood there and watched, he hurriedly took it and jacked in himself with the cable that was fortunately two or so meters long. The wired connection warning popped up in his vision, and immediately after it disappeared, a slightly low, husky voice echoed in his mind.

"I didn't mail you because I have info I wanted to tell just you first." Naturally, this was the answer to the question Haruyuki should have asked first. He looked up at her as she leaned back against her bike again and crossed her arms.

He somehow managed to shift the gears in his brain and utter in neurospeak, *"Does that mean you don't want the other members of Nega Nebulus to know I saw you?"*

"That's the end result, yes. It's not that I don't trust your comrades. I just wanted to let you decide what info to pass along."

Unable to immediately get what Leopard was trying to say, he cocked his head to one side. The cable connecting their Neurolinkers shook, and a hazy light slid along the shielded, braided wire.

They might have been in the narrow lane beneath the tracks, but they were still in full view of the north side of the sidewalk. Haruyuki wondered what people made of the high school girl in a sailor-style uniform leaned up against a large motorcycle with a short, round junior high boy, directing and staring at each other first thing in the morning. Old, young, boy, girl—the people passing by gazed at them freely, and frighteningly, he glimpsed Umesato uniforms among them, but the words Leopard uttered next contained enough of a shock to send all these scattered thoughts easily flying.

"Silver Crow. There's a movement to ask a PK group for your immediate purge."

"What…," he gasped, his real voice slipping out. He staggered for a moment, and then quickly regained his footing. But the sensation that the ground was slowly swaying did not leave him.

Seeing him like this, Pard twitched an eyebrow and stretched out her right hand once more. She pulled on Haruyuki's shoulder and sat him up on the front of the motorcycle seat, immediately to her right. The large bike, firmly supported by a solid kickstand, didn't move an inch even as it took his full weight.

Slightly regaining his calm from the reliable feel of the machine he had ridden several times, Haruyuki finally sent his next thought through the cable. *"Purge... This is because of the Armor of Catastrophe thing, right? But at the Meeting of the Seven Kings, they said I'd have this whole week."*

"Yes. However, the ones talking the extreme talk aren't the kings, but some of the key Burst Linkers under them. They're insisting... that you're the source of the infection of the 'dark power' that's been spreading through the Accelerated World these last few days." Even the indomitable Pard showed the merest hint of hesitation before speaking those words.

However, paying no mind to this, Haruyuki trapped an even larger gasp in his throat. *"That's—N-no, I..."* Reflexively, he looked up at Leopard standing to his left and shook his head violently. *"They're wrong! It's not me! I—I would never make something like that..."*

But even as he protested the idea, a voice came back to life in the distance in his mind. Ash Roller's final words in the closed duel the morning before, very near where they were now on Kannana Street.

"There's more to the rumors I heard. This 'weird tech' Utan and Olive are using...I heard it's a copy of Chrome Disaster's power."

It was true that the shadowy aura emitted by users of the ISS kit and the dark fluctuations that blanketed Silver Crow when he equipped the Armor of Catastrophe did strongly resemble each other. Someone who saw both of them could determine that they were of the same origin. Still, a single day was much too little time for this rumor to race around the Accelerated World and grow into talk of an immediate purge of Silver Crow.

At the same time, though, Haruyuki could see that it wasn't necessarily impossible. For Burst Linkers, a mere 1.8 seconds in the real world was actually equivalent to thirty minutes. If the rumor was spread among the members of the Gallery at the countless duels happening one after another in Shinjuku, in Shibuya, in Akihabara, it was plenty believable that some people espousing strong views on the matter had already appeared. Believable, but in his heart, he simply could not accept it.

Pard watched as Haruyuki opened his eyes wide and shook his head in short, sharp increments, and a faint but definite smile rose up onto her lips. The right hand that had trapped his collar before now patted his back lightly. *"K, got it. Red King and me, we don't believe the ranting and raving. But we can't be optimistic, either. Which is why I came to give you the info."*

Words weren't quick to come out. But the softness and warmth of the hand touching him through the fabric of his shirt pushed back the shock and terror, even if it was only for the moment.

The Red Legion, Prominence, had what was basically a temporary cease-fire with Haruyuki's Nega Nebulus, although this certainly didn't mean they had formed an alliance. When he met the Legion Master, Niko, she had contacted Haruyuki in the real world and forcefully requested their help in subjugating the fifth Chrome Disaster, but she had paid back that debt with interest when they were dealing with Dusk Taker, so at present, their relationship could be said to be completely even. Which was why, for Prominence, there was no longer any obligation to maintain the cease-fire with Nega Nebulus, especially not to the point of incurring the displeasure of the other five great Legions. In fact, it wasn't hard to imagine that some people within the Legion were probably already of the opinion that they should resume attacks in the weekend Territories.

And yet Niko and Pard continued as they had, not fighting, and more than that, they would even go out of their way, like Pard was doing now, to inform him of a direct danger in the real. Probably—definitely as a friend.

"Thank. You." Haruyuki spoke these words alone, not just with his thoughts, but also with his real voice. Using the back of his hand to rub away the tears welling up in his eyes, he got himself back on track. The way to respond to Pard's kindness wasn't to pointlessly freak out and practically cry on her; it was to calmly grasp the situation and handle it in the best way possible. He took a deep breath and switched back to neurospeak.

"But even if they are talking PK, it's not as easy as all that, right? I mean, they have to out me in the real first."

"Yes. The PK groups don't have an inexhaustible supply of points, either, so they can't use extreme methods like Rain did before to get in touch with you in the real world."

"...That's true."

Niko had used the fact that in reality, she was in elementary school and systematically applied for hands-on school visits at the junior high schools in Suginami Ward, where she got temporary accounts on the local nets and checked the matching list to pin down the school Silver Crow was enrolled at. Next, she set up camp where she could look out at the school gates and accelerated each time a student came out on their way home after school to check the matching list, eventually cracking Haruyuki's identity in the real. The number of points she used in the process was not on the level of a hundred or two hundred; this method was impossible for anyone who wasn't a king and no longer needed to be diligent about points to level up.

So then how exactly were the people espousing this strong opinion planning to PK Haruyuki?

He furrowed his brow, and Pard, next to him, also looked as though she was thinking. *"Right now,"* she muttered, *"the only ones outside the current members of Nega who know your real name are me and Niko. That right?"*

He nodded after a moment's hesitation. *"Yeah. You should be."* To be more accurate, if they were talking about "knew in the past," then there was actually one more person. Dusk Taker, the marauder who had appeared at Umesato Junior High as a new student that year and overwhelmed Haruyuki and his friends while Kuroyukihime was away. But Haruyuki and Takumu had defeated him in a decisive battle in the Unlimited Neutral Field, and he lost all his points and had Brain Burst forcibly uninstalled. His memories related to the Accelerated World had been completely erased, and he was currently aware of Haruyuki only as someone he used to play some game with.

Of course, the possibility that he passed along Haruyuki's real-world info to the organization he belonged to, the Acceleration Research Society, was not zero. But if he had, then he ran the risk of exposing his own identity, since they went to the same junior high school. Given how utterly and completely Dusk Taker rejected values like friendships and bonds, Haruyuki couldn't believe he would have trusted the members of his organization that much.

Leopard moved her head lightly. *"You'll just have to trust me and Niko, but if that's all of us, then those hard-liners won't crack you so easily. If you...purify the armor before the Meeting of the Seven Kings on Sunday and the kings confirm it, the idea of purging you will be totally baseless. But there is just one thing..."* Unusually for her, Pard trailed off and turned her whole upper body toward Haruyuki, before continuing in a deeply apprehensive voice, *"There is just one force of concern."*

"Force?"

"We assume there are several PK groups out there, but it's not easy to find out who's in them. Put another way, once they are found out, they're purged with the collective power of all Burst Linkers and lose all their points before they even know it."

Haruyuki bobbed his head up and down. His teacher Sky Raker had also smilingly informed him that she had tossed a Burst Linker who had been identified as a PK deep into the territory of a Legend-class Enemy. PKs were so detestable that even the (supposedly) kind Raker adopted such merciless methods. In which case, how was it even possible in the first place to make a request to these guys to purge Haruyuki? First of all, how did the would-be purgers get in touch with the PK?

Leopard replied to Haruyuki's question with a low, stifled thought. *"There's a group that fancy themselves 'executioners.'*

They're the sole PK group who've made the group name known.
The most malicious and evil physical knockers. Supernova Remnant, Remnant for short."

"Supernova Remnant," he parroted.

"They take on PKs in Japanese yen instead of burst points,"
Leopard added, a faint grimness rising up onto her normally
cool brow. "They have a ton of know-how about cracking the real.
Every Burst Linker they've been contracted to execute has without
exception been taken out with a PK. For them, Brain Burst's not a
game; it's nothing more than a way to earn money."

"Wha..." Once more, Haruyuki gasped in his real voice, this
time unconsciously.

"Why..." A chill running up his spine, he racked his brain as if
to try and fight back. "Why are they just left to do that? If anyone's
going to be purged, shouldn't we start with them instead of me...?"

"Naturally, people have said the same thing many times in the
past. But no matter what anyone does, no one can get ahold of any
of the members. The way you place the order, you send a money
code together with the target's name and information to an anony-
mous mail address. It just might be they don't do normal duels at
all and just level up through PK. In which case, it's totally possible
they are completely mysterious Burst Linkers known to no one."

"Th-that's...So then it's almost like they're ghosts—no, gods of
death, aren't they..." Haruyuki let out this futile thought, back-
side still resting lightly against the seat of the electric bike.

Leopard affirmed his words with a short silence and then gently touched his back again. "This is all still guesswork. You don't
need to be excessively scared. The biggest risk for outing in the real
is information leaked by a 'parent' or 'child,' and you don't have
a child—" At this point, Pard cocked her head momentarily as if
to say, You don't, right? and Haruyuki hurriedly bobbed his head
up and down. "And your parent's the king of your Legion, not to
mention a seasoned veteran. She wouldn't carelessly let something
slip or sell you out. So in such a short time, even for those would-be
executioners, outing you in the real's impossible."

The thoughts flowing through the cable stopped there for a moment. But Haruyuki understood that Pard had chopped just a bit off the end of her sentence. *Outing you in the real's impossible, I think.* That's what she had actually been going to say. Because if she was convinced that it was absolutely impossible, there would have been no need to come all the way over like this and warn him. But she'd made it a declaration, perhaps to give Haruyuki strength.

He tried to bolster himself with this declaration anyway and looked up at the older girl sitting. *"Understood,"* he replied in a firm thought. *"But just in case, I'll be careful on my way to and from school."*

"K. You should walk home with someone else especially when you're going home late. Don't get too close to anywhere the social cameras can't see, either," Leopard added, and the conversation was barely finished before she was yanking the XSB cable from their Neurolinkers. She quickly coiled it up and stuck it in the pocket of her skirt.

Since the directing had been released, Haruyuki opened his mouth to thank her with his real voice. "Oh, uh, seriously, thank—" But he was forced to unexpectedly interrupt himself.

Pard pulled a spare jet helmet out from the luggage space at the rear of the bike and plopped it on his head. After nimbly fastening the strap under his chin, she grabbed her own full-face helmet from the handlebars and slipped it on.

…Huh?

Without giving him the time to even open his eyes wide, the high school rider grabbed both handles from behind Haruyuki as if covering him, and murmured the voice command, "Start." The motorcycle's dash, connected with her Neurolinker, flashed brightly, while the front and rear active suspension raised the vehicle body up in a supple motion, like a leopard about to jump out after its prey.

"Uh, uh, um!"

No way. No. Don't. I'm not ready. Haruyuki's mind raced, and in his ears came a low murmur from the in-helmet speaker.

"I took a fair bit of your time. I'll give you a lift to the school gates."

"I-i-i-i-i-it's okay, y-y-y-y-y-you don't have to."

"NP." She lightly opened the throttle, and the bike sleepily moved forward and out onto the road along the overhead train tracks. She dropped the machine into a right turn, and the front wheel headed in the direction of the station. In the next instant, the two large output in-wheel motors roared ferociously.

"Aaaaaaaaaah!!"

The scream he let out as he clung to the vehicle with his arms and legs was without a doubt heard with a significant Doppler effect by the students walking along the left side on the sidewalk.

Having hit hard with the super technique of riding up to the school gates on an electric bike that the average junior high school boy would call nothing but "super ultra great cool," in tandem with a high school girl in a sailor-style uniform to boot, no sooner had Pard waved lightly and raced off toward Kannana than Haruyuki was activating his special attack Dash and Flee for the first time in a long time to race inside the school.

Begrudging even the time it took to change into his indoor shoes, he climbed up the central stairs of the first school building and arrived at the classroom of eighth grade's C class, where he finally let out a long breath. With a feigned nonchalance, he took his seat and fiddled with his virtual desktop in a purposeful manner.

Slap! At the same time a hand hit his back, a familiar voice rang out. "Morning, Haru."

His shoulders stiffened up momentarily before he awkwardly turned around to return the greeting. "M-morning, Chiyu."

The instant Chiyuri Kurashima—his childhood friend who it was no exaggeration to say he had known since he was born—saw his face, her own went from puzzled to intent stare. "You've got that 'oh crap' look on your face."

"I—I do not. This is just my 'I hate gym first period' face."

"That's tomorrow. First period today's math."

"Oh! Uh, um, then it's my 'I hate math' face."

Here, her expression finally changed from intent stare to eye rolling, and he let out a sigh of relief. Having gotten to class before him, Chiyuri had no way of knowing yet how Haruyuki had come to school, and even if she would find out sooner or later, the best policy at the moment was to avoid it. He shifted his gaze with maximum naturalness, looking toward the rear of the room, and opened his mouth. "Uh…umm, huh? Taku's not here yet? He never cuts it this close."

Noticing that his other childhood friend's desk was empty even though there was only five minutes left before the first bell, Haruyuki made this remark solely to change the subject. But the moment he did, Chiyuri's forehead creased with worry, and now it was his turn to look puzzled.

"So, the thing is, Haru"—Chiyuri glanced back herself and lowered her voice—"Taku's home with a cold."

"What…" Reflexively, he ran his fingers along his virtual desktop and opened the class register in the local-net menu. An "absent due to illness" icon was indeed displayed beside the name Takumu Mayuzumi, class number 31. When he clicked on it, the simple explanation FEVER DUE TO COLD popped up.

"That's weird. That guy getting a cold…" Haruyuki furrowed his brow. Having trained in kendo from a young age, Takumu had always been much healthier than Haruyuki. They had known each other a long time, but Haruyuki couldn't remember any more than a mere handful of times Takumu had been taken down by a cold, and all of those had been in the winter, when it was already going around.

It didn't seem to make sense to Chiyuri, either. She brought her face in close abruptly and lowered her voice even further.

"So, like, last night, he didn't look like he had a cold at all, right? Maybe the fever started after that?"

"Oh, now that you mention it...And if he had been feeling like he was coming down with one, he would've been super careful to try not to give it to us."

Chiyuri nodded deeply. Takumu was the kind of person who would never neglect this sort of consideration. So then maybe he had gotten sick after he'd gone home after ten—

No. A sensation like a sudden cramp ran up the back of his head, and Haruyuki's eyes grew unfocused.

Something Takumu had said at Haruyuki's house, and something in the information communicated to him that morning by Pard. The two combined, and a hazy anxiety began to bloom. Some place deep, deep down where light didn't reach, something was coming. And while he was sitting here, a situation he would never be able to come back from was drawing nearer moment by moment. A premonition-like panic.

"What's the matter, Haru?" As if his unease was contagious, Chiyuri also furrowed her brow.

He brought his eyes back into focus with a gasp and shook his head sharply. "N-no, it's nothing. Right. On our way home, let's go visit him together. Mail me once practice is over."

Chiyuri turned large eyes on him as if trying to see through to his heart, but finally she nodded. "Yeah...Okay. And you have Animal Club stuff, too, right? Tell me when you're done working there."

"Okay, got it."

The first bell rang, and she waved lightly before returning to her own seat. Haruyuki turned to face forward again, and staring at the still-open class list, he fought the urge to mail Takumu right then and there. Currently, all students, including himself, were forcibly cut off from the global net, so there was no way for him to get in touch with Takumu, who was supposedly at home in bed.

It's fine. It's all in your imagination. As of this moment, the only one exposed to any Brain Burst–related problems is me. The Armor of Catastrophe, the ISS kits, Remnant—none of it has anything to do with Taku being absent. I'll buy him some of that matcha ice cream he likes and go see him, and he'll totally be smiling, kind of embarrassed, in his bed, Haruyuki told himself, and promptly swiped the window away with his right hand.

Their homeroom teacher yanked open the front door, and the orders for the day began to echo listlessly through the room.

7

As Haruyuki digested his four morning classes in the same way as always, the bizarre uneasiness just wouldn't fade.

At the chime to signal the start of lunch, which sounded a tiny bit lighter for some reason, Haruyuki stood up. He considered his options, a crease popping up between his eyebrows—should he take care of things the cheap way with bread and a juice box, or dine in luxury in the cafeteria on *katsu* curry?

Regrettably, until the school festival at the end of June was over, lunch in the lounge with Kuroyukihime would have to wait. Given that it was the last big job of the current student council, even Kuroyukihime, who asserted that she'd only joined for the sake of Brain Burst, wouldn't be able to neglect her duties.

When Kuroyukihime's busy, I feel weird with luxury lunch by myself. I'll hold off today, maybe just milk and a katsu *sandwich—no, I could be forgiven for adding* rusk *at least...*Seriously struggling with the issue, he moved toward the rear door.

Clatter! The door slid open with a fair bit of force, and a human shadow took a large step in from the hallway.

Nicely shaped, long legs wrapped in black tights. The skirt was the same gray as the other students', but the short-sleeved shirt above it was jet-black. Even blacker lustrous hair flowed down on both sides of the dark red ribbon indicating that this was a ninth-grade student.

The Umesato school rules prescribed a uniform shirt that was "uncolored and in compliance with the style indicated by the school." And when you put this "uncolored" into a dictionary app, the explanation "a color from white passing through gray to black" popped out. In other words, although it couldn't be said that gray or black was against school rules in the strictest sense, because the manufacturers were given instructions and only white shirts were registered on the sales site, the students had no choice but to buy those in the end. Excluding the sole case where a special order was placed with the manufacturer for black fabric.

There had been only one person in the thirty-odd-year history of Umesato Junior High who had gone to all that trouble, and then coolly used the school rules as her shield against the natural requests from the teachers to fix the situation.

That very person was now standing two meters in front of Haruyuki, hands on hips, head tossed back resolutely, a lovely and yet stern expression on her face—Kuroyukihime.

As the students of class C fell silent, the vice president of the student council took a deep breath and let her dignified voice ring out. "The Animal Care Club president selected from this class is requested to present himself immediately in the student council office!"

A second later, together with a quiet chattering, the eyes of a dozen or so people focused on Haruyuki. By nobly standing and declaring his candidacy—in fact a mistake due to his own carelessness—he had been selected for the Animal Care Club, a fact which was still fresh in everyone's memory. Immediately, the faces of the students around him were practically begging him to explain what was going on, but Haruyuki himself had absolutely no idea.

"Um...o-okay..."

Kuroyukihime shot a look at Haruyuki. "You, then? Fine, come with me."

You, then? She already knows that I'm the Animal Care Club president and all that, and anyway, I'm her child and her Legion member and stuff...

Even as his thoughts raced, confusion reigning in his brain,

Kuroyukihime whirled around, the hem of her skirt flipping up, and started marching down the hall at such a brisk pace that somehow her rubber-soled indoor shoes mysteriously clacked against the hard floor. After standing there stock-still for a second and a half or so, Haruyuki hurriedly chased after her.

As they went down the stairs and headed west in the hall on the first floor, Kuroyukihime did not look back once. They passed the ninth-grade classrooms and finally arrived at the student council office in the depths of the first school building. When Kuroyukihime waved a hand abruptly, he heard the weighty sound of a lock being released. The student council vice president opened the door and disappeared inside.

He gulped loudly before stepping over the door's sliding track himself. The door closed on its own behind him and locked itself once more.

When he had come here the day before yesterday, the orange light of the setting sun had given the room a warm hue, but under the gray light spilling out from the cloudy sky, even the air itself felt cold. Having advanced to the center of the room with the lights dimmed, Kuroyukihime finally turned around and looked at Haruyuki with stern eyes.

"Uh, um," he said in a very thin voice, as a weak smile started to grow on his face. But before it could, he pulled his lips down firmly.

After school was possibly a different story, but there was no way Kuroyukihime would mix work and her personal life by using the student council office for private business over the lunch break. In other words, this was an official request from the vice president of the student council to the president of the Animal Care Club to present himself. He knew it; without even being aware of it, he had messed up some part of his club duties.

In which case, he could at least accept any reprimands seriously. Having resolved this in his heart, Haruyuki waited for Kuroyukihime to speak.

A few seconds later, she pursed her lips and puffed out her cheeks. At the same time came her voice, peevish. "I heard about it, you know, Haruyuki. This morning, you rode up to the school gates on a motorcycle with a beautiful, cool older woman, didn't you?"

"...Huh?" Haruyuki asked in response, his eyes, mouth, and even nostrils opened up into wide circles.

The look on Kuroyukihime's face grew even more fiercely sulky. "What, are you planning to lie to me even now? Let me just tell you, I am able to reference a video recording of the period of time in question. And you! I don't want to watch such a thing, and you—"

"Oh! No, that's—um, j-j-j-just hang on a minute!" Haruyuki earnestly interjected, alternately shaking his head and waving his hands. He followed this with a timid question. "Um, so the 'official request to the president of the Animal Care Club'...?"

A faint red rose up in Kuroyukihime's cheeks, and she jerked her head to one side. "That was just an excuse to call you here."

Whoa! This is super mixing business and personal. He staggered but somehow managed to get his footing before opening his mouth once more.

"Uh, umm, so this is about the motorcycle. Maybe you haven't met her in the real, but that was one of Promi's senior members, Blood Leopard."

"...Oh?" She twitched a single eyebrow.

"This morning, on my way to school, she came to warn—or, I guess, give me some information," he explained, intently glancing at her face to check in with her mood. "And then we ran out of time, so she just gave me a ride. And, uh, I tried to say no, but she's, like, super impatient."

As Haruyuki continued speaking, the look on Kuroyukihime's face changed microscopically, but in the end, she pursed her lips once more and uttered something entirely unexpected. "No fair."

"...Huh?"

"Haruyuki, the last time you and I met as just the two of us was already ten days ago! With all the student council things and what have you, I've been patient all this time, while you go taking care of animals and exploring the Castle with Uiui, and now a girl from another Legion."

"I-I'm sorry." It wasn't entirely clear to him at that moment what exactly he was apologizing for, but even still, Haruyuki reflexively bowed his head.

Kuroyukihime stepped over to him, dissatisfied look still on her face, and stopped right in front of him. "If that's how you feel, then give me one burst point and 1.8 seconds of real time as a present."

"What? O-okay." He nodded, puzzled.

Kuroyukihime flashed both hands with a whirl, and the plugs of the black XSB cable she had picked up at some point were inserted into the direct terminals of each of their Neurolinkers at lightning speed. For the second time that day, a wired connection warning flashed before his eyes, and he unconsciously traced the lustrous lips on the other side of that warning to shout the command.

"Burst link."

Skreeeeee!! The familiar sound that accompanied the world freezing blue around him came on quickly.

Haruyuki, in the form of his pink pig avatar, smaller even than his real-world self, took a heavy step forward. He raised his eyes, and a fairy princess avatar with a black spangle butterfly motif stood silently before him, essentially the same height as she was in the real world. The nature of it might have been different, but the beauty of that face was unchanged. A hue of dissatisfaction drifted across it somewhere even now, but as he raised his face, heart pounding, that hue disappeared into a faint smile.

The relief he felt as he sighed was fleeting. Approaching him silently, Kuroyukihime leaned over and stretched out hands encased in long gloves and slid them under Haruyuki's avatar's arms.

Gah?! He barely had time to think before he was raised up and pulled in tightly against her chest.

"Uh, uh, um um um, K-K-K-K-Kuroyukihime!" he cried shrilly.

A smiling murmur reached his ears. "If I did something like this in the VR space of the local net, much less the student council office in the real world, it would be a clear violation of school rules, but those foolish laws don't apply in this world. Or would it be better if we were both our duel avatars?"

He imagined it for a moment and then immediately shook his plump head. When the Black King had previously embraced Silver Crow in a way very similar to this, he had ended up in some serious trouble when, two seconds later, her level-eight special attack Death By Embracing had ripped into him.

"Ha-ha!" Laughing once more, Kuroyukihime squeezed him even harder. "The truth is, I've wanted to do this ever since the Meeting of the Seven Kings was over on Sunday. To tell you that there is nothing for you to be afraid of."

Haruyuki swallowed lightly and pushed out a hoarse voice. "That's...I—I..." *I'm fine.* He tried to finish the sentence, but for some reason, his entire avatar was shaking like a leaf, preventing him from producing normal sound.

At the same time, he understood just how much pressure he had been under with the situation facing Silver Crow. The terror that he might not be able to stay in the Accelerated World, the way it pushed down to the depths of his soul without him being aware of it.

Haruyuki shook even more intensely, and Kuroyukihime, embracing him as though she were trying to wrap up his entire body with her arms, murmured smoothly by his ear.

"It's okay, you're not alone. I'm here. Your Legion comrades are here, too. And the Red King, Rain; Leopard; the Green Legion's Ash Roller; the Blue Legion's Frost Horn and the others; and so many more Burst Linkers are eagerly awaiting your return."

"...Right. Right..." Nodding intently, Haruyuki realized that at some point his own short arms had pulled Kuroyukihime's body closer as well. But he didn't feel any embarrassment anymore. Their thought clocks, moving at a speed a thousand times that of reality, were synchronized; they melted into each other and became a single being, sharing even their emotions.

Several seconds passed, pregnant with curious emotion, until finally Kuroyukihime gently pulled away from him. Her face regained a slight bit of its usual severity, and eyes like the night sky also grew serious. When she spoke again, her words were entirely unexpected.

"Which is why, Haruyuki, there is no need to be afraid of strange rumors. It's not possible that the ISS kits currently spreading the infection through the Accelerated World were generated from you."

After taking a sharp breath of virtual air, Haruyuki asked in a small voice, "Did you already know about them, about the kits?"

"Mmm. Utai explained it to us when Fuko drove us home yesterday."

"She did...huh? I'm sorry I was late to report—"

"No, actually, I should be reproached for not noticing what was happening sooner. After I got home yesterday, I hurried to collect information. Given the method and timing, we should suspect their participation. The Acceleration Research Society, the ones who destroyed the Hermes' Cord race."

As she spoke, Kuroyukihime moved toward a sofa set transformed into blue ice and sat Haruyuki down before taking the seat next to him.

Sitting neatly on his knees, Haruyuki bobbed his head up and down. "Yeah. That's the same conclusion Taku and I came to yesterday. And Taku said he'd do some looking into it himself. But he's actually home sick with a cold today."

"What?" Kuroyukihime furrowed her brow and fell silent for a while, as if in thought. Looking up at that face, Haruyuki felt his earlier irrational unease filling his heart again.

I'll try some tricks of my own to get information on the ISS kit thing.

That's what Takumu had said at the end of their conversation yesterday before going home. *Tricks of my own.* Did that mean connections he alone in Nega Nebulus had—the pipeline with his old Legion, the Leonids?

The instant his thoughts reached this place, Blood Leopard's words from that morning came back to life in his ears: *The biggest risk for outing in the real is information leaked by a "parent" or "child."*

"Ah!" Haruyuki cried out, snapping to attention, and Kuroyuki-hime turned surprised eyes on him. Staring at her face, he gave voice to the idea welling up inside him. "Um...Kuroyukihime, Taku's parent was someone fairly high up in the Blue Legion, but they're already gone from the Accelerated World because of a Judgment Blow, right?"

"Oh, mm-hmm. I believe the one who reported that to me was you yourself. For the offense of distributing the backdoor program Takumu once used, that Burst Linker was beheaded by Blue Knight, the Blue King. I remember finding that altogether natural, since Knight's very fastidious about such things."

"Right. But I'm pretty sure at the time, they didn't know who the first one to use the backdoor program was. In which case, maybe they're still alive and well in the Accelerated World." He broke off and squeezed Kuroyukihime's hands tightly with his own hooves before continuing. "The problem is...the guy who created the program and gave it to Taku's parent, he maybe cracked Taku's parent in the real in the process. And if he did, it's possible his reach would extend to Taku, who was at the same school and on the same kendo team."

"That is a possibility, but it's already been eight months since that incident. If whoever it was intended to out Takumu in the real, wouldn't they have made some kind of move a long time ago?" Kuroyukihime's argument was exceedingly reasonable.

But Haruyuki slowly shook his head and announced in a trembling voice the only bit of information Kuroyukihime likely didn't know. "This morning, the reason Pard came to see me was to warn me. She said Supernova Remnant, the worst of the PK groups, might have their sights set on me."

"What?!" Kuroyukihime's eyes flew open, and she stretched out her arms as if to cling to him.

Haruyuki focused on forcing his frozen mouth to move. "If...if Taku faked sick to skip school and go to Shinjuku...and if those Remnant guys found him and attacked him outside the view of the cameras..." He blinked hard once. "Kuroyukihime, I have to leave school early and go look for Taku! Even if they try to steal his points with a direct duel, it'll still take a fair bit of time to take them all. If...in the worst case, he has been attacked by a PK, I might still be in time if I go now—"

"You mustn't!" She grabbed his shoulders as he stood up, about to shout the "burst out" command. "It's too dangerous for you to leave school right now!"

"B-but Taku's—! If he has Brain Burst force uninstalled, I—I—!"

"Calm down, Haruyuki! We have to first confirm the situation! He might really simply have caught a cold and be home in bed right now!"

"But to check that, we have to go outside the school and connect globally..."

"Don't worry about it. The fixed terminal here in the student council office can connect to the global net if you make a request. First, we'll try to get in touch with Takumu using that line. If we can't connect with him, then...I will go to Shinjuku to look for him. If I bow my head to Knight, he should at least mobilize his subordinates for me."

Surprised at these words from her, Haruyuki's avatar froze.

The Blue King had been the sworn friend of the first-generation Red King, Red Rider. Haruyuki heard he had been incredibly furious when the Black Lotus took the Red King's head in a surprise attack. At the Meeting of the Seven Kings the other day, the Blue King had maintained a calm demeanor, but deep down, he had to still be hiding hard-to-control feelings toward Kuroyukihime.

If she went to him with a request to help a member of her own Legion, Haruyuki very much doubted it would be taken care of by her simply bowing her head. She would definitely be asked to pay a price the help merited. Kuroyukihime was implying that she was prepared even for that.

Having instantly grasped all this, Haruyuki forced himself to hold strong against the urge to start running recklessly. He absolutely could not lose his cool here. Kuroyukihime's hand still pressing down on his shoulders, he let out a deep breath and nodded. "I—I understand. First, we'll try to contact him."

"Mmm. All right, then, let's stop accelerating for the moment."

They stood facing each other and shouted, "Burst out," at the same time. As soon as they returned to their real-world bodies, Kuroyukihime pulled out the direct cable and ran over to the work desk at the back of the student council office. She touched the extremely thin panel monitor there and tapped her fingers lightly along it. Bringing up the rear, Haruyuki stood next to her, and she grabbed at the cable still dangling from his Neurolinker and inserted the connector into a terminal embedded in the desk. When she did, a system message to the effect that Haruyuki was now connected globally scrolled past his eyes.

"You're good."

He nodded and moved his frozen mouth as fast as he possibly could. "Command, voice call, number zero three."

A calling icon immediately started flashing in his field of view. At the very least, Takumu's Neurolinker was online. If he was accelerating, though, message mode would answer, so Haru still wouldn't know whether Taku was being attacked by PKs—or if it was all already over.

Sweat oozed from the palms of his hands, and he stared intently at the icon. It flashed five, six times...On the seventh time, it picked up.

"T-Taku?" he said hoarsely, nearly crushed by an enormous sense of dread. Whether he liked it or not, the conversation he had had with Dusk Taker, aka Seiji Nomi, after the other boy lost Brain Burst came back to life in the back of his mind. The first thing he had done was look at Haruyuki—who he had met and spoken with on any number of occasions—with an expression of doubt, as if to say, *Who's this again...?* Related memories were erased together with total point loss, and Nomi hadn't been able to remember Haruyuki right away, given that the majority of their interactions had been through the Accelerated World.

Of course, Haruyuki and Takumu were childhood friends; they

had known each other a long, long time before they both became Burst Linkers. So even if he lost his memories of the Accelerated World, he shouldn't completely forget who Haruyuki was.

Haruyuki understood this, but he couldn't help being afraid. Takumu's reply came a mere two seconds later, a span of time that felt light years longer.

"Haru? What's up?"

"Oh...um..."

His friend's voice, complete with its totally normal, amiable tone, echoed in Haruyuki's brain. He almost staggered backward, his relief was so great. "I-it's just, it's weird for you to miss school. So I was wondering how you were feeling," he replied awkwardly, putting a hand on the desk.

"Sorry to make you worry. I'm fine. It's nothing big."

Listening very, very carefully to Takumu, he could actually hear that his friend was not quite his usual lively self. But if he was sick, then that was only natural. Haru got worried about the cold again. "You have a fever? You gotta really rest. No moving around. Are you at home right now?"

"Ha-ha! Of course I am. I'm not like you, Haru. I took some medicine, and I'm resting like a good boy. I'll never forget that time when you had the flu ages ago, and you had a fever of thirty-nine degrees, so me and Chii went to see you, and you were pretending to sleep but actually playing a full-dive game."

"Well, you *should* forget that," Haruyuki replied, and then, just in case, instructed, "Stay away from duels, and just work on getting better. After all, we have an important Legion mission again tomorrow."

And there was the slightest pause before Takumu replied, "Yeah, I know. I'll totally be better by tomorrow. It's still lunch break, isn't it? Thank Master for me, too, for letting you use the global connection."

The person he referred to as "Master" was, of course, Kuroyuki-hime, the Legion Master of Nega Nebulus. In other words, this made it certain that he hadn't lost his memories of the Accelerated World or anything.

Haruyuki breathed a sigh of relief. "What, you figured it out? Got it. I'll tell her. Okay, see you tomorrow. Get better soon."

Reluctant to make Takumu talk any longer when he could tell his friend was exhausted, Haruyuki cut the connection there. He lifted his face and turned to Kuroyukihime, next to him, with a sheepish smile.

"Uh, um. It looks like Taku really is resting with a cold. I'm sorry—this is all me jumping to the wrong conclusions."

"No need to apologize." Kuroyukihime shook her head with a warm smile. "I'm just glad it was nothing. But…" Her expression changed slightly, and when Haruyuki handed her the cable he had pulled from his Neurolinker and the desk, she continued as she put it away. "We can't close our eyes to the fact that those Remnant Linkers might be moving. At the very least, here in Suginami, I don't think they'll have such an easy time of finding you or us in the real, but just in case, we should refuse standby duels for a while. And even when it comes to challenging someone, it would be better to refrain with opponents we don't know very well. After all, it's not necessarily the case that your real can't be cracked from the position your avatar appears in."

"Yeah. I'll tell Chiyu and Taku."

"Please. Well then, shall we have lunch? We should eat in the lounge together from time to time." She patted him on the shoulder, and Haruyuki nodded, his face softening finally. Kuroyukihime also smiled brightly, and added casually, "We have to thank Blood Leopard for the information as well. In that case, perhaps it wouldn't be a bad idea to meet in the real. You, set that up for us soon."

"Okay…o-okay?" After he had already nodded in agreement, he imagined just what the mood would be at such a meeting and threw his whole upper body back with a start. "U-uh, I—I—I don't know about that?" A shrill tone slipped out as he trailed after Kuroyukihime toward the door.

While they were having this back-and-forth, Haruyuki could feel that the strange uneasiness still hadn't completely left him, perhaps because there had been a slight echo of something not normal in Takumu's voice. If he had a cold and was just feeling sick, then that was only natural. But the weight in that voice, it sounded less like poor physical condition and more like a sort of emotional fluctuation. An instability that somehow made Haru remember Takumu from a certain period the year before.

It was just his imagination. Takumu was now an unshakable pillar supporting the Legion with his intellect and cool composure.

Reassuring himself with this thought, Haruyuki wiped the slight sweat coming up from the palms of his hands onto his pants once more and followed Kuroyukihime out of the student council office. Instantly, his apprehensions grew distant at the hustle and bustle of the lunch break that slammed up against him and the smell of spices coming down the hall from the distant cafeteria.

However...

A mere three hours later, Haruyuki was made aware of the fact that his apprehensions had been qualitatively correct to a certain extent. But quantitatively, they were wrong. The situation had already reached a point far beyond his or Kuroyukihime's expectations.

The one bringing this directly to his attention was the youngest member of the Legion, come to Umesato Junior High to feed Hoo the northern white-faced owl after school: Utai Shinomiya.

After two afternoon classes, which gave him the chance to nicely digest the curry he'd had for lunch with Kuroyukihime, Haruyuki called, "I'll mail later," to Chiyuri on her way to practice and slipped outside. Although up until a week earlier he had raced to escape school and connect his Neurolinker globally so he could devour net information instead of a snack, he couldn't do that now that he had been officially appointed the president of the Animal Care Club. That said, he was strangely not annoyed by it. In fact, he could even believe he was looking forward to his club work.

The sky above was cloudy as usual, but fortunately, there was no rain in the forecast again today. He should be able to finally bag up the mountain of leaves he had swept out of the animal hutch and put them in the garbage.

He went around the second school building and came out in the north yard at its back. Stepping along the mossy ground, he set his sights on the natural wood hutch in the northwest corner. The majority of the yard got no sunlight, but the school building ended and became a low grove of trees to the south of the hutch, allowing sunlight to reach in through the chicken wire.

There was no sign of anyone else at the hutch that came into view in front of him. The Animal Care Club also consisted of a boy, Hamajima, and a girl, Izeki, in the same grade as he was and selected by drawing lots, but Haruyuki currently had their participation set to voluntary. He had decided that rather than force them to work, it would be better to wait for them to join in of their own volition. He expected to be waiting a fairly long time.

When he arrived at the hutch, the white-faced owl with the rather cheap name of "Hoo" was taking a bath in the gold tray on the floor. He spread his wings fairly wide and pitched forward, sinking his chest up to his face in the shallow layer of water. He soon pulled himself up again, folded in wet wings, and rubbed them in tiny increments. Haruyuki couldn't stop himself from laughing at this mannerism, so like a person washing their body.

"Ha-ha! That looks like it feels good."

When Haruyuki spoke to him, Hoo whirled his head around and looked at his caretaker, a somehow awkward look coming across his face. He shook his whole body fiercely and sent droplets of water flying before taking off from the water. He carved out several large circles in the hutch and then landed on the left perch, apparently his preferred position, where he promptly began to smooth down the feathers on his chest.

There was a pressure sensor in that branch that could measure Hoo's weight. Haruyuki manipulated his virtual desktop to open the club business tab from the local net browser and display the linked sensor value.

At that moment, a request window for an ad hoc connection

popped up in his field of view. Looking to his right, he saw a small girl standing there smiling, clad in a snow-white dress-type uniform, brown backpack on her back.

"Oh. Hi, Me—I mean, Shinomiya."

It was weird, but when he saw her like this in the real world, he always accidentally almost called her by her duel avatar name, and when they were in the Accelerated World, he almost called her by her real name. On the verge of referring to her as "Mei," short for Ardor Maiden, but catching himself, Haruyuki tapped the Yes button with his right hand as he scratched his head with his left.

The chat tool launched automatically, and Utai began to type on her holokeyboard at her usual speed of ultra. UI> Hello, Arita. How is Hoo's weight, then?

"Oh! Um…It's within normal range, but a little on the low side?"

UI> It is immediately after his living environment changed, so there's no avoiding some amount of stress. I brought a bit on the extra side for today's dinner. Did you want to watch the feeding from close up?

"Y-yeah, totally!" he replied. Before he closed the browser window, he checked the club tab one more time. The only duty assigned by the system was normal cleaning of the hutch, with one person required. He went through the motions of checking Hamajima's and Izeki's names, but as expected, the status shown for both of them was Departed.

Swallowing a sigh, Haruyuki watched as Utai unlocked the large electronic lock. Her small hand beckoned him over. They opened the chicken wire door the barest minimum and hurried inside.

After she shut the door and slid the inside lock closed, Utai took off her backpack. She first pulled out a light-brown leather gauntlet—no, glove. When she put it on, it covered her left arm up to her elbow. She reached into her bag once more, this time taking out a small cooler. She popped it open with her left hand, and he saw what appeared to be thin strips of raw meat inside.

Whoa, total bird-of-prey stuff.

As Haruyuki watched, impressed, Utai stood and held her left hand up toward the perch. Hoo spread his wings, like he had some kind of telepathic connection with her, and flapped them to move to her hand. Reddish-gold eyes open in perfect circles, he pushed his beak forward, practically telling her to hurry up.

Utai went to lean down to the cooler on the floor, so Haruyuki hurriedly lifted it up and held it in both arms. Utai smiled and plucked a strip of the dark-red meat from the cooler.

When she brought it near Hoo's face, he quickly pecked at it with his sharp beak and ate it, basically swallowing it whole. It was utterly unlike pigeons or chickens pecking at food on the ground. Haruyuki was once more impressed, while Utai offered pieces of meat one after another to be promptly dispatched to Hoo's stomach. Although he wondered what kind of meat it was; having never cooked in his life really, Haruyuki couldn't tell just by looking.

In no time at all, the cooler, which looked like it held a lot in comparison with the owl's twenty-centimeter body, was empty. Utai stroked his face as if to say, *That's all*, and Hoo moved his head around, looking satisfied, before flying up to return to his original branch.

After Utai took off the glove and accepted the cooler from Haruyuki, she went outside the hutch and began to wash up with the tap attached to the hutch. While she did, Haruyuki changed the synthetic paper spread out around the perch. In the era when the daily news had been delivered on paper media, they had apparently used the stuff, known as newspaper, for this purpose and then thrown it away, but natural-fiber paper was now an expensive luxury item. He took turns with Utai, using running water to wash off the paper mats dirtied with Hoo's droppings and then hanging them on the small hanger on the side of the hutch.

Once the job was finished, Haruyuki asked the question he had been dying to for a while now. "Hey, Shinomiya? What kind of meat was it you gave Hoo there?"

The fourth grader smiled and her hands flashed. UI> PLEASE TRY TO GUESS.

"Huh? Umm, chicken?"

Utai pushed at a spot in the air with her fingertip; *Bzzt!*—the sound of a wrong buzzer echoed in his hearing, the chat tool's sound function at work.

"O-okay, then, pork?"

Bzzt!

"What? It can't be beef?"

Bzzt!

"L-lamb?"

Bzzt!

"It can't be fish?"

Bzzt!

Here, Haruyuki threw up his hands in surrender.

Utai tapped out unexpected words, smiling somehow meaningfully as she did. UI> WELL THEN, TOMORROW I WILL SHOW YOU FROM THE POINT OF DRESSING IT. A CERTAIN AMOUNT OF MENTAL DAMAGE CAN BE EXPECTED, SO PLEASE PREPARE YOURSELF.

"Uh…dress?"

UI> NOW THEN, BEFORE IT GETS TOO LATE, SHALL WE TAKE CARE OF THESE LEAVES? THEY APPEAR TO BE COMPLETELY DRIED. She grinned at him once more, and unable to pursue the matter further, he nodded.

"Y-yeah. I'll go get some garbage bags." He began to trot off toward the toolshed in the courtyard as he glanced at the inside of the hutch; the owl, belly full, had his eyes closed, seemingly asleep in his usual pose: ear coverts down, standing on one leg.

The work to stuff the old leaves piled up in the yard into semi-transparent garbage bags, the design of which had not changed in who knew how many years, took nearly thirty minutes. If they could have built an enormous bonfire and roasted sweet potatoes and things over it—he had seen scenes like this in old movies and manga—then it might have been a fun and delicious process, but if a fire was set on school grounds, an alarm would sound, fleets of emergency vehicles would swarm the place, and with no exaggeration, the fire starter would be arrested by the police. But even before that, it was next to impossible for anyone underage to get ahold of any kind of fire-starting device like a lighter. The gang that had bullied Haruyuki so mercilessly the year before apparently never managed the Eternal Legend–level act of delinquency of smoking on school grounds.

Thus, they had to drag the eight bags they had worked hard to cram full of leaves over to the collection area in a corner of the front yard. When this task was complete, the time was 4:20 PM.

"Phew. Finally cleaned all that up, huh…"

UI> THANK YOU FOR YOUR HARD WORK.

They looked at each other and smiled before washing their hands in turn. And with that, the day's duties were complete. He had promised to go visit Takumu with Chiyuri, but her practice usually ended around five, so he had a little time.

Just as he was wondering what he should do, Utai, having finished neatly drying her hands with a snow-white handkerchief, cocked her head lightly to one side and clicked on space. Manipulating a window with her right hand, she tapped deftly at her keyboard with just her left. UI> IT'S A MAIL FROM FU. IT'S TAGGED AS URGENT, SO I APOLOGIZE, BUT I'LL JUST TAKE A MOMENT TO READ IT.

The "Fu" Utai spoke of was Fuko Kurasaki, aka Sky Raker. He asked himself why she would be able to get an e-mail from Fuko, who attended a high school in Shibuya Ward, while on school grounds, before quickly answering his own question. When Haruyuki's Neurolinker was connected to the Umesato local net, he was automatically disconnected from the global net, but Utai was treated as a guest user of the Umesato net, so that restriction didn't apply. And because she used a brain implant chip for normal networking, even if she left her connection to the global net open, she wouldn't be registered on the Brain Burst matching list.

"S-sure, go ahead." Haruyuki nodded, and Utai quickly opened the mail and ran her eyes over it.

Instantly, her large eyes, irises tinged with a faint red, opened as wide as they could. Her lips sucked in air as if gasping and trembled lightly.

"Huh? Wh-what's wrong?!" Stunned, Haruyuki took a step toward her.

The girl shifted the focus of her eyes from her virtual desktop to Haruyuki and tapped at her keyboard with fingers that were the slightest bit clumsy. UI> ARITA, DO YOU KNOW ABOUT SUPERNOVA REMNANT, JUDGED TO BE THE WORST OF THE PK GROUPS?

"......!!" He did know them. To be more precise, it was only that morning he had learned of them, but in the eight hours since, that name had been burned into Haruyuki's brain together with an overwhelming terror. "Y-yeah...what about them?" he asked in a hoarse voice, a very bad feeling crawling up his spine.

UI> THIS MORNING, FOUR HIGH-LEVEL BURST LINKERS ASSUMED TO BE MEMBERS OF THIS REMNANT ATTACKED A LONE BURST LINKER IN THE UNLIMITED NEUTRAL FIELD IN SHINJUKU WARD—

Haruyuki screwed up his face and stared at the cherry-colored font scrolling across the window. *It can't be. No way.* The thought chased out all others as it whirled around in his brain. *It's not Taku. I mean, Taku answered when I called at lunch and everything. And he totally remembered me and Kuroyukihime, didn't he?*

However, the several characters displayed in his field of view in the next instant gave an even more enormous shock, throwing him deeper into confusion.

UI> —AND APPARENTLY, THEY INSTEAD WERE *COMPLETELY DESTROYED.*

"Huh? D-destroyed?" Haruyuki parroted, dumbfounded, unable to grasp her meaning immediately. "Destroyed...So the worst PK Remnant was...done in by one person...?"

UI> IT APPEARS THAT WAY. AT THE TIME, THERE WAS A LEGION CAMPING OUT NEARBY ON A LONG-TERM ENEMY HUNT. THE BATTLE EFFECTS WERE SO VIOLENT THAT THEY NOTICED THE FIGHT AND WENT TO INVESTIGATE. WHILE THEY WATCHED, THE FOUR, WHO WERE ASSUMED TO HAVE BEEN THE SIDE TO ATTACK FIRST, WERE KNOCKED DOWN ONE AFTER ANOTHER, AND WHEN THEY DIED, IT WAS APPARENTLY A FINAL DISAPPEARANCE. IN OTHER WORDS, THE FOUR BURST LINKERS AND THE LONE BURST LINKER

ARE THOUGHT TO HAVE WAGERED ALL THEIR POINTS ON A SUD-DEN DEATH DUEL CARD.

"Uh, um. So is it like this? The four members of Remnant attacked someone in the real, threatened them to get them to agree to Sudden Death. But that someone fought back and brought them all to total point loss in one go?"

UI> THAT WAS THE HYPOTHESIS FU ALSO NOTED.

"Wh-who on earth could turn things around like that? One of the kings? A king used themselves as bait to call out Remnant and finish them off?" That was as far as Haruyuki could manage to guess.

But Utai, face still frozen, shook her head slowly from side to side and tapped at the air with even more awkward fingers. UI> NO. THIS LONE PERSON THE ENEMY-HUNTING LEGION SAW WAS A HEAVYWEIGHT CLASS WITH LIGHT-BLUE ARMOR, EQUIPPED WITH AN ENHANCED ARMAMENT WITH PIERCING CHARACTER-ISTICS ON THE RIGHT HAND. HE CARRIED THE LAST MEMBER OF THE GROUP HE WAS FIGHTING, SPEARED BY THE STAKE IN HIS RIGHT HAND, OVER TO THE WITNESSES AND ANNOUNCED THAT THIS BURST LINKER WAS A MEMBER OF SUPERNOVA REMNANT BEFORE STRIKING THE KILLING BLOW AND LEAVING THROUGH A PORTAL. FU SAYS IT MIGHT BE

After a moment's hesitation, she continued, and the final words scrolled slowly before Haruyuki's eyes.

UI> CYAN PILE.

8

Haruyuki ran.

He went out the school gates and turned east on Oume Kaido, directly to the north. He often kept going in this direction on his way home from school, all the way up to Kannana Street, but right now at least, time was his top priority, and he went back the opposite way along the road to school that cut diagonally through a residential area.

Since the shortest route between Umesato Junior High and his own condo was approximately 1.5 kilometers, running the whole way nonstop was quite the trial for Haruyuki. However, just this once, he felt practically none of the pain of the torture of being made to run long distances in gym class. A fathomless impatience spurring him on, he pulled air into his lungs one breath after another and kicked at the pavement.

A few seconds after he had been made aware of the content of the urgent mail Fuko Kurasaki had sent to Utai Shinomiya, Haruyuki had gone into action. First, he submitted the Animal Care Club daily log to the in-school net and sent a mail to Chiyuri Kurashima, who was still at practice, saying, "I'm going to head over to see Takumu now." Then he asked Utai to tell Kuroyukihime in the student council office what she had just told him, and he himself had flown out the school gates.

"…Taku…why…what…" Between gasps for air, broken words slipped out of his throat. The sweat pouring down from his forehead got in his eyes, and he wiped it away with clenched hands.

The information communicated by Fuko itself was not critical. Because Takumu—Cyan Pile—had won the fight of one against many and safely left the field. This was clear also from the fact that he had actually answered the call Haruyuki made to him over lunch.

But there was a "something" that happened before this situation arose. He had no doubt about that. Supposedly home in bed with a cold, Takumu had crossed swords with a PK group in Shinjuku, an already abnormal situation. And there was one other mystery that he didn't want to think about but couldn't ignore, either.

How did he win?

Cyan Pile was currently at level five, just like Silver Crow. While he couldn't be called a newbie, he wasn't exactly a veteran, either. In contrast, the members of Remnant all had to be level six at least, given that they were described as "high level." A perfect victory taking on four such Enemies at the same time—and in the Unlimited Neutral Field, where anything could happen—would have been absolutely impossible, for Haruyuki at least.

Of course, he could definitely vouch for Takumu's physical attack abilities, and he simply could not compete with his friend's cool or his resourcefulness. Still, slaughtering four Burst Linkers at a higher level than he was and all at the same time was not normal. After all, Kuroyukihime herself had said that she had once fought five kings, all the same level as she was, and had not been able to bring down even one of them.

"Something." An abnormal "something" that Haruyuki couldn't begin to imagine was distorting the rules of the game. And he was sure it was still around. Takumu's voice during the call at lunch had held the faintest hint of a hollowness. That was probably not because he had a fever.

"…Taku…"

When he turned left onto Kannana from the path along the elevated Chuo Line, the familiar figure of his destination appeared, the multiuse skyscraper condo.

Best friends. Not that bond. That at least should still not be lost. At the same time as he sent up this fervent prayer, Haruyuki also understood, whether he wanted to or not, that the fact that he'd run so desperately all the way here was proof that he had unconsciously felt that at that moment, even that bond was rocked, unstable.

The condo that Haruyuki, Chiyuri, and Takumu lived in was a combined facility, with a large shopping mall taking up the space from the basement to the third floor. Although the mall, which housed all kinds of shops handling groceries and daily necessities, clothing, and electronics, and even a cinema complex—albeit a midsized one—increased the added value of the condos, naturally, it wasn't only residents who came to shop there. Thus, a strict security gate stood in the area that was the boundary between mall and condo. If even residents, much less visitors, were not recognized by the biometrics in their Neurolinkers, they could not pass.

At the gate before the elevator hall, Haruyuki waited impatiently for the few seconds it took for the indicator displayed in his field of view to change to green. The instant the metal bar bounced up, he dashed through and blocked an elevator door that was about to close with his body before jumping inside. A housewife who apparently lived there frowned, but he simply bowed lightly and turned to face forward.

Haruyuki's apartment was on the twenty-third floor of the eastern B wing, and Chiyuri's was on the twenty-first floor of the same B wing, but Takumu lived on the nineteenth floor of the A wing, built separately to the west. Haruyuki naturally got into the A-wing elevator, and as he listened to the somehow slightly different sound of the motor, he stared at the ever-increasing floor display, willing it to go faster.

When he was little, no sooner had he set down his backpack

after coming home from school every day than he was flying out of the house to play until dark in the amusement area of the mall or at a park nearby. When they went home, stomachs rumbling with hunger, the three of them would wave at one another on the first floor of the mall, and Haruyuki and Chiyuri would head toward the B-wing elevator hall on the right, while Takumu went over to the A-wing hall to the left. If he had turned around in front of the security gate, Takumu's eyes would have seen the backs of Haruyuki and Chiyuri running for the elevator.

What had he felt then?

What if whatever it was that had been building up in his heart over the years had made him decide to confess his crush on Chiyuri just a little early, when he was still in fifth grade?

It was in the evening of a cold, cold day, when the first snow fell, a little slushy.

Naturally, their usual outdoor fun had been called off, and Haruyuki was playing video games by himself at home. The doorbell rang, his full dive was automatically canceled, and when he sullenly opened the door, Chiyuri was on the other side of it. Cocking his head to one side at his childhood friend, who didn't look like her usual self, Haruyuki showed her to his room. She sat down on the bed, and then after a brief silence, she announced it finally in a thin voice.

That Takumu had told her he liked her. And that she didn't know what to do about it.

There was no way that eleven-year-old Haruyuki could know, either. As he stared at the dumbfounded Chiyuri's profile, listening with equal parts surprise and confusion, he was intuitively certain of one thing at least. If Chiyuri turned Takumu down, he would pull away. They would lose their time together after school, so filled with golden light, and they'd never get it back.

When Chiyuri asked him what he thought she should do, a helpless look on her face, Haruyuki replied, half reflexively, "You and Taku'd go good together. And I won't stop being your friend even if you guys start dating."

Chiyuri hung her head deeply and wiped at the corner of her eye with her hand before lifting her face and smiling with a "Right, got it."

In the end, however, Haruyuki's words turned out to be a lie. He distanced himself little by little from the new couple, Chiyuri and Takumu, and by summer vacation of sixth grade, the three of them almost never hung out together anymore.

When they were moving up to junior high, Takumu apparently recommended that Chiyuri take the test for the same school in Shinjuku as he had. But she had made her decision long ago and chose Umesato Junior High, which was so close to home.

She was probably trying to at least maintain the circular shape of the ring the three of them made, which was starting to break. However, this declaration of intent chased Takumu further away. He tried to get the power to secure his connection with Chiyuri through Brain Burst, given to him by the captain of his kendo team. Although he had managed the brilliant accomplishments of the top grades in his year and winning the municipal kendo tournament through the power of acceleration, the burst points he needed to maintain this status dried up, and he succumbed to the temptation of a forbidden cheat tool, the backdoor program.

Once he set up the program in Chiyuri's Neurolinker by directing with her, he used her as a stepping-stone to infiltrate the Umesato local net, found the name Black Lotus there, the Burst Linker with the largest bounty in the Accelerated World, and tried to hunt her. And then...

The elevator came to a stop with a gentle sense of deceleration, and Haruyuki lifted his gaze from the floor. On the other side of a holotag indicating that this was the nineteenth floor, the door opened. The legs that had so earnestly raced all the way to the condo felt heavy now for some reason. Spurred on by the apparently intentional cough of the woman behind him, he stepped out into the hallway just as the door was about to close.

He knew Takumu's apartment was number 1909, but he could count on his fingers the number of times he had visited it. Takumu's parents were very passionate about the education of their only son, and they never looked pleased when his friends came over to play. When Takumu decided to transfer from the famous school he was attending in Shinjuku to Umesato Junior High this year, they had apparently made quite a fuss. For Haruyuki, the very person who had seduced their son away (or so he assumed they thought), this raised the barrier to entry in this apartment even higher than it had been in the past, but fortunately, both of Takumu's parents worked, and they shouldn't be home for a while yet.

He had walked only a few meters when the name plate MAYU-ZUMI leapt into his field of view, altogether sooner than he remembered it being. Standing in front of the door, a different color from those in the B wing, Haruyuki drew the curtain on his interrupted thoughts.

A lot of stuff's happened, and I've made a ton of mistakes. But in that fight in the Purgatory stage, me and Taku got to come up against each other's true feelings, putting it all out there in our fists. That time was probably when we finally became true friends. No matter what happens, that fact alone can never change.

Taking a deep breath, he raised his right hand and touched the call button displayed in his view.

After a slightly long wait, the voice that answered was indeed not that of a parent, but Takumu himself. "Come on in. Sorry, but can you just come straight to my room?"

He had likely confirmed that it was Haruyuki with the camera embedded in the door, but even so, he spoke as though he had almost been expecting this visit, and the door was unlocked. Haruyuki pulled on the door handle, muttered, "I'm coming in," and crossed the threshold into the entryway.

He took off his sneakers, lined them up neatly, and stepped up into the hallway. He advanced, following a distant memory, and knocked on the second door on the right. After hearing a real voice from inside tell him to come in, he turned the knob.

The lights had been dimmed, and only the dusk light coming in through the west-facing window weakly illuminated the room.

Takumu, in jeans and a jersey shirt with three-quarter-length sleeves, turned toward Haruyuki from where he was seated on the bed, a small smile on his face, half sunk in shadow.

"Hey, Haru. Don't just stand there, sit down."

"Oh, right."

Haruyuki stepped awkwardly into the room. Some of the furniture was the same as it had been when they were in elementary school; some of it was new. However, two things were unchanged: there were overwhelmingly fewer things than in Haruyuki's own room, and it was neatly tidied. He cut across the blue-gray carpeted floor and set his bag down before sitting down about eighty centimeters to Takumu's right. The folding bed creaked, and the very springy mattress sank down nearly halfway.

He had run all this way, spurred on by an impulse, but now that they were face-to-face, he didn't know how to get the conversation started.

Takumu hung his head once more, left hand on his right arm and both on his knees; he looked different somehow from when they had said good-bye at Haruyuki's the day before. He was certain of it. But the information he was getting was too complicated, and Haruyuki almost couldn't grasp the situation he had been put in now.

After sitting in silence for nearly ten seconds, Haruyuki finally remembered that he had originally been planning to come and pay a visit to the sick Takumu. "Uh, so, like...You were sick with a cold today, so...how are you feeling?"

"Ohh...Right, that's right." Takumu laughed softly, and shrugged his shoulders lightly. "It's true I had a bit of a fever this morning. Otherwise, there's no way my parents would've let me stay home from school. But I'm fine. I took the medicine the doctor gave me, and my fever went down."

"You went to the doctor?" In which case, maybe Haru was leaping to conclusions?

No, it was a fact that this afternoon, a lone Burst Linker had destroyed the PK group Supernova Remnant. But maybe that had been someone else who just looked like Cyan Pile. After all, if Takumu was getting checked out at the doctor at that time, he wouldn't have been attacked in Shinjuku—

"Yeah. The doctor where we can use my dad's insurance is in Shinjuku, right? I got a ride over there this morning." Takumu's words cut off Haruyuki's half-hopeful thoughts.

"Sh-Shinjuku?" Haruyuki repeated tensely.

"The exam itself was over pretty quick, right?" Takumu's ever-calm voice reached Haru's ears in reply. "My cold wasn't such a big deal, and since I'd gone all the way over there, I figured I'd gather some info in the Shinjuku area. I mailed a member of the Blue Legion I used to be pretty friendly with way back when. Of course, we weren't so friendly we met in the real or anything. We decided to meet up on the local net of a little arcade near the station...I never dreamed he'd sell me out to a PK group."

Haruyuki stared, dumbfounded, at the shadowed profile of Takumu as he laughed softly.

Curling forward farther and tightening the hand that gripped his right arm, Haruyuki's best friend continued, voice gradually growing lower. "Somehow those PK guys got the real info of the Burst Linker who was my parent, and following that lead, they narrowed down students who could be candidates for Cyan Pile. These four guys—they looked really rough—they shoved me into a group dive booth at the arcade and told me to choose one or the other, flashing this knife that looked like a toy. Either have my points carved away bit by bit in a direct duel or die once and end it all in the Unlimited Neutral Field. They seemed really shady, like they would really use that knife if I fought back." Takumu's shoulders shook as he laughed. His voice contained a faint echo of a distortion Haruyuki remembered hearing somewhere, sometime before.

"Naturally, I chose the Unlimited Neutral Field with all its irregularities. But as befits anyone with the title of 'worst PK,' all of them were way above me in strategy and ability. I struggled desperately while they tortured me mercilessly and tried to kill me—"

"Incarnate?" Haruyuki interjected hoarsely, no longer able to stand just sitting there and listening to the chill-inducing monologue. "Did you beat them back with the power of the Incarnate System? I—I mean, I'm not blaming you or anything. I'd probably use it without even hesitating in that situation."

But Takumu shook his head slowly. "Naturally, I used it right away. But they were masters of Incarnate use. My baby power expansion Cyan Blade was useless against their negative will."

"So then…how…? How did you annihilate Supernova Remnant?" Haruyuki's question sank heavily to the bottom of the small room colored with twilight.

It was a dry recollection that came via a long-ish silence and one that didn't end up directly answering the question. "I caught a cold because last night, I lied to my parents that I was going to go observe a cram school where I could prep for high school, and I went for a walk. My parents don't trust the full-dive long-distance lessons, so they've been bugging me for a while to go to a real cram school. I headed for the so-called empty area in the south of Setagaya, but it was kind of drizzling there, so…"

Having listened silently, and somewhat confusedly, to Takumu up to that point, a chill ran up Haruyuki's spine. "The empty area in Setagaya," he repeated in a hoarse voice. Very recently, someone else had referred to that place. Right. He was sure Ash Roller from the Green Legion had mentioned it the previous morning in their closed duel. He had said there was a rumor his little brother Burst Linker, Bush Utan, and Bush Utan's partner, Olive Grab, had used some strange power and won in the empty areas of Setagaya and Ota.

And it had been Haruyuki himself who had given Takumu that information. Yesterday, after everyone in the Legion had gone home, he had asked Takumu to stay and talk. About the mysterious Enhanced Armament silently spreading through the Accelerated World, the ISS kit. And he would have told Takumu at the same time that the infection was progressing mainly in the Setagaya, Ota, and Edogawa areas.

So then, after that, Takumu had gone home briefly before going out again and heading for Setagaya by himself. He had indeed said when they parted that he would use his own tricks to get some information. But still, why would he suddenly do something as reckless as going off by himself into a danger zone like that...?

Haruyuki twisted his upper body to behold his friend and opened stunned eyes wide.

As if trying to escape his gaze, Takumu hung his head even farther. From his mouth, hidden behind the line of his strong shoulder, an endlessly calm and yet almost inflectionless voice spilled out. "I just wanted to see it with my own eyes. Whether or not this Enhanced Armament really existed, something that broke even the absolute limits, the basic principle of the Accelerated World that Scarlet Rain taught me; you absolutely can't gain power that goes against your avatar's attributes."

"...Taku..."

"Haru, I'll say this because it's you. My duel avatar Cyan Pile is unfortunately a *failure*. Like a build error in those online RPG games you always used to play."

Haruyuki immediately started to open his mouth the instant he heard this matter-of-fact statement, but Takumu moved his left hand slightly to dismiss his objections. "I'm not sitting here crying over it or anything. After all, I'm the one who made Pile like that. That avatar was generated as a fairly pure close-range type, but then more than half its potential was poured into a long-distance Enhanced Armament. I explained it before as being because of the trauma that caused me to excessively fear piercing attacks, even though I'm a kendo player, but...but I'm sure that's not the whole story."

At some point, Takumu's profile had fallen completely into shadow as he continued speaking, face turned to the ground, and Haruyuki could no longer see his expression. Even though it was June, the air that filled the room was cold and dry, and it stung his lungs.

Takumu's voice grew gradually hoarser and lower. "This is just my own personal theory, okay? The mental scars that are the mold for a duel avatar—the strongest memories and emotions linked with them...I feel like people who are turned vaguely toward the whole world tend to end up red types. And the people who have those emotions focused on a clear target end up blue types. In which case, Cyan Pile's base form without a doubt includes my desire for revenge against the older students in kendo class who bullied me so harshly when I was in elementary school. But when I really think about it, there were people back then who were even more important to me and for a lot longer...you and Chii. There's no way my feelings for the two of you wouldn't be a source for my duel avatar."

Here, Haruyuki finally managed to push a few words out of his completely dry throat. "That...I mean, it was like that for me. I mean, inside me—Silver Crow is full of feelings for you and Chiyu."

"Yeah. I guess so, huh, Haru? But the thing is...unlike you, born without a weapon, I was born equipped with that sharp iron spike, Pile Driver. The power of the contradiction of being close-range and also long-distance...That's because my feelings toward you guys are full of contradictions. And what those are...I won't say right now. But..." Takumu abruptly sat up and turned his face slightly toward Haruyuki, leaving it still half-colored with shadow. "But I'm pretty sure that feeling is why I suddenly told Chii I liked her three years ago. Almost like I was testing you two. No, not just that. The fact that I set up the backdoor program in Chii's Neurolinker last year, the fact that I could was because of that, too. Half of me wanted to keep the circle of the three of us, while the other half wanted to destroy it. Always. Just me alone. And that contradiction distorted my duel avatar."

"...T-Taku..." His best friend had just made a confession as if spitting up blood, but all Haruyuki could do was say his name.

With a look somewhere between crying and laughing on his face, Takumu pushed on, his voice cracking. "Haru, have you ever thought about why Chii's Lime Bell was born with that power, the seriously real power to turn back time? I'm sure… it's proof that in the bottom of her heart, she wishes we could go back to how it used to be. Back to when we used to play every day until it got dark outside…And I'm the one who gave Chii that sad wish. I'm the one who destroyed this circle of the three of us she wanted to last forever. And I did it twice."

Takumu turned his whole body and sidled up to Haruyuki. Haruyuki could only stare wordlessly at the faint dampness of his best friend's eyes behind the frameless glasses.

"I thought I could make up for it. We were miraculously given this new circle, Nega Nebulus, and I thought that supporting and protecting that with everything I had was the final penance I could do. But…Cyan Pile is the realization not of a simple wish, like your avatar or Chii's, but rather a distortion…I just know that at some point it's going to be the Legion's weak point. No, it's already becoming that. So…before that happened, I thought maybe it'd be better to disappear…so I…"

"…So you what?" Haruyuki opened his mouth, unable to stand listening to any more of Takumu's heart-piercing words. In a whisper, he hazarded the guess that had been steadily approaching certainty as they spoke. "So you went looking for an ISS kit?"

A few seconds later, a feeble smile rose up on Takumu's lips, and he nodded gently. "Yeah. In Setagaya area three, I waited for a long time in duel standby mode until a Burst Linker finally challenged me…After they made me switch to closed mode, they told, if I wanted, they'd share the power. But it's not like I was just looking for power right from the start. The ISS kit was sealed in an item card at first, like a lot of unused Enhanced Armament. So I thought I'd save it in my storage and have Master and the others analyze it at the next Legion meeting. But…when I was attacked in the real this morning by those Remnant guys…I was useless against four opponents. So I made up my mind. If I was going to be taken out, then that had to be better…"

An expression so appalling it almost took his breath away flitted across Takumu's well-ordered face. As his trembling lips formed a self-deprecating smile, he spat out in a husky voice, "Before I knew it, I was shouting the command to activate the ISS kit I'd been taught. And from there...To be honest, I don't really remember. Just...The one thing I'm sure of is that I didn't just defeat those guys. Ten times—no, a hundred times more horrible, crueler than what they did to me, I tormented them, I tortured them, I slaughtered them. I kept the last one just barely alive and carried him over to where I saw this Enemy-hunting party off in the distance. I made him spit out everything about the PKs, and then I finished him off...The Burst Linkers watching were more afraid of me than them."

"Heh-heh." Chuckling dryly, Takumu moved even closer to Haruyuki. His smile twisted. An almost soundless voice traveled the extremely short distance to Haruyuki's ears. "Haru. I got it wrong again. And all I wanted...was for Chii to be able to keep smiling for a little longer at least...or that's what I thought, but..."

"Wh-what are you talking about, Taku? You...you only used the kit once, right? As long as you don't equip it again...Or if you just get rid of it in the shop, then," Haruyuki said earnestly, but Takumu shook his head quickly back and forth.

"*You can't get rid of it,*" he replied like a groan. "Once you equip it, it disappears from your storage and fuses with your avatar. No, not just that...It's almost...almost like it's gotten into myself in the real world even..." Takumu broke off and abruptly stretched out his left hand to grab Haruyuki's right shoulder tightly.

"T-Taku?" Haruyuki called his friend's name in a hoarse voice, but Takumu didn't reply; he simply tightened his grip.

Unable to completely support the weight of the larger Takumu, Haru fell back onto the bed. But the hand on his shoulder didn't go away. He opened both eyes wide and tried to get up, but with the taller and more muscular Takumu pushing him back, it was impossible.

Takumu leaned over directly above Haruyuki, as if he was about to crawl on top of him. "Haru, destroy me," he said, sounding weaker and more helpless than ever before.

"Huh?"

"Please...wreck me. If you don't, I'm...I already can't properly remember what I wanted, even, what I wished for..."

At some point, Takumu's right hand had come to hold a thin black line. About a meter long—an XSB cable.

Still holding Haruyuki's right shoulder down with his left hand, Takumu first plugged it into his own blue Neurolinker. Next, he slid the cable between sturdy yet lithe fingers and grabbed the plug on the opposite end. He brought this toward the direct terminal on Haruyuki's Neurolinker.

With the slight sensation of pressure, the crimson wired connection warning blinked in Haruyuki's field of view and then disappeared.

Takumu's trembling lips took in air to shout the acceleration command.

Before the single drop spilling out of the corner of Haruyuki's left eye could fall onto his cheek, the thunderous roar of acceleration echoed in his ears, and the world went dark.

9

Although it also depended on the attributes of the stage, the Brain Burst program generally made duelers appear a minimum of ten meters apart at the start of a duel, even if they might be glued together in the real world. Thus, when Haruyuki came down to stand on the virtual stage as Silver Crow, a duel avatar with silver armor, the figure of his good friend was not immediately before him.

At his feet was scorched, cracked concrete. The walls of the condo were all gone, and only thick pillars with carbonized surfaces supported the floors above and below. The wall behind him was completely transparent, and he could look out on the streets of north Koenji, soot-stained as though ravaged by super-high-temperature flames.

A Scorched-Earth stage. All the terrain was more brittle than that of a Twilight stage, but smashing it didn't charge special-attack gauges by any real amount. Without even any objects or critters that could be incorporated into a battle strategy, it was truly a barren world.

Having checked the attributes of the stage right off the bat, as his Burst Linker instincts compelled him to do even in this situation, he turned his gaze forward once more.

Ten meters away stood a large silhouette, arms dangling by his sides, head hanging limply. The armor that encased the sturdy limbs was a light blue of a slightly low saturation. A face mask with several rows of narrow, horizontal slits. And equipped from the elbow of his right arm, an Enhanced Armament in the shape of a gun barrel—Pile Driver.

It was a figure he had seen countless times, first as an Enemy, and then as his partner on the front line in the Legion. But there was no way Haruyuki could not notice the unfamiliar air of intimidation emanating from the heavyweight avatar now. Just going by size alone, there were more than a few duel avatars larger, starting with Frost Horn. This highly concentrated power, however, was likely head and shoulders above any other avatar. At the very least, Haruyuki couldn't feel any kind of weakness stemming from the contradiction between the attributes of the main body and the Enhanced Armament, as Takumu had assessed himself earlier.

Haruyuki took a deep breath beneath his silver mask and, steeling himself, took a step toward Takumu—Cyan Pile. "Taku."

Normally, calling an opponent by their real name within the duel, even if it was a nickname, was taboo, but this was a direct duel, and there wasn't a single person in the Gallery. Which was why Haruyuki dared to use the same name he did in the real world and let his confused thoughts simply spill out of him. "Taku. What...Why do we have to fight? I know your strength better than anyone. We don't need to test it now, after all this time—"

"No, Haru," Takumu interrupted, standing off in the shadows and moving his head slowly from side to side. "What you know so well is not my strength but my limits...In the Suzaku mission yesterday...and the final battle with Dusk Taker...and the mission to subjugate the Armor of Catastrophe, I couldn't even manage to stand by your side right up until the end, could I?" His voice was dispassionate, without even a hint of self-deprecation. But Haruyuki faintly felt the existence of something pushed deep down, whirling around, seeking release. "After all this time, I have no intention of denying the principle of same level, same potential. You and I have been the same level all this time, almost six months now. So I'm sure there isn't too huge a difference in the abilities of our duel avatars. What's missing is not the avatar's strength but that of the Burst Linker himself. The strength of your heart to grit your teeth and stand up, no matter what the crisis, no matter how big a difference there is between you and your opponent's battle abilities...I don't have that in me. That's right. I see it. I've always been jealous of you. Of you in that form, the realization of a wish almost too pure; of hope, that power, the way you defy the impossible..."

Takumu moved his left hand and grabbed the Enhanced Armament of his right hand, a gesture uncomfortably like the way he had sat on the bed in the real world mere minutes earlier.

Once again, a low, suppressed voice. "That 'darkness'...The ISS kit pushes into gaps like this in your heart and puts down roots. It's not a simple Enhanced Armament. It's pure negative will made into an object somehow. It pollutes the heart of the wearer and overwrites it. And then it eats negative feelings and grows and multiplies...Haru, I'm already...I can't tell myself anymore...how much of this black feeling is my own... and how much of it is induced by that thing," he finished, almost groaning.

Haruyuki was sure he saw a weak, shadowy aura momentarily envelop Takumu's entire body. Clenching both hands into tight fists, he took another step forward.

It was no illusion anymore; he felt an intense pressure blowing coldly up against the front of his avatar. Never before had Cyan Pile given off this kind of power. In a certain sense, Takumu was indeed no longer the him he had been before. Haruyuki recognized this, but he still faced the boy the same age as him, the boy who had to be his best friend still, and held nothing back.

"Taku...I'm sorry." Rather than thinking, he let the feelings filling his heart become words and spill out. That way, at least, he couldn't lie to Takumu. "All this stuff you're thinking about, all the stuff that's weighing you down, I basically didn't even try to understand it. I just thought you're always so cool, always so calm, you're never shaken, you're always supporting me. But...I didn't want to see. I mean, you had to have something...You were aiming for yourself..."

He cut himself off for a moment and turned clenched fists toward Takumu.

"But, okay? I'm just gonna say this. Taku, you...you're my hero, my goal. Ever since I can remember, I've wanted to be like you. Before, you were talking like your power wasn't enough, so you gave in to the temptation of the ISS kit, but that totally can't have been it. I believe that no matter how dire the situation, you can get through it with your own power."

He took a deep breath and put every ounce of feeling he had into his eyes and his fists. "So that's why...I'll fight you now to show you that. I'll go up against you with everything I've got."

Exactly.

Once you accelerate to the battlefield, all that's left is to simply duel wholeheartedly. All the answers lived there. That had been the first teaching of the person he loved and respected more than anyone else.

As if feeling the heart coming from Haruyuki's fists, Takumu lifted his head. Beneath the slits cut into his face mask, sharply shaped eyes flashed bluish white.

Slowly, Haruyuki stretched his fingers out from tightly clenched fists. His tapered fingers drew out a straight line like a sword. The clear metallic hum of vibration was accompanied by a glittering silver shooting up over the tip of this sword. The light extended about fifteen centimeters from his fingertips and made the virtual air shudder. Haruyuki's Incarnate attack, Laser Sword.

"Full throttle right from the start. Taku! Come at me with everything you've got!"

As if in response to Haruyuki's call, Takumu also wordlessly raised the Enhanced Armament of his right arm. He slid the left hand pressing down around his biceps and grabbed on to the iron spike peeking out from the barrel. Which was immediately followed by the attack name, quietly: "Cyan Blade."

Gashkt! The pile was shot forward violently. Impressively, Takumu caught the momentary flash of light like lightning in his left hand and carved a pale arc out in the sky. At the same time, the Enhanced Armament of his right arm disassembled, and his free right hand also wrapped itself around the light, stopping it precisely on the median line. Appearing from within the scattering light was a large, close-range weapon with a blue blade, enveloped in an aura of the same color—the Incarnate sword Takumu had made materialize through his training with the Red King.

Bathed in the red twilight, the two friends stared at each other for a while, standing on the scorched floor.

The time counter in the top of his field of view, which had started at eighteen hundred seconds, was already cut down to fifteen hundred. Twenty-five minutes left. But if they were both exchanging Incarnate attacks right from the start, the battle would likely be decided in less than half that time.

In exactly the same magnificent, upright pose as when he clutched a bamboo *shinai* sword in kendo, Takumu readied the sword at midlevel with both hands. There wasn't a hint of an opening in that stance. But Haruyuki had already decided it would be hard for him to get in the first blow. Going from Silver Crow's abilities, his usual strategy was to be on the defensive for the first half and build up his special-attack gauge to then attack in the second half and finish it in one go from the sky, but in this fight, there was no need for such shrewd calculations. This wasn't about his average win score. The do-or-die contest here was the soul of a Burst Linker, to simply burn the flames of his heart wholeheartedly and give it everything he had. Throw cleverness to the dogs, as she had once resolutely declared.

Gradually dropping his hips, he pulled the light sword of his right hand up behind him. The tension filling the space increased geometrically, and tiny sparks bounced off the air itself.

"Ngaaaaah!" Haruyuki kicked at the ground as hard as he

could. In an instant, he had closed the mere ten meters between them. He concentrated the momentum of the dash and the torsion of his entire body in the tip of his right hand and layered on it the light speed of his imagination.

Shweeeenk! Together with a high-pitched, crisp sound, the Laser Sword extended more than a meter and struck at Cyan Pile's left shoulder. Since Haruyuki's technique belonged to the range expansion category of the four basic types of Incarnate, its special characteristic was that the blade only stretched out at super speeds when he was attacking or defending.

Thus, the person facing off against him had an extremely hard time reading the distance between them. Even Dusk Taker hadn't been able to see the tip at first sight.

However…

Takumu shifted the angle of the blade in his hands the slightest bit and wonderfully caught the irregular track of Haruyuki's slash from above and to the right. The high-pitched *screech* of impact echoed throughout the stage, and beams of silver and blue light scattered. The swords shrieked as they slid along each other, and in the blink of an eye, Haruyuki's blade, once on top, had been pushed down below.

"Ngh!" He lifted his left hand reflexively at the terrific pressure. A sword of light stretched out from this one as well, and he crossed this to make an X with his right hand—an attempt to double his resistance to Takumu's two-handed sword.

But he was able to compete for only a mere half second. As soon as the blue aura of the two-handed sword spread up the sturdy arms, the weight of the blade doubled instantly. Takumu's experience—the countless times he had locked swords and pushed with his whole body like this in kendo practice and tournaments—strengthened his imagination. Exposed to extreme pressure, Silver Crow's elbow and knee joints creaked and squealed, orange sparks dancing up.

Using all of the modest gain in his special-attack gauge he had gotten in exchange for the few pixels of damage carved out of his

HP gauge, Haruyuki momentarily flapped the wings on his back. He pushed back slightly at the blue blade with the thrust this generated and used the reaction force to race backward. He put some distance between them and once again faced his opponent.

Not having moved a step from his starting point still, Takumu readied his sword at midlevel and murmured, "Haru, you have absolutely zero chance of winning in a stupid straight-up contest of strength. What I want isn't that kind of fight."

"Yeah, I know." Nodding, Haruyuki casually raised the sword of his right hand. "That was just me saying hello. Next, I'll show you the power and technique of me." Admittedly, this was a bit of bravado, but it was at the same time an accelerant to cheer himself up.

Takumu's sword handling was backed by his skill and talent in the kendo that he had spent nearly six years practicing. Even if Haruyuki had challenged him to a normal contest, he wouldn't have had a hope of winning if each of them had been gripping *shinai* in the real world, much less sword against sword in the Accelerated World.

But Haruyuki now had a technique for changing the attacks of a more powerful opponent into his own strength.

Guard reversal—the "way of the flexible" Kuroyukihime had shown him through her own actions, and which he had been practicing ever since—a high-level technique to pull an opponent's attack into your own movements, blend with it, and release it, rather than crash up against it or repel it.

Haruyuki guessed that to some minute and curious extent, the Incarnate System was at work when he used this technique. It wasn't so strong that it generated a visible aura—an overlay—but it did influence reality through the imagination, operating only on the trajectory of the attack power.

In which case, he had to have faith in this important point. It was paradoxical, but he believed in his Enemy's attack and accepted it. If he simply met it with hostility, he couldn't create the image of fusing with it. He wasn't trying to aggressively repel the attack; he only wanted to gently follow along with it. Which was why this was the way of the flexible.

Only ten days had passed since Haruyuki started practicing this technique. He had barely used it in actual battle—only a few times, including the fight with Bush Utan. And it went without saying that this was the first time he was trying it with a swordsman, and in an Incarnate fight. But he had promised to go up against Takumu with everything he had. He couldn't allow himself to hold back or make any excuses here.

After taking a deep breath and then expelling it, Haruyuki contracted the sword of light housed in his right hand until it was just the overlay covering his five fingers.

Takumu's eyes narrowed sharply beneath the slits. But he seemed to take this to mean that Haruyuki was throwing in the towel; the glittering aura around his right hand condensed and grew stronger.

"Here I come, Taku!"

"Bring it, Haru!" Takumu's reply to Haruyuki's shout was almost an invitation.

Haruyuki sank down slightly before kicking fiercely at the floor and charging ahead in his second dash. This time, Takumu brought his own attack to meet him to speed the whole thing up. Many blue Burst Linkers were equipped with sword-type Enhanced Armaments, but almost none of them had experience in kendo. Takumu's technique was on a completely different level, right from the speed of his launch.

Just like a punch in boxing, there was no obvious preliminary movement in a truly refined technique. Unlike the other Burst Linkers, who brandished their swords above their heads or brought their arm down before their sword in a slashing cut, the tip of Takumu's sword had no sooner twitched than it was already closing in on his opponent. If this had been the real world, Haruyuki would have had a fresh new lump on his head before he could even figure out what was happening.

However, his perceptions and reaction speed in the full-dive environment were about the only abilities Haruyuki had that he was proud of. Not relying solely on his sight, he used all his senses—and maybe even his intuition—to focus on the tip of the Cyan Blade pressing ever closer at ungodly speeds, threatening to slice into the forehead of his helmet.

Rrrrrring! He heard the sound from off in the distance. The color of the world changed. His perceptions became super accelerated, and the speed of the blade was just a very tiny bit too late.

Now!

Haruyuki gently ran the fingers of his right hand along the ridged side of the lethal sword, the area that had little ability to generate damage.

Even up against the flat of the blade, if Haruyuki's hand hadn't been guarded by the overlay, it would've gone flying at that moment and disappeared without a trace. That was the power of the Incarnate surpassing all physical laws within the game. However, the speed of light enveloping his right hand guarded against the image of Takumu's severing.

That said, the blade would still indeed cut him if he tried to catch it on the leading edge. Because while Haruyuki's Incarnate was a range expansion, Takumu's was a power expansion. This was why Takumu had asserted earlier that Haruyuki didn't have a hope of winning a contest of strength. Thus, he was trying to catch and return it through the way of the flexible.

Of course, Takumu's dauntless noble blade would not be bent so easily as that. Rotating the attack vector a hundred and eighty degrees the way Kuroyukihime had shown him would be absolutely impossible. But in the fight with Bush Utan, Haruyuki learned that if it was just a matter of averting the power and avoiding a lethal blow, a bit of interference much smaller than he had imagined was enough to do the job.

Gently, softly, he put his strength into the fingers touching the ridges of the sword. Both overlays were compressed at the contact point, sending sparks flying. He couldn't be repelled here.

The image of Ardor Maiden catching and sending back Bush

Utan's Dark Blow with the palm of her hand the other day flashed in the back of his mind. That hadn't been the way of the flexible, but there hadn't been any hostility or malice in her flame aura. He had felt only the intent to purify as she accepted the raging will of her opponent, quelled it, and tried to heal it. He hadn't trained anywhere near as much as she had, but even so, there was not a shred of animosity toward Takumu in his heart. He simply wanted to show him how much he, Haruyuki Arita, believed in this person Takumu Mayuzumi.

The aura snaking around the blue blade seemed to be replete with Takumu's confusion and fear, his regret, and also his longing.

As if to draw closer to those feelings, Haruyuki lightly brought his hand, from the pads of his fingers up to his palm, in contact with the sword. He pulled himself in with the image and pushed outward with his movement.

Skrreeenk! A sound like metal impacting a hard surface echoed inside his head, and orange sparks flowed out in infinite lines in his vision. The tip of the two-handed sword scraped off the left side of Silver Crow's helmet and slipped off, to the rear.

Undaunted, Haruyuki took the hand that had been touching the sword and, directing it toward his own shoulder, launched the rest of his arm forward.

Unexpectedly, the blow, very much like a Chinese Kempo elbow strike, exploded into the base of Cyan Pile's left shoulder. *Thud!* A weighty resistance. Upper body shaken, Takumu tried to bring his sword back up as he braced himself.

Most likely, the guard reversal he had just used wouldn't be so neatly decided like that again. Takumu would no doubt have guessed at the logic of what Haruyuki did in an instant, and would formulate a response to it immediately. Which was why he couldn't let Takumu get any distance between them now. He had to cling to him—he could only rush him now!

"Aaaah!!" Haruyuki howled. Spending the charge from this clean hit in his special-attack gauge, he fluttered only his left wing with all his might. The explosive propulsion whirled his body around to the right, where his opponent was. Using this force, he delivered a knee kick to Takumu's side, which was open now that Takumu's sword was in the air.

Another hard blow.

"Ngh!" Takumu let out a low groan. Being the experienced swordsman that he was, however, he didn't stop moving, but instead tried to launch a blow at Haruyuki's helmet with the pommel rather than the blade of his sword. Naturally, this attack didn't fit into the kendo system, but there was apparently this sort of blow to vital points in the art of other swordsmanship.

His timing was exquisite; Haruyuki wouldn't be able to dodge in any direction in time. However, Haruyuki deliberately slid the sole of his right foot, which had acted as his pivot before, and dropped his entire body perpendicularly. The hilt of the two-handed sword barely scraped his brow and deflected behind him.

Takumu seemed momentarily confused by Haruyuki's evasion with a literal sacrificial throw. In kendo, lower-third attacks essentially did not exist. That said, if Haruyuki kept falling and hit the ground, he would inevitably be immobile, if only for a mere instant. Perhaps intending to pin him there, Takumu raised his right leg.

But as he fell backward, Haruyuki released thrust from his wings in the direction of his head, just barely above the ground. A sudden slide, as if he were being pulled along by an invisible rope. By the time Cyan Pile's foot came down heavily on the ground, Haruyuki was springing up in a backward somersault. Haruyuki kept going, intent on a strike to his opponent's back with the tips of his toes as he vaulted over him.

Takumu staggered and tried to turn around, while Haruyuki used the momentary flapping of his right wing to slide-dash into his opponent's blind spot and finally launch a piercing attack with his right hand.

The strike, colored with the light of the Incarnate, hit Cyan Pile's left shoulder and ripped the thick armor like it was made of paper.

This three-dimensional maneuvering, making use of one or both wings for instant slides, was the other technique Haruyuki had been practicing this last while—Aerial Combo. As long as his special-attack gauge was charged up about 10 percent, he could activate the technique and connect the combos endlessly as long as his attacks continued to land. And his movements were extremely irregular, so at first glance, it was basically impossible for an opponent to respond meaningfully. Even the Black King herself had been forced into a defensive battle for nearly a minute.

"Unhgaaaaah!" With a sharp battle cry, Haruyuki dialed up his combo speed.

Of course, being a nearly pure-blue type, Cyan Pile's HP gauge was still more than 70 percent full, even as he took all these clean hits. Silver Crow was basically full, but trying to face his opponent with this kind of rush attack took a delicate timing.

But Haruyuki had decided to throw away any and every calculation for this fight. Full throttle from start to finish. There were things in the Accelerated World that couldn't be communicated any other way.

As his brain shifted to higher and higher gears, Silver Crow's maneuvering accelerated. His small body danced through space dizzyingly fast, his limbs drawing out an infinity of flowing lines in the air. Sometimes, the Laser Sword and Cyan Blade would crash into each other, and an enormous shock would shake the stage, but Haruyuki still hadn't taken a clean hit.

Takumu gradually started responding to the rhythm of the Aerial Combo, but attacks he couldn't dodge peppered his large body and tore into him. His HP gauge continued to drop until finally it dipped below 50 percent and changed to yellow.

In the height of the fierce battle, Haruyuki felt like he heard a whisper echoing directly in the back of his mind.

…Aah…Haru…It's beautiful. Your fighting is stunning…

Behind the slits cut into Cyan Pile's face mask, both eyes narrowed like threads. The pale light weakened and began to blink irregularly.

...But that beauty...It's too dangerous. It stirs my spirit. Crush me, make your violence more, more overwhelming. Otherwise, I'll...
    I'll want to destroy you.

Fwshk! His eyes glittered fiercely, and pointed warheads appeared from several holes on Cyan Pile's chest plate.

"Ngh!" Haruyuki immediately slid to the right.

But as if seeing through his dodge, Takumu also quickly whirled his body around. "Splash Stinger!!"

As Takumu shouted the technique name, several pencil missiles were launched before Haruyuki's eyes. At this close range, completely avoiding all of them was impossible.

Dashing backward at high speed, Haruyuki cut down one missile after another with the light swords of both hands. Since this attack wasn't Incarnate, the missiles themselves couldn't break Haruyuki's light aura, but there were just so *many* of them. By the time he had knocked all the guided missiles out of the air, a gap of nearly fifteen meters had opened up once more between him and Takumu.

The wind in the stage immediately blew away the black smoke from the explosions. On the other side of it, Cyan Pile stood with his arms dangling by his sides and his head hanging, just as he had at the start of the duel. The aura around the Cyan Blade in his right hand flickered irregularly, indicating that its imagination element was starting to take hold.

And then Haruyuki noticed another new phenomenon.

Something like a thin shadow twined itself around the blue-gray avatar's entire body and rose up toward the sky. He had seen that color before. There was no mistake; it was the same dark aura that had enveloped Bush Utan in the tag-team duel the other day.

Which meant it was finally waking up. The Enhanced Armament that lived inside Cyan Pile and had granted him the power to simultaneously slaughter the four members of Supernova Remnant.

Haruyuki took a deep breath. "Go ahead, Taku," he said clearly. "Use it."

Takumu silently raised his head. Haruyuki stared directly at that face and continued. "Use up everything you have. Right? That's *your* power now. If you don't come at me with your all, this fight won't end. So use it! The ISS kit!"

Takumu seemed to smile faintly, and started to nod.

Haruyuki prayed in his heart the words he couldn't say out loud: *Taku, I believe in you. No matter how this fight ends, I believe you can overcome that dark power.*

His friend nodded again, almost as if he were able to hear even this silent prayer.

The flowing two-handed sword, the materialization of the positive will of the second quadrant, disappeared from his right hand. Blue light encircled his arms once more and turned back into his original Enhanced Armament, Pile Driver.

Takumu brandished this arm high in the air and sang out quietly yet resolutely, "ISS mode activate."

The darkness spilled over.

10

Compared with its awesome power, the mysterious ISS kit Enhanced Armament was extremely small as an object.

It was a black half sphere about five centimeters in diameter, which also looked like a social camera somehow. Bush Utan and Olive Grab had equipped it in the center of their chests. But after Takumu shouted the activation command, the half sphere popped up on the back of his Pile Driver hand. With a snap, a horizontal line ran through the center of the sphere. From there, the surface split into top and bottom, and a single orb appeared from within, reminiscent of the eye of a living creature. It shone wetly, a deep red, the color of blood…

The light of an overlay of terrifying density and scale then gushed up in a vortex from Cyan Pile's feet. But it couldn't actually be called light; it was stained a rich, inky black. No longer the hazy shadow that had enveloped Bush Utan, this was an almost pure aura of darkness.

Haruyuki desperately braced legs that threatened to crumble under him.

The force of the gushing aura was also well beyond anything Utan had produced. As proof that this was no mere light effect, cracks radiated out in circles on the floor from where Takumu stood.

...Taku...

"Haru," Takumu responded gently, perhaps hearing Haruyuki unconsciously calling to his friend in his heart. He indicated the floors above and below and the smattering of pillars with his left hand. When he continued speaking, his voice was quite different from before summoning the kit. Dark, desolate, tinged with a metallic effect. "If we stay in this tiny place forever, you won't be able to use your full strength, either, right?"

"Y-yeah. You want to move outside?" Haruyuki judged that somehow Takumu didn't seem to be experiencing the same level of interference with his mind that Utan and the others had and let out a quiet breath as he asked the question.

But...

"No, there's no need for that," Takumu murmured and turned the Pile Driver, complete with ISS kit, casually toward the floor. Immediately after that came a level voice, almost entirely without fight, with the technique name.

"Dark Shot."

Instead of the iron spike, a dark beam shot out. In an instant, it had gouged a ten-centimeter hole through the floor and disappeared into the lower floors.

One, two, three seconds later.

Haruyuki felt a tremendous vibration pushing upward from directly below him. Before he had a chance to even swallow, the floor cracked into tiny pieces, and a torrent of energy that could only be described as black flames jetted out through the gaps.

"Hungh!" Gasping violently, Haruyuki reflexively deployed his wings and dashed straight backward. Flipping his body midair, he charged toward the opening to the outside of the condo, flying at top speed with both hands thrust forward. The shock wave pressing up against him from behind shook his body as he managed to leap into the air and soar in a straight line through the sky of the Scorched-Earth stage. Once he confirmed he had gotten ten more than enough distance, he flipped himself around once more and looked back.

"Wha…," Haruyuki gasped, astonished.

He watched as the thirty-story tower that was the A wing of his condo in the real world shattered into pieces from the ground floor and collapsed.

It was true that the terrain objects in the Scorched-Earth stage broke fairly easily. But even so, there were limits. Because the destruction of an enormous building like that would rip a duel strategy up from the roots, the system was set up to make such an act take a suitable amount of time and effort. As far as Haruyuki knew, the only Burst Linker capable of destroying a massive building in a single blow was the Immobile Fortress, aka the Red King, Scarlet Rain, when all her Enhanced Armament was fully deployed.

Unable to believe the sight before his eyes, he blinked repeatedly. But the condo collapsed completely in mere seconds and became an enormous mountain of rubble.

As if compelled, he checked Cyan Pile's HP gauge in the upper right of his vision. Despite the fact that Takumu had been pulled into a collapse of this magnitude, it was still just under 40 percent full, right where the damage from Haruyuki's Aerial Combo had left it. And although this was the Scorched-Earth stage, where the bonus for terrain destruction was weak, his special-attack gauge was at once fully charged.

Shifting his gaze back to the mountain of rubble, Haruyuki saw a mass of objects on the peak of the pyramid blown off from directly below.

Appearing from within the smashed rubble was Cyan Pile, in an even more concentrated aura of darkness.

"Taku," he murmured hoarsely. But no other words came out.

This was nothing short of overwhelming, enough to make even shock and fear disappear. After activating IS mode, Bush Utan had also shown a terrifying leap in battle ability, but Takumu's changed appearance far and away surpassed that. Which meant that this was how deep he had pushed into his heart a pain and suffering that was almost maddening.

So Haruyuki absolutely couldn't lose here. If he did nothing, daunted by the power of the ISS kit, the darkness that held Takumu would only increase in strength. Takumu might step into the bottomless hole in his heart, the dark side of the Incarnate that Kuroyukihime, Sky Raker, Niko, and Blood Leopard had warned them about.

Ever since the backdoor program incident, Takumu had been earnestly trying to get back to his old self. He had transferred from the university-track school in Shinjuku with its cutting-edge education and high-level information to the frequently analog Umesato Junior High, and taken one step after another at his own pace. Haruyuki couldn't let the malice someone was deliberately spreading interrupt that journey. Somehow, he had to drag Takumu out from the interference of the kit and sever its control over him. And to do that...

He would win this battle. It was the only way.

He would win and show Takumu. The power of the positive will. Of the light of hope shining modestly but stronger than anything else.

Hovering at an altitude of seventy meters, Haruyuki materialized the Laser Sword in both hands.

Below, Takumu stood at the peak of the rubble mountain and raised the Pile Driver with the ISS kit in it in a leisurely motion, setting his sights on Haruyuki.

The dark shot released from that barrel before had been tremendously powerful. He wouldn't be able to repel it with his light swords the way he had Bush Utan's technique of the same name. But if he could see the launch position and timing, it should be possible to deal with it. His only hope was to dodge it at a distance where he just barely avoided damage and settle this fight in a counter–dive attack.

Haruyuki stopped his virtual breathing and concentrated all his mental energy on the barrel of the Enhanced Armament Cyan Pile had raised.

Which was why he was late to notice. That together with Takumu's whisper of the technique name, the special-attack gauge, not used normally with Incarnate attacks, went from fully charged to completely spent in an instant.

"Dark Lightning Spike."

His friend called out a technique name he had never heard before, and at the same time, it seemed like the barrel of the Pile Driver flashed with black light for an instant.

That was all. The massive beam that had destroyed the condo, the thunderous roar, the shock wave—none of that. The dry wind of the Scorched-Earth stage blew drearily, and a light sensation stroked his left shoulder.

"…?"

Haruyuki suddenly felt his body shaking lightly. At the same time, several small lights cut across the bottom edge of his field of view. Shifting his gaze, he noticed strange objects falling toward the surface of the ground. A silver pole, a few thin panels. *What?* He strained his eyes and—

"Ngh?!"

The moment he realized what those objects actually were, Haruyuki could do nothing but open his eyes wide, dumbfounded, and suck in air. It was—an arm. And a wing.

Belatedly, he looked at his left shoulder. There was nothing there but a smooth cross section, as if it had been processed with a precise mirror finish. Silver Crow's left arm and metal wing had been completely removed from the base.

His body listed heavily. Unconsciously, he increased the thrust from his right wing and tried to maintain his altitude, but this move actually left him unbalanced, and he plunged into a tailspin. Carving out a spiral like the leaf of a tree, he began to plummet toward the earth.

Just as he was on the verge of crashing into the ground, he recovered from his daze and tried to counterbalance the rotation with his wing, narrowly succeeding in landing on his feet. Still, he was unable to entirely absorb the impact; violent sparks flew from the joints in his knees and ankles. Losing his left arm and

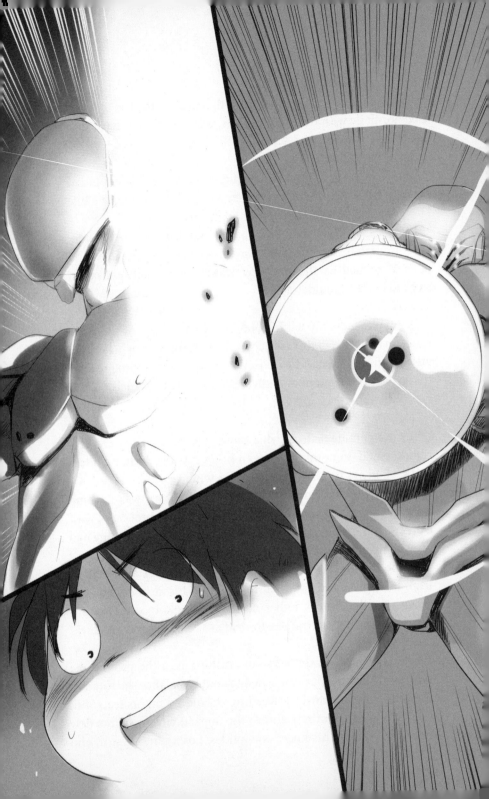

wing wholesale caused his gauge to drop 50 percent all at once, dyeing it yellow.

But more than the amount of damage, Haruyuki felt a massive shock at the thing that had done the damage itself.

He basically hadn't seen it.

He had managed to notice that the shooting effect had drawn a black cross over the barrel of the Pile Driver. But he hadn't been able to perceive the body of the projectile itself, which had to have crossed the seventy meters between them.

There had been a time when Haruyuki struggled forward with absurd special training to avoid a bullet launched from close-up in a VR program he'd made. The result was that currently, as long as he could see the shooter, he could evade even snipers with large rifles fairly consistently. Put another way, if he hadn't been able to do at least that, he wouldn't have been able to fly at all, given that there were no obstacles in the sky. And yet not only had he not been able to avoid this shot, he hadn't even been able to see the projectile's trajectory. It was completely unbelievable.

The shock was exceedingly massive, but Haruyuki's stupefaction there on the ground lasted a mere half second.

One of a Burst Linker's most critical abilities was to immediately get their thoughts together and shift their focus to their next move, however unexpected the situation they found themselves in. Haruyuki pushed his surprise aside for the time being and tried to rebuild his strategy for the current situation, in which he was essentially robbed of the ability to fly. In this case, the only chance of winning he could see was to once more bring the fight up close and personal, make it a close-range battle, combining guard reversal and Aerial Combo, even if he just had the one arm and one wing.

First of all, move!!

Rebuking himself, Haruyuki stood up to run from the courtyard of his fallen condo to the still-standing B wing.

However, once again, he was faced with the unexpected situation.

Whump! The sound of impact shook the ground, interrupting his dash. Staggering, he turned his eyes toward the source of the sound, to where a large avatar had landed on the ground a mere ten meters away. Takumu, who should have been at the top of the mountain of rubble, had leapt down to the courtyard in one bound.

Heavyweight avatars like Cyan Pile and Frost Horn had the special characteristic of being able to produce a shock wave in the Field by stomping, which obstructed the movement of light-weight avatars. However, the shaking now was less a shock and more a large earthquake. Haruyuki's feet got caught in the cracks racing out in all directions, and he stumbled while Takumu closed in from behind him in the blink of an eye with a high-speed dash—also nonstandard—and stopped a very short distance away.

His overwhelming sense of presence, almost as if the duel avatar itself had gone up a full size, froze Haruyuki in his tracks.

Beneath the slits lined up on his face mask, there was a low sound, and Takumu's eyes flashed. But the color had changed from the light blue of a little earlier to a dark purple. He stared quietly from his higher position at Haruyuki standing stock-still in an unsteady posture.

"Sorry, Haru." A voice tinged with a distorted effect flowed from his mouth.

"...Taku..." All Haruyuki could do was call the name of his best friend, almost soundlessly.

"I'm sorry." Takumu slowly took another step closer. "I—I knew it'd be like this. I knew it'd end up like this. And yet I pushed you. I forced you into a duel. I guess...there's no helping it if you think I just wanted to beat you down like this..."

Thud. He narrowed the distance between them by another step, and now Cyan Pile's massive body was directly before Haruyuki. A thick, jet-black aura poured ceaselessly from the enormous rocklike avatar, gushing up toward the sky. Takumu glanced down at its source, the black eyeball parasitizing the Enhanced Armament of his right arm.

"I heard that the deeper the darkness of the owner's heart, the more terrifying the power this ISS kit manifests. So you see...I'm this kind of person. I realized this while I was massacring those four PKs with this power—though the truth is maybe I knew it right from the start. After all, I only became a Burst Linker to get good grades, win tournaments, and hold on to Chii."

"Taku...Taku."

You're wrong. You're wrong. Wrong, wrong, wrong, wrong!!

This word alone swirled around in Haruyuki's heart. But he didn't know how to say it so Takumu would hear. His vision shook, rainbow-colored and blurred. Haruyuki belatedly realized he was shedding tears under his helmet.

As he looked down at Haruyuki, meager particles of light spilled out from Takumu's eyes as well and evaporated instantly.

"Thanks, Haru." The gentle voice of his best friend reached his ears. "I'm glad my opponent in my final duel was you...Thanks."

"...F-final? What...are you talking about...?" Haruyuki asked in a trembling voice.

"When this fight is over," Takumu replied quietly, "I'm going to go take a stab at the Acceleration Research Society."

"...What..."

"They're the ones making and handing out this kind of terrible Enhanced Armament. I don't think I can beat the top-level guys. But once I reach the infection route, I should be able to figure out the ones at a certain level. I'll invite them into the Unlimited Neutral Field somehow and get all the info I can from them. Even—" He cut himself off momentarily, but soon continued again with certainty. "Even if I lose all my points doing it and Brain Burst force uninstalls, I'll definitely tell you everything I learned. After that, it's up to you to stop them, Haru. This kind of...power—taking advantage of the mental scars that all Burst Linkers have to mislead them—shouldn't exist. The Accelerated

World is a place for people like you and Chii and Master, people who change that pain to hope and move forward."

"Taku...But you...I mean, you, too..." Haruyuki was frustrated and annoyed by his own inability to do anything but stammer like this.

But it seemed that his childhood friend of more than ten years still understood Haruyuki's feelings. He felt a gentle smile beneath the mask.

"Haru, I have to thank you for one more thing." In contrast with the dark aura streaming from his body, even more wildly, his voice was nothing but gentle. "That time...at the end of our first fight, thank you for forgiving me. The eight months from that day to today, fighting as a member of the new Nega Nebulus, have been so much fun, it's like I've been dreaming. Thanks, Haru. It's too bad I got knocked out in the middle of your purification mission and the Legion's work to reach the ending, but...tell Master, Raker, and Maiden thanks for me. And...tell Chii I'm sorry."

"Don't say that! Don't talk like that, Taku!!" Haruyuki screamed, suppressing a pain like his heart was being ripped in half.

He clenched his remaining hand into a fist and focused on the glittering Incarnate lodged there. Reflecting his violently shaken emotions, the light flickered irregularly, but even so, the dark color winding around the two of them weakened the tiniest bit.

"Chiyu's gonna cry if you leave the Legion, you know! She'll totally cry! You wanna make Chiyu cry, Taku?!"

Takumu hung his head slightly. Finally, an even more gentle voice. "Yeah, she probably will, huh? But...I know she'll get over those tears and keep moving forward. After all, I'm the one who's been making her want to go back to the past. Haru, please. Look out for Chii."

Grinning, Takumu clenched his enormous left fist tightly in front of Haruyuki.

The condensing dark aura roared ferociously. The midnight

black, absolute as a black hole, easily overwhelmed the modest silver light in Haruyuki's right hand.

"Okay, let's finish this, Haru. You don't have to look so sad for me. This darkness was inside of me right from the start. You just have to make the opposite choice you did eight months ago. I'm making you do it."

Perhaps due to the concentration of such enormous power, an infinite number of sparks shot into the air from his left fist as Takumu slowly pulled it back.

As if to comfort Haruyuki, to encourage him, the call of the technique name was somehow kind. "Dark Blow."

Haruyuki tried to guard with the silver light of his right hand against the fist, which shot down at him with pressure akin to an enormous meteor pouring down from space.

However, an impact unlike any he had ever felt before, as if the world itself were exploding, made his entire body dance. Meager though it might have been, if he hadn't had his Incarnate defense, his avatar would have been blown to bits instantly.

He managed to avoid annihilation, but, very much unable to stand his ground, Haruyuki went flying backward toward the condo's B wing at a terrifying speed.

He flew for half a second or so, parallel to the ground, before his back crashed into the exterior wall of the building. His body gouged out a large hole in the scorched concrete, and he still didn't stop but plunged inside. Only once he had smashed through the next wall, and the next, and then yet another, was his momentum finally diminished. After bouncing once on the floor of a large, empty room, Haruyuki tumbled onto his back, arms and legs splayed.

Something was flashing red in the top left of his vision, sunk into gloom from the intense impact. His brain had basically stopped working, but even still, Haruyuki understood that this was his HP gauge, reduced to a few pixels.

The power imbalance was enough to make him lose hope. And

here, for the first time in all of this, Haruyuki felt despair filling his heart.

How conceited he had been to think that he'd win using his full force on Takumu, and then he'd save him. After all, right from the start, Takumu's abilities far exceeded Haruyuki's in all things. That's why he looked up to him. That's why Takumu was his hero.

If this Takumu had pushed himself up against this wall and made up his mind, then what on earth could Haruyuki do, with his sole power—his wings—taken from him...

He felt a heavy vibration from off in the distance. Takumu was coming straight for him, punching out the walls of the condo as he did, to finish this duel.

Beneath his cracked helmet, Haruyuki's eyes once again filled with tears. He never thought it would end this way. He had really believed that he, Chiyuri, and Takumu would be able to hang out together forever. All this time, he had believed that Brain Burst, the Accelerated World, existed precisely for that reason.

"That's right."

Abruptly, someone's voice echoed inside his head.

He absently opened his eyes. Against the scorched, bleak ceiling, he saw a strange sight: another human form gently slipping away from Silver Crow's body on the floor and standing up silently.

Haruyuki had no idea who this someone was, faintly transparent, basically a hallucination.

A slender girl-shaped avatar. The design, with the flower petal motif at the shoulders and hips, resembled Chiyuri's Lime Bell somehow. But the short hair on her head, ends flipping up, and her armor color were totally different.

A bright, golden yellow that reminded him of spring sunlight.

This unnamed someone sat down on a pile of rubble beside Haruyuki, flat on his back, and spoke once more. *"It's just as you* say. *Brain Burst doesn't exist simply to fight and hate each other. We can join hands; we can build bonds."*

"...Who are you...?" Haruyuki asked vacantly. "Why are you here...? This is a direct duel field..."

The ephemeral, transparent someone smiled lightly. *"I'm...a memory. A tiny fragment of a thought living in a corner of the enormous body of quantum information that makes up a certain object registered in the central system."*

"...A memory..." The instant he murmured this, Haruyuki felt a prickle stab his own memory somewhere.

I know her. We've never met, and I don't know her name, but still, I know this person...

Almost as if to affirm this thought, the golden yellow avatar nodded lightly. *"Because you traced a past memory in the Castle, the system circuits were temporarily activated, and I'm able to talk to you like this. But I'm sure it won't last long."*

The girl broke off and then announced in a voice with increased strength, *"There's still a way to help your friend."*

"What..." His eyes flew open. Supporting himself with his battered right arm pressed against the floor, he desperately struggled to sit up. "Wh-what? Are you saying there's something else I can do?"

"You still have power inside you. The lone power that can resist the deep darkness penetrating your friend," the golden girl murmured, smile fading.

After a moment's confusion, Haruyuki intuitively grasped what she was getting at. Reflexively, he shook his head.

"N-no way. I can't use *that*. If I summon that again, I definitely won't be able to come back from it ever again."

That. The cursed Enhanced Armament parasitizing Silver Crow deep inside, currently returned to a seed state by Lime Bell's Citron Call Mode II.

The Armor of Catastrophe.

A somehow sad smile rose up onto the golden yellow girl's face. *"It's not as though the armor was born crowned with the name*

Catastrophe, you know. So many sad, sad things happened, and its form was distorted."

"The form was...distorted..."

"I've been waiting all this time in a little corner of that armor. Each time a new owner came along, I prayed, 'Please, let this be it.' The appearance of someone who could remove the curse of it. I've waited all this time for someone who could heal his fury and sadness..."

Nimbly standing on the pile of rubble, the girl knelt down in front of him and touched the injured silver avatar gently with her slender right hand.

"And you. You're so much like him, I'm sure you can do it. It might take some time, but someday, I just know it. So don't give up here. For the sake of your friend, stand up just one more time."

The girl's figure became even more transparent. As she changed into a hazy silhouette, she stepped back inside Haruyuki.

In his head, far, far away, the last of her voice: "Now, remember. Call that name...the name of the armor before it was twisted into the Disaster...You should...already know it..."

Abruptly, a scene rose up on the screen of his memory. The pedestals of the Seven Arcs they found inside the Castle. The metal plate adorned with the name of the zeta star of the Big Dipper, *kaiyou*.

And at the very bottom, several roman letters. He had indeed felt something when he saw that. A tiny throbbing something deep in his soul. Like it called to mind a sad memory from a long, long time ago.

Thud. The heavy vibration came to him through the floor, and Haruyuki lifted his face.

Takumu had apparently arrived in the next room or the one beyond that. Now matter what attack Haruyuki faced next, the remaining pixels in his HP gauge would be easily blown away.

Can the me I am now stop Takumu? He's brooded over it so deeply; what words could I say to bring him back?

A cold despair threatened to fill his heart once again, but Haruyuki gritted his teeth and shook it off.

Not words.

Feelings. With fists containing feelings. Me and Taku are both Burst Linkers. So then there's only one thing to tell him, only one way.

"Go at each other with all we've got. Right at the beginning, I did, you know, Taku," Haruyuki murmured in a low voice, and intently forced his battered avatar to stand. Fragments of his cracked armor fluttered to the floor.

There was no longer any fear, any panic.

Staring through the large hole in the wall, Haruyuki quietly gave voice to the name that had come to life from the depths of his memory.

"Equip...the Destiny."

To be continued.

AFTERWORD

Reki Kawahara here. I'm bringing you the first book of 2011, *Accel World 7: Armor of Catastrophe.*

Thinking back on it, in the afterwords I wrote for the books from two years ago until last year, I have simply apologized intently and earnestly. Thus, my goal this year is to not apologize in the afterword. Or at least that's what I thought, but…I'm sorry, please allow me to apologize out of the blue…I am already apologizing for the apology itself. (lol)

What?! I continued the story into the next volume again! I'm so sorry! Honestly, after dragging it out in book six like that, I resolved to neatly tie things up in book seven. And then, amazingly, I created this very detailed plot, and just as planned! That was how I was supposed to write it, but…Takumu worked so much harder for me than I was expecting…(lol)

B-but he almost never got the chance to come onstage in books five and six, so as the writer, I'm relieved that he's really pulling his weight here. And I guess you could say, if the story's continued this far, the only thing to do is let it go where it goes; I'll just have to move forward following the demands of the characters. As of the time I'm writing this afterword, I've already begun work on the next book, and my heart is pounding as I type away at the keyboard, eager to see how the duel that didn't finish this time is going to be resolved between Takumu and Haruyuki. I hope you'll wait a little longer until I can deliver it to you in the form of a book!

Now, here, I'd like to write briefly once again about the outlook for 2011.

Since I've already (promptly) failed at my first goal to not apologize (lol), I'd like to at least meet my second goal of continuing to write without any big problems…Suddenly getting a bit raw here, but—no, but, I've been idly thinking lately that continuing to write at any rate is maybe the most important ability in this job of "writer." To make an analogy with car racing, let's say it's something like rather than recklessly launching a do-or-die attack, you pick out the next hill, the next stage; you leave your assistants and continue cruising along…Although naturally, even still, there will definitely come some point where you have to fight for the finish line, sprint for the most important goal. So right now, I'd like to keep solidly turning that crank while not letting the timing for that sprint pass me by.

Volume 7 also slid into home just barely in time, and so to my long-suffering editor, Miki, and illustrator, HIMA, I am going to work hard in 2011 to be a good little boy and meet my deadlines. I hope you'll stick with me!

To all you readers who were attacked with "to be continued" in the very first book of the new year, I humbly bow my head to you and entreat you to somehow please join me with a magnanimous spirit this year as well!!

Reki Kawahara

On a certain day in 2010 still, but it feels like 2011

THE CHART-TOPPING SERIES
THAT SPAWNED THE EXPLOSIVELY
POPULAR ANIME ADAPTATIONS!

SWORD ART ONLINE, VOL. 1-4
LIGHT NOVEL SERIES
SWORD ART ONLINE © Reki Kawahara
KADOKAWA CORPORATION ASCII MEDIA WORKS

SWORD ART ONLINE, PROGRESSIVE I
LIGHT NOVEL SERIES
SWORD ART ONLINE: PROGRESSIVE © Reki Kawahara
KADOKAWA CORPORATION ASCII MEDIA WORKS

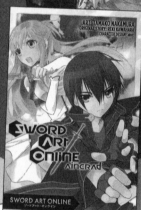

SWORD ART ONLINE, PROGRESSIVE I
MANGA SERIES
Sword Art Online: Progressive
© REKI KAWAHARA / KISEKI HIMURA
KADOKAWA CORPORATION ASCII MEDIA WORKS

SWORD ART ONLINE, VOL. 1-4
MANGA SERIES
SWORD ART ONLINE: Aincrad
© Reki Kawahara / Tamako Nakamura /
KADOKAWA CORPORATION ASCII MEDIA WORKS

SWORD ART ONLINE, GIRLS' OPS, VOL. I
MANGA SERIES
Sword Art Online: Girls' Ops © REKI KAWAHARA /
NEKO NEKOBYOU
KADOKAWA CORPORATION ASCII MEDIA WORKS

VISIT YENPRESS.COM
TO CHECK OUT ALL THESE TITLES AND MORE!

www.YenPress.com